LOCKED IN SILENCE

A Novel by

Natalie Zellat Dyen

Black Rose Writing | Texas

ISBN: 978-1-68513-363-4
LIBRARY OF CONGRESS CONTROL NUMBER: 9781685133634
PUBLISHED BY BLACK ROSE WRITING
www.blackrosewriting.com

Printed in the United States of America
Suggested Retail Price (SRP) $21.95

Locked In Silence is printed in Baskerville Old Face

*As a planet-friendly publisher, Black Rose Writing does its best to eliminate unnecessary waste to reduce paper usage and energy costs, while never compromising the reading experience. As a result, the final word count vs. page count may not meet common expectations.

This book is dedicated to all those who discover what they love to do, regardless of how old they are.

PRAISE FOR

LOCKED
IN
SILENCE

"A haunting and gripping tale of a woman's unrelenting search to shatter the silence imposed upon her while locked within the cells of society's injustices."
–Janis Robinson Daly, author of *The Unlocked Path*, a #1 New Release for U.S. Historical Fiction

"Natalie Zellat Dyen hits a raw nerve here: a 19th century woman is incarcerated for an unspeakable crime that she's confessed to committing but has no recollection of it having ever happened. She has little will to live, and with the loss of her only child, an infant victim, there's little for her to live for. The truth will set you free, if only she can get to it. A great premise, a gripping, powerful mystery, and powerful prose."
–Chris Bauer, author of *COBALT* and the *Blessid Trauma Crime Scene Cleaners* trilogy

"Not even Charles Dickens can save her. A poignant nineteenth-century historical drama of a young woman locked away in total silence in Philadelphia's notorious Eastern State Penitentiary. Natalie Zellat Dyen writes of an injustice that will keep the reader turning pages."
–Don Swaim, author of *The Assassination of Ambrose Bierce: A Love Story*

"*Locked in Silence* is a powerful portrait of resilience and love. Natalie Zellat Dyen has a unique and beautiful insight on the human spirit, and brings it to life within the vibrant chaos of pre-civil war Philadelphia. A joy for any historical fiction reader."
–LCW Allingham, Executive Editor - Speculation Publications

"1848. Secrets, lies, solitary confinement, Quakers, The Underground Railroad, and a young woman named Lizzy O'Meara who shows courage in the face of betrayal, strength when it seems all is lost, and shining hope in the darkness. This poignant novel will stay with you long after you've turned the last page."
–Dawn Beecroft Teetzel, author of *My Mary*

"With its twisty plot, admirable heroine, rich historic details, and cameo appearances by Charles Dickens, *Locked in Silence* takes readers on a fascinating journey into the past and explores the timeless themes of love, forgiveness, and redemption."
–Jill Caugherty, author of *The View from Half Dome* and *Waltz in Swing Time*

LOCKED IN SILENCE

PART I: CHERRY HILL

CHAPTER 1

Years ago, my brother Aiden and I stood outside this solid stone fortress, scarcely a mile from our home in the Moyamensing section of Philadelphia. I held Aiden's hand and trembled as he told me about the prisoners who were executed here and the misery of those locked within its walls. I was thankful I would never see the inside of such a place.

But then three months ago I was brought here as an inmate. The warden said I should be grateful, should thank God for the blessing of being here—even as they stripped me of my name, telling me that henceforth I was to be addressed as B358, not Elizabeth O'Meara; even as they stripped me of my clothing, bathed me, and gave me new clothing with my new "name" sewn into the cloth; even as they threw a sack over my head so I would not see anyone or anything as I was led to my cell.

The warden said I should sink to my knees and give praise to my Maker that I was at Eastern State Penitentiary (which was called Cherry Hill for the cherry trees that once grew on this spot), and not in Moyamensing Prison, where I would have been packed tight with a multitude of sinners—pickpockets, thieves, drunkards, murderers— drowning in their odors, deafened by their cries, suffocating in my own wailing, as bodies pressed and hands probed.

"Look here," said the guard who had brought me to my cell and removed the hood. "You have a toilet that is flushed a few times a week—not many people have even seen such a thing—and a skylight that lets you tell day from night. This is your home now. You will not see any other prisoners or hear their voices, for that would be a distraction. From now on you must listen to God's voice."

I shall try to give thanks for the blessings bestowed upon me here at Cherry Hill. Surely, the Quakers, upon whose principles this penitentiary was founded, will protect me from the men who in that other prison could take advantage of me with the same impunity as *he* did.

•   •   •

Sarah. My child. I knew her name before she was born. Now I must think about her and the crime of which I am accused. I must look into my heart and repent, for that is why I am here at Eastern State Penitentiary in this year of Our Lord 1848.

The Quakers say uninterrupted repentance will save me. They believe all people are good, everyone has an inner light, and by reflecting in solitude, the sinner will discover this light and uncover it to the world. But how can I repent for a crime I never committed?

Even before the cruel twist of fate that brought me here, I was not a stranger to injustice. I had been surrounded by it—all those poor souls imprisoned by the color of their skin, struggling to be free. Although I was once a part of the movement to right that injustice, I am now a prisoner myself. I am but eighteen years of age, and all the time in God's great universe would not be enough to bring back the memory of something that never happened. My baby is dead, but I did not kill her.

I have now spent three months confined to this cell, but it already feels like forever. The walls are so thick I hear no sounds, no voices of the other prisoners. The meager furnishings—bed, clothes rack, stool, table—and the shattering silence are my only companions. I have not yet grown accustomed to the stench of human waste, but I imagine I will in time.

I grow fearful of losing my memories as they become increasingly torn and frayed. I long to talk to my dear brother, but no outside visitors except the priest are allowed here. No letters from home, no newspapers. My personal contact is limited to the prison staff: the guards, the matron who takes me to the bathing stalls every two weeks, a Quaker morals instructor, and the warden, who calls on me from time to time. Aside from these brief visits, there is no respite from the unremitting strangulation of total silence, save for the sound of rodents burrowing inside the walls in the dead of night. On more than one occasion, I have seen a rat scamper across my cell. I'm thankful they ignore me—not seeking sustenance from my body—and hope they continue finding food elsewhere.

Today, as every day, I read the Bible to pass the time, even though it is the King James version and not the Catholic bible. I don't know the difference between the two, but it was important enough to many people—so many, in fact, that it sparked a bloody riot between Protestants and Catholics four years ago.

Later on, in my mind's eye, I conjure up the faces of my family, my friends, the violence that has shaken my neighborhood, the hatred of the former slaves and freemen who live among us. When Jesus said, "Inasmuch as ye have done it unto one of the least of these my brethren, ye have done it unto me," did He not count the Negroes as his brethren? I must speak to the priest about this.

This afternoon, I am startled by a knock on the door. I rise abruptly from my chair as a man enters my cell bearing writing paper, a pen, and an inkpot. I am confused, but then remember that after a few months of confinement with only the Bible as distraction, we are allowed writing and reading material. For the first time since my arrival at the penitentiary, my spirits are lifted at the prospect of setting my thoughts down on paper.

My visitor is a short man, hardly older than me, with a round face and body. His features are ordinary save for the large bushy mustache that turns down at the ends. Mustaches are not in fashion, and I find it difficult not to stare. There is also something odd about his mouth. He sets everything down on the little table and turns to look at me. My fingers are itching to wrap themselves around the pen.

"Th...thank you, sir."

"So...you know how to read and write." His speech is slurred, as if he is intoxicated, although I smell no alcohol on his breath. He pronounces the word "so" like "show," and I realize the reason for the mustache. He has a harelip.

I clear my throat. "Yes sir, I do know how to read." I point to the Bible lying on my bed.

"Everyone here gets a Bible, but not many know how to read it. I'm surprised you can, being a girl...and Irish and all."

I should be offended by his assumption that I am unschooled, but I will not hold it against him, because he has shown me kindness.

My primary school teacher told me that speaking well would open doors, so I wouldn't have to make my living by cleaning houses. In an effort to speak properly, I practiced reading stories and poems aloud, imitating the words and phrases I learned, and in time I sounded more like my teachers than my classmates. This pleased me, although my manner of speech was often a source of ridicule. "Who do you think you are? The Queen of England?" my schoolmates would taunt me. "You're acting all high and mighty, but you ain't no better than us." And that was true. In many ways, I was no better than anyone else. I just sounded that way. And what was wrong with that?

"Well, sir," I respond to this kind gentleman who brings me the writing materials, "I do know how to read and write. And I am grateful for what you have brought me."

"I must tell you that it is highly unusual for a prisoner to request writing materials, even when they're permitted to have them, since most here have not learned to read or write."

He stands close, and I take a step back, wary of his intentions. After all, he is a man. He must sense my discomfort, for he steps back as well.

"I must say I'm surprised that your demeanor is so...normal. Most prisoners start to take leave of their senses after only a few weeks of isolation."

I say nothing, but think: *If only you had known me when I was free and headstrong, before everything turned against me.* I may have retained a remnant of that strength, and that has kept me from going mad until now. But there are so many more months of solitude yet to endure, it is unlikely I will keep my sanity.

"You are free to write whatever you like," he says.

"I am grateful, sir."

"We hope that you will write about the terrible thing you did. What you've learned from your solitary contemplation. How you are repenting for your sins, asking God for forgiveness."

The word "sins" sounds like "shins" when he says it. At times he sounds like he is speaking through his nose, and he substitutes puffs of air for certain sounds.

I nod. "That is what they told me when they brought me here. They told me..." He is so sympathetic that I am tempted to tell him everything. Why I don't belong here—give voice to my frustrations. But to what end? So I hold my tongue.

"As I said, you are free to write whatever you wish. We will not read it."

I do not know whether to believe him. "Can I write a letter to my brother?"

"Yes, of course. Whatever you wish."

A pleasant surprise. "When I arrived, they told me I would not be allowed to send or receive letters."

"That is true. There is no communication allowed with anyone outside these walls. Your letters will not leave these confines."

Ah, nothing has changed. But I won't allow myself to linger over my disappointment, as I have learned that it is futile to waste my energy on dashed hope.

"A question, sir. Is that all the paper I am allowed?" He had brought only a few sheets.

"My, you are ambitious." He chuckles. "I'll make sure you get as much paper as you'd like. A journal, perhaps." Do I detect a hint of sarcasm in his voice, or is it admiration?

"Yes, thank you. I would dearly love a journal."

"I will bring you a sheaf of hand-sewn papers that can serve you as a journal."

"That would be wonderful."

"I'm afraid mine will be the last voice you'll hear for a long time, except for that of your priest, your morals instructor, and the warden who will look in on you regularly," he says as he leaves my cell.

I sit on the bed, reliving the unaccustomed experience of communicating with another human being. But not for long. There is much to be written. I pull up my chair to the little table and grasp the pen, but find myself momentarily frozen, my mind a maelstrom of swirling memories, bits and pieces of conversations, images, and sounds. No matter. I will write everything before my thoughts disappear into the mists of solitude.

The tip of my pen connects with the paper, and the words explode on to the page. I write quickly, afraid some of it may be illegible, even to me. But I cannot stop to correct spelling, grammar, or incomplete thoughts. I sing with my pen, although it is a song only I can hear.

CHAPTER 2

Every month, a Quaker lady comes to give me moral instruction. A tall, angular woman with brown hair pulled back into a tight bun, she sits inside my cell and reads passages from the Scriptures. She talks to me about my inner light and the healing power of silence. She uses "thee" and "thou" as if I were holy, for where else do those words appear other than in the Bible? I beg her to call me by my name, but she insists on addressing me as B358. She explains that shedding our former identities while we are in prison enables us to emerge from confinement both reformed and transformed.

And once each month, I am also visited by a priest. The first time he came, he reminded me so much of Father Brennan that I cried from homesickness. We talk about spiritual matters like repentance, forgiveness, and the grace of God. That's when I dare to ask him about why the Church does not speak out against slavery, and why slaveholders are welcome to attend Mass. Before my incarceration, I dared not question a man of God; but it appears that prison has unexpectedly liberated my tongue. As he is a priest, I am sure he will state his opposition to slavery, but he does not.

"Slavery is an unfortunate institution," he says, "which is why it has been outlawed in Pennsylvania. But remember what Paul said in

Ephesians, 6: 5-7. 'Servants, be obedient to them that are your masters according to the flesh, with fear and trembling.' And you know, my child, Africans have been made to know their Savior through the means of slavery. Africans were heathens in their own countries. Here they are learning important lessons about self-control and obedience." He pauses and looks directly into my eyes as he adds, "Something we would *all* do well to practice."

"But Father, how can it be that—"

"It is God's will, my child. It is not for us to question."

"But—" I was going to ask him why the Quaker God looks at slavery so differently from the Catholic one, since the Quakers don't believe in slavery, but he stops me.

"Enough, my child. It's time to talk about the sin that you have committed."

"Forgive me, Father, but I did not commit murder."

"My child, it is a sin to lie. The judge found you guilty. There was a corpse. Your baby's corpse. Let me remind you that..." He provides details. He cites witnesses. It is a sad story he tells, but it is not mine, because if it were, I'd remember some of it, wouldn't I? I will listen no more.

Since I do not confess to the sin of murder, he gives me my penance for the sin of lying.

After he's gone, the guards pass me the dinner and supper trays at the appointed times, but I eat nothing. Instead, I lie in my bed repeating the Our Fathers and Hail Marys the priest has assigned as my penance. "Holy Mary Mother of God...Mother of God...Mother..."

That night, the nightmares begin.

My baby is close, just out of reach. I can't see her, but I know it's my Sarah. I hold out my arms. "Please let me hold her." Why are they so cruel? "Please let me hold her."

I wake up screaming.

CHAPTER 3

Something has awakened me. I sit up in bed, heart pounding, confused, but the fog slowly clears as I look around. In the six months since I was given writing materials, nothing has changed: the heavy oak door with the food slot; the cold-water tap; the heating pipes; the clothes rack; the toilet; the iron bedstead; the wooden table and chair.

And there's the stench. The ever-present stink of human waste. Even after they flush the funnel-shaped toilet every two or three days, the smell remains, having seeped into my clothes and my skin and penetrated the thick stone walls of my cell. I am most aware of it when I awaken, after which its effect on me lessens, but it's always there.

Silence reigns within these walls. But...what is that sound in the corridor? Something creaking, like the groan of the loose floorboard on the steps of the rowhouse where I live...lived...like someone opening the privy door in our yard. I take a moment to realize that I'm hearing the food cart being rolled down the corridor. Normally, the wheels are covered with leather to muffle the sound, but the covering must have slipped off. It is as if everyone and everything in this wretched place has taken a vow of silence.

A tap at the door announces the arrival of breakfast, and I hurry over to receive the bowl and plate that are slipped through the food slot by a gloved hand.

There can be no touching here. I remember how I once enjoyed the tender touch of the man I loved. Thomas. I allow myself to remember how the edges of his mouth curved upward every time he caught sight of me, as if every meeting was our first.

The morning meal is coffee and cornmeal mush, but I might as well be eating straw. I will eat their tasteless food and try to remember how I feasted on the nourishing light of the sun, the cool blue of the sky. I will try to remember when the world was my breakfast, supper, and dinner, and the taste of freedom was sweet. And I will try to remember dear Thomas, my first and, I fear, only love, because the promise of true love was forever lost when I was soiled by the Master—the reason I distanced myself from Thomas, determined not to bring shame upon him.

CHAPTER 4

It is painful to write about this, but when I was given this journal, I promised myself I would record everything. So, I write.

·   ·   ·

Robert Northam was the master of the house on Lombard Street, where I spent my days dusting, sweeping, and polishing. The man who saw fit to call me an "Irish wench," while he used me for his personal satisfaction. He told me I was his possession because, he said, if I denied him his due—or worse, if I whispered a word about what he was doing to me—he would fire me, claiming I was a whore. Which would ensure I would never get another respectable job in all of Philadelphia. Since my family needed my income to survive, I endured his abuse.

He insisted I call him "Master" since he was master of the house, and I served at his pleasure. For months he didn't notice me, his attention focused instead on the cook's assistant, a true "Irish wench" if ever there was one, recently arrived from Ireland. Erin was about the same age as me, with a mischievous laugh, creamy skin, generous hips, and ample breasts that were barely constrained by her thin cotton dress. When the Master's eyes traveled the length of her body, she smiled at him brazenly, encouraging his advances. With Erin in the house, I could attend to the silver, china, vases, and gilt-framed mirrors uninterrupted. But—after she left suddenly—it wasn't long before he set his sights on me.

I avoided being in the same room with him as long as I could; but one afternoon when the Mistress was out with the children, he pushed me against the wall of the pantry and lifted my skirts. I struggled to get away from him—pushing and pummeling his chest with my fists—but he held me fast. I managed to scrape the side of his face so fiercely with my fingernails that they drew blood.

"Bitch!" he called me when I cried out, then covered my mouth with his sweaty hand. "Scream again and I'll tell everyone you're a whore." When he was sure that had quieted me, he removed his hand and unfastened his trousers. Then he penetrated me, covering my mouth once again to stifle my cries as the pain cut me to the quick.

"You temptress," he said, and thrust until I could feel blood trickling down my thighs. "It's been so long since I had a virgin. It feels so..." He thrust harder.

Will this never end? My voice screamed inside my head.

"You want it too," he hissed in my ear, "or you would have pinned that hair tighter. You must know that red hair inflames a man." With his hand over my mouth, I could not dispute his lies as he tore me apart.

Afterward I shook with anger and humiliation. He had grievously wounded me, and while I had only inflicted a deep gash on his cheek, it gave me great satisfaction to have left my mark. I hoped the scar would be permanent.

After that first time, the Master found ways to take me in the shadows, surrounded by the smells of the kitchen, while his children played in the next room, or when his wife entertained guests in the parlor. When he was away, which, mercifully, was a good deal of the time, I was free to work unmolested. But when he returned, I was once again his possession. At times I felt sorry for his wife, and at other times I cursed her stupidity and ignorance.

And I cursed myself for not leaving. But he was a powerful man who could ruin my reputation with a few words and deprive me of my livelihood.

CHAPTER 5

At the back of my cell is a locked door that leads to an exercise yard. The space is the width of the cell and is enclosed by four brick walls. I am allowed an hour a day outside, and every day I wait for the guard to unlock the door, so I can breathe fresh air, if only briefly. The walls surrounding the yard are too high for me to see over, but at least this enclosure is open to the sky. Even a hot breeze is refreshing compared to the oven that is my cell.

I had hoped there would be other prisoners outside exercising in their yards, and I would be able to talk to them. But they must stagger the exercise times, for I never hear anyone else outside. Still, I want to yell out over the wall, but my voice is weak, and I don't even know what I'd say.

One day I can no longer stand the silence, so I summon all the breath I can muster and shout "Hello!" once, twice, even though I risk punishment. I am starved for the sound of a voice, even if that voice is my own. "Is anyone out there? Can you hear me?" When the guard comes, he calls me a she-devil and pulls the hood over my face as punishment. I struggle against him and scream myself hoarse, but my anger makes him laugh. After that, I decide to keep my wits about me and stay quiet, not wanting to risk the same punishment. But there might come a time when I will no longer be able to contain myself. More and more, my mind has a mind of its own.

Every day I tread the same path. Ten paces along one side of the yard, six paces across the far end, ten paces down the other side of the yard, and six paces across to complete the circuit. I walk clockwise, raising my face to the sky, inhaling for two steps, exhaling for two, and imagine I'm sharing every breath I take with the people I left behind who breathe this same air—my friends, my brother Aiden, my departed father, my dear Thomas.

I jump and hop to exercise my limbs when I am able, but my body has weakened much over time, and the effort is becoming more and more difficult. I have been in prison over a year now and have tread the same path through scorching summer days, when crisp autumn breezes blow, and even in winter, when my woolen clothing and yarn stockings provide little protection from the cold. So I wrap my blanket around my shoulders and continue to walk a path that ends where it begins.

Today as I circle the exercise yard, a flock of geese passes overhead, lifting my heart, reminding me of...of...what? I cry out in frustration—another memory gone. Or maybe not. Perhaps I can coax it back to life.

Back in my cell, I pick up a piece of charcoal and draw the bird on the wall. The tip of the charcoal skips over the cracked plaster. The result is more bird-*like* than bird—a raggedy, stretched-out M. No matter. I draw the bird again and again until a section of the wall is covered with my primitive designs, and the charcoal is worn to a nub. Then I sit on the bed and gaze at my handiwork until it grows dark.

Perhaps when I wake up the next morning, the sight of all those birds will bring back the memory. When that doesn't happen, I open my journal and write: "My memories are a patchwork, like an unfinished quilt." And just like that, I remember where I saw those birds. On a quilt. So I continue to write.

·   ·   ·

"Red. Hey, Red. Over here!"

I was on my way to the store to buy thread for Ma when I heard a familiar voice and shuddered. Timmy Doyle, schoolyard bully and ruffian, calling out to me from across the street. We both went to the Ringgold School, which most of the Irish children in the neighborhood attended. Timmy was almost twelve, a year older than me, so we were in different classes. Still, he never seemed to miss the opportunity to rub up against me in the hall with a self-satisfied smile, just to let me know it was not accidental. And sometimes I caught him looking at me, smirking and winking, which never failed to send a chill down my spine.

I'd rather be across the street from anyone other than Timmy, with his close-set eyes, pug nose, thick lips, and greasy black hair. Timmy, who never failed to remind me that his cousin was William (Bull) McMullen, already well known in Moyamensing and Southwark for roughing people up.

"Red, you're the prettiest girl in all of Philadelphia, and I want you to be my girlfriend. So come here—there's something I want to show you."

He was halfway across the street before I could get my legs to move. Then, heart pumping, powered by fear, I ran as fast as I could. The people on the street paid me no mind, since there were always children running in the streets. I dodged street peddlers, and women holding babies, and men coming out of bars. I stayed ahead of him for a time, but he finally caught up with me. Grabbing my shoulder, he dragged me into an alley, which was as dark and empty as the street was busy. He laughed triumphantly as he shoved me against the wall. I pushed back, but he was stronger.

"What do you want from me?" I gasped, still struggling to free myself from his grip.

"Just a kiss, Red. C'mon...please...," he begged.

"Get awa—" I screamed.

That's when he pressed his mouth against mine so hard I could hardly breath. As I squirmed, he took one of my hands and tried to jam it down his pants. *What was he doing?* I kicked him and he yelped, loosening his grip on me. I pushed him out of the way and ran like the wind, up one street and down the next, crying out for help. But Timmy was not far behind, shouting, "Stop her. Gotta catch my little sister or my ma will give me hell." People must have believed him since they ignored my cries for help.

I turned a corner on to a block I'd never been down before. I stopped and bent over, gasping for air. Timmy's shouts were getting closer. I noticed the houses were not unlike those on my block, the only difference being the skin color of the people who lived in them.

"Come with me, child," said a voice above me.

I looked up to see a heavyset Black woman in a print dress, with a mass of curly hair piled high on her head. She took my hand and led me up the front stoop and into her house. Before she closed the door, I heard Timmy yell, "I seen where you gone, Red. You'll pay for what you did to me."

"Come sit down, child. You're safe now."

"Thank you, Mrs...."

"Washington. And you are—?"

"Elizabeth...Lizzy O'Meara."

"You looked scared to death, Lizzy. Poor dear. You're still shaking. Come, sit down here," she said, pointing to a green velvet chair, "and let me get you some water."

Yes, scared to death. Who knows what would have happened to me if she hadn't taken me in. I remember that parlor, the maroon curtains with tassels, the sofa with carved wood and maroon cushions, the loveseat. All the furniture was brightly polished, and the smell of freshly baked bread filled the room.

Ma often said that Blacks were dirty n——s, and until I met Mrs. Washington, I had no reason to doubt her. As far as I knew, most of the colored people in the neighborhood were jammed into makeshift houses situated in a cobweb of alleys a few blocks south of our house. Ma said "those people" preferred it that way, and even if they had decent houses, they wouldn't know how to keep them tidy. But there I was in a house that was cleaner and much finer than mine.

When Mrs. Washington went to the kitchen to bring me some bread, my eyes were drawn to a large quilt hanging on the wall facing me. I'd never seen anything like it. There were red and white stripes, black silhouettes that looked like people, black wings against a light blue background, and a wavy blue stripe along the bottom.

"I saw you looking at that quilt," said Mrs. Washington, handing me a plate of warm, buttered bread. "There's a story behind it. Would you like to hear it?"

As I nodded, I couldn't help but wonder why a colored woman would want to tell a story about a quilt to a stranger. A white girl at that. When I asked her, she laughed and said, "Well, you ran right into my arms. Who better to tell?"

Although Mrs. Washington talked for a long time, most of the details of the story are lost to me now; but I remember just enough. She said that the quilt told the story of slavery. There were blackbirds flying unshackled, high above the troubled world. No one had clipped their wings, she said, and they were free to fly with their children and parents and grandparents, all together. The white stripes represented the lines of cotton the slaves picked in the hot sun. And the red stripes represented the bloody backs of the men and women who were whipped. The wavy blue patch at the bottom of the quilt was a river of tears, and the black figures on the banks were the slaves who cried the river into being and were about to cross it to freedom.

I closed my eyes in an effort to rid myself of the thought of men and women being lashed until their backs were bloody and scarred, but the image stayed with me.

When it was time to leave, Mrs. Washington offered to accompany me home, but I told her I'd be all right walking alone. I would have loved her protection, but walking home with a Black woman would raise all kinds of questions. Before I left, she said she hoped I'd come back to visit when her daughter was home. "You'd like her," she said. Then she hugged me, and I lingered a moment in her warmth before running off.

The memory of the bloody stripes conjures up another incident that followed not long after Mrs. Washington's kindness to me.

My mother was weaving straw into the braids she sold to a hatmaker, and complaining to her friend Mrs. Moore about how good, hardworking Irishmen were losing jobs to n——s. Mrs. Moore was a large woman with unkempt brown hair and a permanent scowl etched by deep lines that extended from the sides of her nose to the corners of her mouth. Her craggy voice matched her face. They talked about how it disgusted them to see whites and Blacks mixing and said it shouldn't be allowed.

Did they know slaves were being beaten bloody? I wondered. Did they care? When Mrs. Moore squeezed my arm affectionately before leaving our house, the touch of her calloused hands sent a shiver down my spine.

CHAPTER 6

Blood. Pooling between my legs, staining the sheets crimson. A woman with thick fingers is holding my baby just out of reach. I cannot see her face, but I can make out her form in silhouette—tall and broad. Like Mrs. Moore, but not Mrs. Moore.

The dream feels so real, I am surprised my sheet and nightshirt are not bloodstained. I soothe myself by imagining Aiden handing my baby to me. He was living at home with Ma and me when I was waiting to give birth, and I have no doubt I'd still have my Sarah if he'd been there when she was born. He told me why he had to leave, but I can't remember what he said. And he promised he'd return before the baby came, but he never did, leaving me there alone with Ma, whose anger boiled over when she was with me. Aiden probably had a good reason for his absence, but now I'd probably never know.

I long for the sound of my brother's voice, because I was closer to him than to anyone else. I smile, remembering how hard it was for him to lie. His untruths were unmasked by the scarlet that bloomed like roses on his cheeks. Like the day we met Lucy Washington, who was to become my best friend and change my life in so many ways.

I open my journal and pick up my pen.

• • •

"Mrs. Murphy saw you two playing with two n——s the other day," Ma said, confronting us one morning as we were headed to school. I was almost eleven and on the brink of womanhood, and already I was the same height as my mother. Aiden, who was two years older than me, towered over her. "Is that true?" she asked, looking up at him.

"No, ma'am," he answered. His face flushed red as the blood of Jesus on the cross, but Ma was already glaring at me.

"No, ma'am," I repeated emphatically.

"Well, don't you be playing with those n——s."

"No, ma'am," I repeated, avoiding her gaze.

As she turned back to Aiden, I jabbed my elbow into his side.

"We promise," he stammered, looking down at the floor to hide the red bloom on his cheeks, knowing it was a promise we had no intention of keeping.

Although I'd intended to visit Mrs. Washington soon after I met her, six months passed before I saw her again. And it was only by chance that Aiden and I found ourselves on her street, which is when we met her daughter Lucy.

We were walking to school as usual, when we were blocked by an overturned horse and cart, vegetables strewn everywhere. So we took a different route and turned a corner on to her street.

"Aiden, this is Mrs. Washington's street. Remember I told you about the day I met her?"

I had told him everything about meeting Mrs. Washington—except the part about my encounter with Timmy Doyle. I would never tell my brother or anyone else about what had happened in that alley. Although Timmy hadn't touched me after that, he'd taken to staring at the place where my breasts were beginning to bud, telling me he'd "wait for me and stay pure for me." I didn't know exactly what he meant, but his smirk conveyed something that was far removed from purity. And there was a hunger in his eyes that scared me.

"That's her house," I said, pointing to it as we passed by.

A girl in a faded cotton dress was sitting on the bottom step of the stoop watching a dark-skinned boy playing the cup-and-ball game in the street. The girl's skin was light—darker than mine, but not by much. Her hair was curly and reddish-blond. When I extended my hand, she took it.

"Hi, my name's Lizzy. What's yours?"

"My name's Lucy. Pleased to meet you, Miss Lizzy."

"Just Lizzy. All right?"

She smiled. "Pleased to meet you, Lizzy."

Although it was possible she had never shaken hands with a white girl before, there was nothing awkward in her movements. And there was nothing awkward in my movements either, since I'd already hugged a Black woman. Mrs. Washington was right when she said I would like her daughter.

"This is my brother, Aiden," I said as he stuck out his hand like I had done.

Lucy shook his hand, "Pleased to meet you, too." She pointed to the boy in the street. "That's my cousin Isaac Freeman. Come here, Isaac, and introduce yourself proper."

Isaac stopped playing and joined us on the sidewalk.

"My daddy's friend smuggled him up from Virginia," said Lucy. "He's only staying with us till his father and mother buy their freedom."

Like the slaves on Mrs. Washington's quilt, waiting to cross the river of tears, I thought.

Isaac looked at Aiden and me, then quickly lowered his eyes and backed away.

More than once I'd seen a white man refusing to yield to a Black man in his path, waiting until the Negro stepped aside to let him pass. If the Negro took too long, the white man would say, "Move, n——," or even push him aside. My teacher said that according to the Constitution, a Negro was counted as three-fifths of a white man. I remember wondering at the time how one man could be counted as three-fifths of a man? Didn't they know their arithmetic? Three-fifths did not equal one.

"Don't be afraid, Isaac," said Lucy. "You are in Philadelphia now, not in Virginia."

He looked relieved, and then came closer to shake hands with Aiden and me. "I be twelve," he said.

"I *am* twelve, Isaac." Lucy looked at him sternly. "You have to practice what they teach you at school." She turned to us. "We go to the Lombard Street Colored School, but most of us call it the Bird School, 'cause the principal's name is Mr. Bird, and everybody likes him. Some people say it's the best school in Philadelphia, even though all the teachers except Mr. Bird are colored. Isaac, you must keep working hard to sound like a free man, because that's what you are. Isaac *Free-man*."

We all giggled.

"How old are you, Lucy?" I asked.

"I'm ten."

"You're only a year younger than me," I said, pleased at the thought. "You know, Lucy, I was in your house once, and your mama gave me a slice of delicious bread and told me—"

"You know what happens to n— lovers?" yelled a boy from across the street.

"We'd best go into the house now," Lucy said to Isaac, and they hurried up the steps and went inside as the boy and his friends cursed and threatened them.

"You're worse than them n——s," one of the boy's friends called out to me and Aiden. "They can't help what they are, but you can keep them in their place."

"They can't scare us, Aiden," I said with a lot more confidence than I felt.

But Aiden was no longer standing next to me; he was at the curb, staring at the boys on the opposite side of the street. I recognized them from our school, and I knew they were a year or two older than my brother, but Aidan was at least a head taller than they were. They got quiet for a moment before resuming their taunts. I joined Aiden at the curb.

"I got knuckle-dusters in my pocket," he said loudly, within earshot of our tormentors, "and I know how to use them." He put one of his hands in his pocket and took my hand with the other. "Let's get these feckin' Irish thugs, Lizzy," he said.

How I loved him at that moment.

The two of us headed across the street, me trying to look cocky as my knees threatened to buckle. If those boys had had knuckle-dusters or knives or some other weapon in their pockets, the good Lord knows what would have happened. But God was on our side that day, and after one of them shouted, "N—— friends," they swaggered off.

I had never seen Aiden stand up for himself like he did that day; and I believe that experience taught him something about his own strength, just as I had learned something about my own.

Before we exited the block, I took a last look at Lucy's house, and there in the window was Mrs. Washington waving goodbye. And although we were too far away to see her face, I was sure she was smiling.

As Aiden and I walked the rest of the way to school—his arm around me—I felt relieved. And powerful.

CHAPTER 7

Although it is difficult to measure the passage of time, I think I am somewhere into my second year of imprisonment because I arrived in the summer, and another summer has passed. I break up the hours by reading or writing, and recently a matron came to teach me how to stitch properly. I have been given needles, thread, a thimble, and a workbench, and I stitch fabric into shirts. In my other life I would not have been drawn to such work since I do not have nimble fingers, but I am learning. I must concentrate or I might prick a finger and ruin the fabric, for which I would undoubtedly be punished. I'd like to think that focusing on a task such as this will strengthen my brain and improve my memory, but I remember less and less.

Today my eyes are tired from the hours spent sewing in this dim light, so I lie down on the bed and gaze up at the skylight. The guard who brought me to this cell told me that having a skylight was a privilege for which I should be thankful. But my Quaker instructor tells me that the skylight is more than just a window on the world. It is the "eye of God," and it should be a constant reminder that even when no one's here, God is always watching. Today I feel God's eye upon me, judging me. I meet His gaze and He blinks. Is it a real eye? It's getting harder for me to know what is real and what is not. But there, He blinks again. I am sure it is a real eye, a monster eye that never lets me out of its sight. What is He telling me? That I am guilty of the crime of which I'm accused? That I am the monster? No, that cannot be.

Now the sky is dark, but I still feel His eye on me as I fall asleep.

I see a monster with an eye for a face. The eye-face blinks, and when it opens, I am on that bloody sheet, reaching out to hold my baby. The woman who is big like Mrs. Moore but is not Mrs. Moore holds my baby above me, squeezing her tiny arms with her rough hands. Why can't I see my baby's face?

I awaken to another day of silence. Above me, clouds block the light, and the gloom weighs me down like a heavy cloak. Desperate for sounds of life, I try to imagine myself back home: horses *clop-clopping* on cobblestones; the joyous singsong of the peddlers, "Here's milk, ho," "Buy any peaches?" "Bake pears," "Oysters, oysters, here's your fine fat salt oysters"; children chanting "Oranges and lemons"; mothers calling their children in to dinner; babies crying. (No! That is a sound I cannot bear.)

Later in the day, the clouds disperse, and the circle of sky is as bright and blue as my father's eye. And I hear Da's voice—so sweet when he would hold me on his lap and sing songs from the old country.

In Dublin's fair city

Where the girls are so pretty

I first set my eyes on sweet Molly Malone

As she wheeled her wheel barrow

Through streets broad and narrow

Crying, "Cockles and mussels, alive, alive, oh!"

I must write quickly before I forget his voice and how much he loved me.

•   •   •

Da died six years ago, yet I still miss him so. He was barely forty-six years of age. Such a gentle man. And handsome. Square-chinned with a prominent cleft and reddish-brown hair.

Each night, Da would come home sweaty, smelling of the Baldwin Locomotive Works where he worked. Ma said it was a dirty odor and couldn't wait to scrub it from the house on bath day, but to me the scent of smoke and ash was perfume because it smelled like Da. I never tired of hearing him tell me about the fiery hot liquid he poured into giant molds, and the metal he hammered, and the huge gears and shafts and pistons. I begged him to let me visit, but he said it was no place for a girl. Although I couldn't go inside, I could see the factory from almost anywhere on Broad Street if I looked north—the huge brick buildings stretching for two blocks, flames and black smoke billowing from their chimneys like the fires of hell.

I was so proud of Da, building locomotives that carried people along Broad Street, east on Market Street to the Delaware River; south to Grays Ferry, and farther still, to Germantown and Norristown and New York and Washington, and places I could only imagine. And whenever a train passed, I liked to think that Da had made a piece of it.

One night after Da came home from work, he was called in by the sheriff to help control a riot that had broken out a couple of blocks south of us. Da was a volunteer policeman, and when the night watch couldn't control the fights between Protestants and Catholics, or whites against coloreds, the sheriff called in volunteers and deputized them. And if the watchmen and volunteer policemen couldn't control the violence, the sheriff would call in the militia.

By the time they came to summon Da, flames and smoke were already rising high in the night sky. "It has to be the shanties," said Da. "All that fire."

The shanties were wooden shacks on both sides of the narrow alleys, built onto the backs of the regular houses that faced the street. No windows, only holes next to the door to let light in and smoke out. The hose and engine companies were already on their way, each one eager to be the first to arrive, roaring down our street.

"Didn't you ever want to be a fireman, Da?" said Aiden. "It looks so exciting. I'd like to work for one of those hose companies when I'm old enough."

"Not for me, lad. Nor for you."

"But—"

"You know those street gangs—the Killers, the Rats, and the like? Well, once they started running with the hose companies, the whole lot of them were after fighting each other instead of fighting fires. You wouldn't want to be one of those hooligans, now, would you, lad?"

"No, Da."

"That's me boy."

"But Da," I asked, "why do they have hoses and pumps if they don't put out fires."

"Perhaps I exaggerated a wee bit. Of course, they put out fires, but mostly when it's white people's houses that burn. Many's the time I've seen them stand there watching a colored family's home burn to the ground. I've seen the Moya lads turn their hoses away from them and towards the ones that belong to whites, to protect *them* from the fires. And then laugh at the houses that are on fire and the people running for their lives. And they've been known to set fires of their own, just to see the colored people run."

Ma called from the kitchen. "And there you be, Brendan, unarmed, risking your own life for what? Sometimes I suspect you care more about *them* than about us."

"'Tis not true, Katie. When I'm called to do a job, I do it."

Ma came out of the kitchen and stood at the front door, blocking Da.

"'Tis not worth your life, Brendan. Let the militia take care of it."

"Och, 'tis me job, Katie, so please get out of the way, woman, and let me do it."

In the end, Da always got his way.

Everyone called Black people n——s: Ma, the neighbors, the boys and girls at my school, everyone. They spit the word out like rotten meat. Everyone but Da. I sometimes wondered if Da was the only person in Philadelphia, besides Aiden and me, who didn't say n——.

"Why don't you ever call them that?" I asked him one night as he tucked me into bed. "Everyone else does. Even Ma."

He pulled up a chair next to my bed and told me a story. I've forgotten most of it now, but what I do remember is something about a Black neighbor saving his life when he was fresh off the boat—a time when Blacks and Irish lived in the same neighborhood because they were all poor back then and had nowhere else to go. Da said that when someone does you a kindness, even if he talks or looks different from you, that someone becomes a person. And you owe him a kindness in return. Do unto others.

I have forgotten so much already. Why bother writing when there are so many holes? Once again a dark cloud hangs over the skylight, and there is not enough light to see the page, so I put down my pen. Soon the rain comes. The skylight glass is thick, blocking the sound, but I see the first drops hit, then more drops, like tears in God's eye.

I ache from the pain of my father's absence and soothe myself by singing his favorite song, "The Parting Glass." I sing it softly like a lullaby.

And all I've done for want of wit

To mem'ry now I can't recall

So fill to me the parting glass

Good night and joy be to you all

I hope the rain will stop and there will be enough light to continue writing. If not, I'll have to wait until the sun rises tomorrow.

CHAPTER 8

It's cold in the cell today, and I wear my woolen coat as I go about my business. As I am finishing a shirt that I've been stitching for most of the day, I prick my finger, ruining the garment with my blood. I've never done such a thing before, but I'm sure I will suffer the consequences when they come to collect my work. A bloodstained shirt.

A bloodstained sheet.

I squeeze my pricked finger releasing more blood onto the white shirt. Not enough. I prick my finger again and again, and soon the white shirt is covered with red spots.

I am lying on a bloody sheet, reaching out for my baby. I grab the big woman's arm, squeezing it to release her hold on the baby and...

But it is not an arm I'm squeezing. It is the ruined shirt I crumpled into a ball. I fling it against the wall, where it leaves a red blotch before dropping to the floor. I pick it up and bang it against the wall, crying, "No more, no more!"

"I saw that," says someone through the food slot, and I drop the shirt. "Anger like that is not tolerated in this institution."

Even in our solitude we are not alone. As if reading my mind, he says, "We can look in on you at any time, so mind what you're doing. Oh, the things I've seen. Men performing unnatural acts on themselves...you know what I mean." He chuckles. No, I don't know what he means, but he continues as if I did. "Men will be men, even if the act is sinful. And they are punished, as you will be for what you have done."

I hear him opening the door to my cell. As he enters, he hands me a hood and says, "Put this on."

I protest that I am not required to wear a hood inside my cell, but he insists.

"Bloodying the shirt by accident would not alone have been worthy of punishment. But I saw what you did and heard what you said."

I wait in silence for my punishment.

"Take off your coat."

"I don't understand."

"You understand English, don't you? I said: Take—off—your—coat! Or I'll do it for you."

I remove my coat and he grabs it. "Now you will spend the next twenty-four hours in this cell shivering as you think about what you did."

I hear the key in the lock, and I am once again alone in my cell. The cold has not yet penetrated my body, but even when it does, I'm not sure it will be enough to cool my anger. Do the kindly Quakers know about what goes on inside their wretched institution?

He may still be watching me, so I keep my mouth shut. But I need words, so I remove the hood, sit down at my table, and open my journal. I'll need to write quickly, for the cold is making it difficult to hold a pen steady.

I write about the bloody shirt, the punishment, what they are doing to me, all of it—and I forget about the cold, if only for a few minutes.

CHAPTER 9

The matron brings me a list of books from the prison library. When I first arrived, the only book they allowed me was the Bible, but they became more lenient over time. I love to read and was told in school that I was a fine reader, because I read a lot, including books assigned to older children. But I had never heard of any of the books on the list. The first one I chose was by James Fenimore Cooper. The Mohican story was a little hard to follow, but I persisted; so when I got to the end, I reread it and enjoyed it immensely. Scattered among today's list are several primers, probably intended for those prisoners who have not yet learned to read. Today I select one of them—*McGuffey's Second Reader*—hoping it will spark memories of my school days.

When the book is delivered, I leaf through it, and it has the desired effect. I am immediately transported back to my old schoolyard, where I would sit alone on the ground with my back against the fence, reading while the other children played. I was more interested in the words and illustrations on the page than in doing whatever the other girls were doing—more often than not playing house and tending imaginary babies. My schoolmates would make fun of me—even Aiden did from time to time; but he admitted he was jealous of my memory, which rarely failed me, and he predicted I would probably be famous one day. My brother didn't take to reading and spelling the way I did, but he excelled at arithmetic and was always at the top of the class. He was lucky, because math is a quiet skill, so no one made fun of him.

I turn to a page with a poem I remember well.

"Hark! My mother's voice I hear,

Sweet that voice is to my ear;

Ever soft, it seems to tell,

Dearest child, I love thee well."

Above the poem is an illustration of a mother seated in a chair, holding a little girl on her lap. In what world were there mothers who held their children and whispered loving words to them? Not mine, although I did have a vague recollection of Ma's fingers stroking my hair before I went to bed, and memories of her singing a lullaby, but that might have been true only in my imagination. In any case, when Da died, Ma's affection for me died with him.

The little girl in the illustration is cradling a doll in her arms. I remember I had a doll, but I never held it like that little girl held hers. I remember. With the *McGuffey's* open on the table, I pick up my pen and write in my journal.

•   •   •

Dolls are stupid. That's what I thought when Ma gave me a rag doll for Christmas one year, although I never would have said it aloud. Why did she think I would want that? The doll wore a blue calico dress, a gingham apron, and a bonnet to match. She even had little shoes made of leather. Of course, I thanked Ma when she gave it to me and told her it was beautiful, and she said it was important to play with dolls to learn how to be a good mother.

I lied when I told Ma the doll was beautiful. In truth, I hated it. Ma had drawn red hair like mine on her head, red patches on her cheeks, dots for eyes, and a sad little bow-shaped mouth as if she was scolding me. I took a piece of red chalk I'd found outside the Fine Arts Academy and drew a smiling curve of a mouth. I gave her a name (which I forget now), hoping I would love her if she had a name. But I didn't. I left her under my bed when I went out to play, but when Ma found out, she retrieved the doll and told me to take her outside and play with her, so I did. I sat on the stoop and rocked her.

I recall putting the doll down on my lap and covering my ears when I heard the knife grinder's cry on our street: "Any knives, razors, scissors to grind?" I prayed he wouldn't stop near our house because the sharpening wheel he used sounded like the scream of a tortured animal. Thankfully, no one needed his services that day.

I pretend-fed the doll leaves and grass and combed her make-believe hair, but it was no fun, so I took her for a walk down Sixth Street to the Washington house. I knew Lucy would like my doll, so I would give it to her, and that was that. On the way, one of the neighbors smiled at me when she saw the doll in my arms and told me I'd make a fine mother someday.

When I got to Lucy's house, Mrs. Washington opened the door and enfolded me in a warm, comforting hug. I'd been to their house many times, and Mrs. Washington's welcome was the same each time. She told me once that Aiden and I were the only white children who played with Lucy and Isaac. She said usually they were chased, spat on, and called names, especially Isaac, who had dark skin like hers.

I held the doll behind my back when Lucy came down the steps, and I told her I had a surprise for her.

"What is it?" she said eagerly.

Would she be disappointed by my primitive, raggedy doll? Once we were settled outside on the stoop, I showed her the doll, and was relieved to see how her eyes lit up.

"You like her?"

"Um hum. She's beautiful. Can I hold her?" I gave her the doll and she cradled it in her arms. "What's her name?"

"What do you think it is?"

"Abigail," she said without hesitation.

"How did you know that was her name? Would you like to keep her?"

Lucy nodded, clutching the doll even closer. "I want to show Abigail to my cousin Georgianna Purvis. She's seven and she loves dolls. Do you want to come with me?"

As we held hands and skipped most of the way to Ninth and Lombard, Lucy told me that Georgianna wasn't her real cousin, and her aunt Harriet and uncle Robert Purvis weren't her real aunt and uncle, but they were very friendly with the Washington family.

"My auntie and uncle are very famous," said Lucy.

"I never heard of them."

"They help slaves get free."

"They're abolitionists?"

"Um hmm. My mama says that if we lived in Charleston, where Uncle Robert came from, we'd be slaves. I'm glad I'm not a slave."

"I am, too. Glad *you're* not a slave, that is."

The Purvis' impressive three-story brick house was situated in the middle of the block. Uncle Robert opened the door. He was a striking man, tall with very light skin, dark wavy hair, sideburns, and a warm smile. He told us Georgianna was away, but he invited us in.

"Aunt Harriet and I have to leave for a meeting in a few minutes, but I always have time for my favorite niece."

Aunt Harriet was adjusting her hat in front of a large, ornate hall mirror when she spotted us. She greeted us warmly and gave us each a slice of bread before we left.

It didn't seem to matter to them that I was white, and I couldn't help thinking how different it would have been if I had brought Lucy to my house.

On our way back to Lucy's, she told me she had a secret, but I had to promise not to tell.

"It's a secret, so of course I won't tell."

"Georgianna's house has a special trapdoor."

"A trapdoor? What do they use it for?"

"Come closer and I'll tell you." When I did, she whispered in my ear, "They hide slaves there who are escaping up north of here. All the way to Canada." Then she took my hand. "Let's take Abigail home."

•   •   •

Later, I will write more about hiding slaves, but now I'm getting tired. As I get ready for bed, I think I should consider myself lucky despite my suffering. For if I survive the rest of my sentence, I will be a free, whole person; but if one of them is caught, he or she will once again be only three-fifths of one.

The knife-grinder is following me down the street. If I do not run fast enough, he will take my doll. The knife-grinder is gone, but a little girl is rolling the screeching wheel like a hoop. When I hand Lucy the doll, she screams because the body is gone, and she is holding it only by its head. "You killed her," she sobs.

Ma says, "Bastard child. Better it was born dead." I am lying on the bed, blood pooling between my legs, staining the sheets crimson. That huge woman with the thick fingers is holding my baby out of reach. I see the baby's face now. It's a little girl. My baby girl is crying for me, for her mother, but they won't let me hold her.

When I wake up, I remember the two dreams. The first is a tangled cobweb, thin as gossamer, already half forgotten, soon to disappear. That is the nature of a true dream. But there is a permanence to the second dream. It does not fade. Instead, each time it comes back, the edges are clearer, more defined, more detailed. That is how I know it isn't a dream. It is a memory of something that happened. Last night I remembered that the baby was crying. *She was crying,* which means I did not kill her. I *am* innocent.

CHAPTER 10

I am fortunate that I rarely awaken during the night to relieve myself, as it is dark as pitch in the cell, and the floor is rough on my bare feet. But I have been feeling poorly of late and must hurry to the toilet so as not to soil myself. Tonight, my belly is aching, and although I am loath to get out of bed, I have no choice. Is the stench inside the cell especially strong tonight, or is it just my imagination?

I step off the bed and shudder as my foot hits cold water, and the shock sends a chill through my veins. I do not know what caused this flood, but I know that if I don't take care of my bodily needs right now, I will end up lying in my own filth.

I take a step toward the toilet and...there's something soft and furry under my foot. I scream and struggle to keep my balance. The creature does not bite or move, so it must be dead—most likely a rat or mouse that drowned in the flood. I shiver so, I can barely stay upright as I take another step, then another. Fortunately, no other creatures lie between me and the toilet, and I manage to do my business and return to bed, drying my feet with a rag I use for my monthly flow, before lying down. I gag from the stench but manage to hold onto the contents of my stomach and get to sleep without further incident.

At first light, I discover the cause of the problem. I had neglected to turn the tap off all the way, and the drain was clogged by a cloth. I hope they do not think I did this deliberately. I turn off the tap, remove the rag, and drop it on the floor. Then, carefully stepping around the dead rat, I dry my feet with a towel hanging on my clothes rack and sink back into bed.

I must have drifted off, for I awaken to an unexpected sound. *Tap. Tap.* The sound seems to be coming from inside the walls, but it doesn't sound like an animal. There is a rhythm to the sound. *Tap-tap-tap... tap...tap...tap-tap...tap...tap...tap.* The pattern stops, then repeats. It must be the prisoner in the next cell rapping against the wall. Yes, that's the only explanation. Is he trying to communicate with me? Does the silence mean he is waiting for a response? The pattern changes. *Tap...tap-tap-tap-tap-tap* followed by one loud *TAP*, as if he is angry because I don't respond.

How can I respond when I don't know the language? For surely this is some kind of code. We are all so starved for human connection I am not surprised that my neighbor has found a way to communicate. If only I knew the secret language. I get out of bed, pick up my tin plate, and bang it against the wall, echoing my neighbor's pattern. When the pattern changes, I do the same. Although I have no idea what the pattern means—if it means anything—I am consoled by the back and forth and knowing I am not alone.

The tapping stops abruptly, and in the silence that follows, I hear the jangling of metal—keys perhaps—in the corridor. It might be a guard walking by. If our jailers had overheard our attempted communication, they surely would have punished us.

I lie down in my bed, blanketed by the silence. I am almost asleep when the tapping against the opposite wall begins again. This time it is a slow, regular rhythm. More a thump than a tap: *thump...thump...thump...thump.* There is something familiar about the sound. Then I remember and write.

•   •   •

I was on my way home from Mrs. Millicent's Hat Shop, where I had just delivered some of my mother's straw braids, when I heard the thump of feet pounding on cobblestones. It was only when I reached Lombard Street that I saw the lines of Negroes, hundreds of them, spanning the width of the street, marching in my direction. They were chanting and waving banners of rising suns and slaves breaking their chains, as well as others that read "Emancipation Day." I hurried across the street to get out of the way. People were streaming out of the taverns and shops, raising their fists, and cursing at the marchers who were now filling the street in front of me. It was a hot summer's day, and sweat glistened on their skin in the merciless heat.

I ran alongside the parade and asked an old woman wearing a head scarf why they were marching. She told me it was to celebrate Jamaican Emancipation Day to mark the end of slavery in the West Indies. Up ahead, a mob of angry people had gathered outside Mother Bethel Church. They were armed with bricks, bats, knives, paving stones, and guns. The crowd grew larger and larger, blocking Lombard and spilling into the side streets. I watched the front row of marchers approach the mob. Now there was no turning back.

The mob roared as one, like an angry animal, some attacking the marchers with bats. Other protesters dug up cobblestones and flung them at the marchers who tried to hide, but there was nowhere to go. Bricks flew and bodies fell. I remember a woman lying on the ground covering her child with her body as a man stood over her with a bat, bringing it down on her back again and again. I screamed at him to stop, but my voice was swallowed up by the noise of the crowd. The cries of the attackers mingled with the wails of the marchers, the sound of breaking glass, and the smell of smoke.

The police had arrived, but there weren't enough of them to calm this furious mob, and they appeared to be unarmed. I realized with a growing sense of urgency that I had to warn the Washingtons. At that moment a boy with wild eyes shouted at me, "Come with us. We're hunting the n——s." When he reached out to grab me, I got away from him into the street as he and his gang ran down the alley. Someone unseen hurled a brick that grazed the side of my forehead, sending a trickle of blood down my cheek. "Sorry, lass," shouted a voice from the crowd—it was the man who had thrown it and was picking up another. "I was aiming for her." He pointed to a woman carrying a bundle of her belongings and dragging her little girl down the street.

"Monster," I yelled, but my voice was drowned out by the clanging bells of the approaching fire brigades. I ran toward the poor woman to help her—while not sure what I could do for her—but she had already disappeared around the corner. I had to get to Lucy's house, but my head was throbbing, and when I put my hand to my forehead, it came away bloody. I got away from the horde of passersby and on to the sidewalk. Squatting, I ripped a strip of cloth from my petticoat and pressed it against my wound, then wrapped the cloth around my head, tying it in the back. Stumbling back to our house, I barely made it through the door when my knees buckled, and I sank to the ground. Ma cried out and I managed to mutter, "Don't worry, Ma, I delivered your hats."

Fortunately, the wound was not deep, but there was no way Ma would let me out of the house in the midst of the rioting to warn the Washingtons.

Later that night, as the battle continued to rage outside, there was a knock at the door—one of Da's companions come to tell him that the sheriff was calling the volunteers into service. Through the open door came the shouts and cries of the pursuers and the pursued.

"Brendan, I'm begging ye," said Ma. "Don't go. 'Tis not our fight."

"Sure, and whose fight are you thinking it is now, if not ours? Everyone knows it's the Irish who are doing this."

"Not all—"

"No, Katie, 'tis mostly our people. Looting the homes of colored people. Setting their homes afire. I'd not be surprised if some of the rioters are our own neighbors, the good folks we see at church. And the fire brigades are not there to fight fires. It's fighting each other, they are. The Moya Hose Company is the worst of the lot."

Da came back that first night unharmed, but on the second night he returned battered and bruised. He told us the mobs had burned down the African church and the abolitionist meeting hall on Lombard. "They turned on anyone who tried to stop them. 'Tis a sin, it is." He wiped his eyes, red from smoke or sorrow or both.

On the last night of the riot, just hours before Da died, we were eating supper. He was telling us a funny story about his cousin, back when they were growing up in County Kerry. We were laughing so hard, we almost missed the first explosion, but the second one was louder and sounded closer. Da opened the front door. Outside, an eerie yellow glow filled the sky, and we could see plumes of orange flames rising from the direction of the shanties. Already the bells were clanging. Da ran to fetch his coat, and Ma, as she did every night, begged him not to go.

"I am getting a bad feeling about tonight, Brendan. Please stay with us. Let them fight it out. You know they'll call the militia, like they have whenever the locals have lost control." She wrapped her arms around him and tried to drag him away from the front door. With her arms still encircling him, he turned and kissed her in a way I'd never seen before. He must have had a bad feeling himself.

"Brendan, please," she called out as he raced down the street, but her voice was drowned out by the furor of the mob.

Ma tried to get Aiden and me inside, but we told her we would stay on the stoop and promised to come inside if the fighting got too close. She must have been too preoccupied with Da to consider the danger we might be putting ourselves in, because she let us stay outside.

Huddled together on the stoop, a part of me longed for the safety of our house, but something stronger kept us rooted to the sidewalk. To watch? To help? We clung to each other as a cloud of ash drifted overhead, causing our eyes to water. The frightful sound of men, women, and children running for their lives echoed down the narrow streets. A Black man with a bloodied head ran past our house dragging a woman with a baby in her arms. Close behind them was a white man waving a club in the air. A young boy hurried past yelling, "Mama, Mama!" The night was punctuated with the cries of desperate people: "Run!" "They're killing us!" "Head north!" "Benjamin! Henry! Where you at?"

Two men carrying bricks chased a barefoot young man in a torn shirt. "Go home, Sambo. Back to Africa, you dirty n——."

I called out to the boy to offer him shelter in our house, but he just kept running. And what would Ma have done if we brought him inside? Aiden and I were both trembling and choking on ashes, but still we watched, covering our noses and mouths with our hands. A few of the other neighborhood kids ignored the pleas of their parents to come inside, and instead ran out into the street, shrieking and laughing as if all the mayhem was nothing more than a game. A fire brigade thundered down the street, whipping the horses pulling them and cursing at the kids to get out of the way. I recognized the Moyamensing Hose Company from their red shirts.

Another thunderous explosion and once again fire and smoke rose high above the rooftops. I started screaming and couldn't stop. Aiden had his arms around me, and I tried to shake myself loose. "Isaac and Lucy," I sobbed. "That's where they live. We must..." Aiden tightened his grip on me and walked me to the front door. "Nothing we can do," he said.

I went upstairs and observed the horrors from the front window. Someone pulled out a gun, shot a young Negro, and left him to bleed. They beat children and shoved women and old men into the street. They grabbed whatever they could—bricks, crates, slop buckets, cobblestones—and fed them to the flames. "Sambo!" they yelled. "Wooly head!" "N——!"

Later we learned the authorities had to call seven militia companies to end the fighting, but by then it was too late for Da. I was just coming out of the privy when I heard someone say my father's name. A group of Da's fellow volunteers were gathered in front of the house. "'Tis a shame it is. Brendan was a good man. Salt of the earth." Then they saw me. "Ah, you poor thing. You're an orphan now."

"What do you mean?" My heart, already grieving, sank in my chest. Although I already knew the truth, I wanted to delay those awful words.

"Your Da is dead," one of them said.

"How do you know that? How can you be sure?"

"Take our word for it. Sadly, it's true," said another.

I could not face them any longer. Chest heaving, I ran to the back door. "Ma!" I screamed as I ran inside. "Aiden!"

I sobbed as Ma hurried down the steps.

"What is it?"

I couldn't get the words out until Aiden came down.

"Da is dead!"

"What is this story you're telling?" Ma said. "How can you say that?"

"Because it's true."

"How...?" was all Aiden could manage.

"They saw it. The men...with him...saw with their own eyes," I said, gulping for breath.

A knock at the door, then a volunteer confirmed the news. Ma collapsed, and we huddled together on the floor, hugging, and crying. This is my family now, I thought.

But after a time, Ma pulled away and jabbed her finger at me.

"You. You. Your fault!"

"What are you saying, Ma? Why?"

"You were on his side when he said he was going outside to fight for those n——s. If it hadn't been for you, he'd be here today, safe and sound."

Aiden had his arms around me. "That's ridiculous, Ma," he said. "Why are you accusing Lizzy?"

"Da always fought for them," I tried reminding her. "He told me the story about the Black neighbor who saved—"

"Enough!" And she turned her back to me.

Was she blaming me for sending him out into the flames? No, it had to be more than that. I think it was the crime I had committed in Ma's eyes—the crime of being born a girl, and compounding that transgression by not being the docile, ladylike, doll-playing little girl I should have been. Once I overheard her telling Da, "Two babes I lost between Aiden and Lizzy. A lad and a lass. God told me the next one would be a lad. But He cursed me with another lass." I think that's why she stopped trying to love me.

With Da's death, the madness set in, and she turned all her anger against me. She kept a tally of my faults, which she would recite whenever she was about to succumb to one of her "spells."

•   •   •

I am done writing, but the tragedy of Da's death stays fresh in my mind and I cannot sleep. So I sing "The Parting Glass," soft as a lullaby. A hymn in his memory.

> And all I've done for want of wit
> To mem'ry now I can't recall
> So fill to me the parting glass
> Good night and joy be to you all

CHAPTER 11

This morning the priest visits me, as he has every month for the past...how long have I been here? I no longer try to number the days. Why bother when each day is indistinguishable from the one before and those that will follow?

"Repent for your sin, my child. The sin of murdering your baby."

It is the same every month. Although his manner is calm and priestly, I sense his impatience lurking under the surface.

"But Father, I cannot confess to a crime I did not commit. Why must I pay so dearly for a debt I do not owe? Why must I pay every day with my life?" I fight to hold back my tears, and he gives voice to his frustration.

"Why do you insist on lying? How can you deny the proof of your guilt?"

He recounts the "facts" of my culpability—the corpse, the witnesses, the...As always, I close my ears to his narrative, but occasionally a word slips through.

"Pillow," he says, and I shudder, for I *know* there was a pillow that night.

"God knows everything that happens on this earth, my child. He knows what you have done."

I am angry with God. I should not be thinking such thoughts, especially in the presence of a priest, but I cannot help it. If God knows everything, He surely knows the truth of my innocence. And if He knows, why does He not tell this priest? Why does He not set me free?

Once again, the priest cannot make me confess to murder, but he will not leave until I confess to the sin of lying, which is itself a lie, is it not? Sometimes I wish I were Quaker, or Methodist, or any religion that does not make you confess your sins, but lets you worship God in peace.

When I was young, I assumed that confession was a part of all religions, but I learned differently one summer morning on the front steps of the Washingtons' house. I was thirteen when Lucy told me she wanted to confess something to me. We were sitting on her stoop, and she was about to tell me what was on her mind, when Timmy Doyle and two of his buddies yelled, "N—— lover" from across the street. I yelled something back at them, and then...Ah, the memory's gone now.

"Lizzy, sometimes I'm ashamed of my secret thoughts—things I've never told anyone," Lucy confided in low tones.

"Not even in confession?"

Lucy looked puzzled. "Confession?"

"You know. In church, when you tell the priest your sins."

"Priest? We don't have priests in our church."

I explained confession to her.

"Do you tell him everything?"

"Maybe some people do. But I keep some secrets, even though he's not allowed to tell anyone what you confess, since it's between you and God."

"But it must be wonderful to have someone listen to your secrets and keep them secret. Will you be my priest, Lizzy? I must confess something I'm so ashamed of thinking."

I laughed. "I can't be your priest, but I can be your best friend. And I promise I'll never tell another soul."

We held hands as I took her confession.

"I sometimes want to run away and pretend I'm white," she said.

I realized then that someone who looked like Lucy could easily be mistaken for white. Her hair wasn't black, but reddish-brown. Her skin was light enough to see freckles across the bridge of her nose, and her eyes could be green or amber depending on the light.

"Sometimes people think I'm white. I'm ashamed to say this, but it makes me feel good to pass for white. How can I feel like that? My parents and their friends are fighting against slavery. And I know I would probably be a slave if I lived in the South, no matter how light I was. Are you shocked?"

"No, I would probably feel the same if I were you."

"What just happened with Timmy Doyle happens to us every day. Sometimes I look at you and dream about how it would feel to live like you. If I told my parents how I felt, it would break their hearts."

As I walked home, I thought about Aiden and what he would have done to Timmy if he'd been with me.

CHAPTER 12

It's early morning, and I'm startled out of bed by the sound of a man's voice. The words are muffled, but the tone is one of desperation. The voice goes silent as I stand barefoot next to my bed, shivering in my nightdress. There it is again. I follow the sound to...the toilet. It's coming up from the toilet! Someone is talking through the pipes, defying the gatekeepers of silence. In all the time I've been here, I've heard nothing like this.

I rush to the toilet and hold my ear to the opening. The words are clear now. "I am Samuel Preston," he cries in a deep voice. "Can you hear me? Can anyone hear me?" The rest is muffled. Then silence.

His cries of desperation loosen something inside me; I cannot stop myself from screaming into the toilet. "My baby, my baby! My little one cries and cries, and they won't let me hold her. They tell me she's a bastard. Help me. *Help me!*"

I don't know how I summon the strength to scream like this. Although I have no idea who Samuel Preston is, and I am a stranger to him, my loneliness pours out of me in a waterfall of despair, and I don't care who hears.

"They tell me I'm a murderer, but I'm innocent. Innocent! I want to die. Please let me die."

Someone grabs me from behind. *"B358. Shut up now, B358!"*

I'd been screaming with such force I missed the sound of the key in the lock and the footsteps of the man I now turn to face—a huge man whose enormous torso blocks everything from my sight. He ties a gag around my mouth, and then a second guard, as skinny as the other one is fat, binds my hands behind my back. The big one steps back and runs his eyes over my body before pushing me down on the bed. I continue to sob, although I'm all used up, and there are no words left.

"Scrawny thing she is. But that red hair...mmm," says the skinny guard moving from behind me, licking his lips. "You can have her first."

The big one moves closer and climbs onto the bed, straddling me.

I close my eyes and my world turns dark. I am once again in the pantry submitting to the Master, but this time I can't even fight back and leave a mark on his face. I try to twist my body away, but my anger is no match for the bulk of him.

"No!" I scream.

He grabs me by the shoulders, lifts my nightshirt, and lowers himself upon me. I feel him pressing against me through the material of his trousers. I feel his hand reach down to unbutton his pants, and my dark world is now red with rage. I struggle to free my hands so I can jab my fingernails into his eyes, but my wrists are too tightly bound.

"Feisty little she-devil," he sneers.

He is breathing hard, and the smell of him is so thick it penetrates the cloth and sickens me. Nausea rises in my throat, and I fear I will choke to death. I gag and my chest heaves.

He pulls away. "Don't want her drowning in her own filth. I could lose my job."

"Yeah," says the other one. "Ain't worth it." He chuckles. "And anyways, you know Irish girls get pregnant if you jes look at 'em wrong."

"I wouldn't want a little Irish bastard of mine running around," my attacker sniggered.

I feel his hands on my neck, tugging the bottom of my hood.

"Of course, the bitch would probably kill it, like she killed her own bastard." He pulls my hood off, spits in my face, and hisses, "Whore!" before leaving with his companion.

I lie gagged and trussed on my bed, staring at the skylight and watching the day fade, the monster's spittle still wet on my cheek. My nausea is gone, but not my anger. I silently curse my lot as a woman. Then I curse the Quakers, those "good" people who walk the streets arm in arm with colored people to show their solidarity. Risking their lives to defend them. Claiming each of us has an inner light, and all we have to do is reflect long enough in our cells, and we'll reveal that soul to the world. What about that filthy man who was about to rape me and who left his spittle on my face as a parting gift? Why must I suffer the punishment of solitude inside a cell while that monster is free to sin without consequence?

I see God's skylight eye above me casting a faint light. Is He watching? Was He watching when the guards attacked me? When the Master violated me? I scream and curse this cruel God, this Quaker God, this Catholic God who loves all sinners, but doesn't love me.

I struggle to free myself till my arms ache, to no avail. I relive the events of the afternoon as the gag cuts into my cheeks. With tears in my eyes, I wait for someone to unbind me. Will they discover me when they try to deliver the supper tray, or have they already been here and gone?

Now it's dark and I'm still bound. Perhaps they've already looked in, seen me in this state, and decided I was deserving of such punishment. I could be here all night like this. Or longer. Once again, I strain against my bindings until my wrists bleed. Will they leave me here to die? I want to believe there are a few kind people in this world. Like Thomas. But Thomas is a Quaker. Would he save me or would he enforce solitary penance like Quakers do? Why am I even thinking about him? I abandoned him, and he has probably forgotten me. I am so weary I finally fall asleep.

I am lying on the bloodstained sheet and Ma is yelling, "Whore," over and over.

A key jangling in the lock startles me awake. It is the kindly guard. As he gently removes the gag from my mouth and the restraints from my wrists, he says he is sorry I had to spend so much time in such a state. I tell him how grateful I am for his kindness. He rinses the gag in the sink and uses it to wipe the blood from my wrists. And then he leaves. How I wish he had stayed just a moment more.

I walk around the cell to restore my movement. I try to concentrate on the guard's kindness, but his soft, endearing voice fades, replaced by the voice of my mother in my dream, yelling "Whore!" And then by the voice of the burly guard who also yelled "*Whore!*" He was a man who knew I'd been convicted of a most heinous crime, but he had called me "whore," not "murderer." "Whore"—as if opening my legs was a far worse crime than taking the life of a child.

It is too dark to write in my journal, so I grab a fresh sheet of paper, but all I can write is WHORE in big, bold letters.

CHAPTER 13

Tonight I am so weary from my encounter with the two guards that all I want is the oblivion of sleep. Instead I am visited by a memory of what happened when Lucy and I sat on her front stoop after Timmy saw us and yelled "N—— lover!" I get out of bed and write in my journal.

•   •   •

"You!" I yelled. "Get out of my sight."

"Not when you and your nappy-haired friend are about to do something interesting. Go on, kiss her. We just love watching women kissing each other, don't we, boys? Go on, Red. Show us how much you love those darkies."

I leapt to my feet, my face ablaze. "Fecking leave us alone." A word that never passed my lips, and there I was spitting it out like spoiled milk.

"Ooh. The girl's got a tongue on her. We like 'em like that, don't we, boys?"

Hands on hips, dizzy with anger, I strode across the street. "I'm going to kill you, Timmy fecking Doyle."

"Listen to that, boys! Red's gonna kill me. I'm quaking in me boots."

We were inches apart when I drove my fist into his eye. He fell back, clutching his face.

"Okay, Red. Now you've done it." He raised his fist, then lowered it, his face crimson. "I'll not hit you back now. I'm a gentleman, ain't I, boys?" His companions imitated his sneering laugh. "But you'll pay for this. Us Doyles, we never forget nothin'. I won't forget that time when you ran away from me neither—we both know what I'm talking about. And someday, when you're least expectin' it—next week, next year, who knows—I'll hurt you so bad, you'll curse the day you did this to me."

When he took his hand off his eye, I could see it was red and starting to swell.

"Us Doyles, we never forget." Then he turned and marched off with his buddies.

•   •   •

Men assault me in my cell and in my memories. I believe I have earned a night of blessed, untroubled sleep.

Pain. It has no beginning and no end. The coarse-voiced, thick-fingered woman is yelling: "Hold her down. Baby's coming fast. It wants to be born." Ma yells, "Bastard child. Better it was born dead." More pain. Sleep. The woman says, "It's a girl," and holds my crying daughter just out of reach. Her hands are covered with blood, so she must be the midwife. "Please let me hold her." I lie helpless and sobbing in a pool of blood. My sobs are drowned out by Ma's voice. "Whore!" she screams. "Whore!" Over and over.

CHAPTER 14

I am sore in body and spirit from yesterday's ordeal. I have no desire to leave my bed, but because I'm hungry, I manage to rouse myself to accept the breakfast tray delivered by the gloved hand. When I set it on the table, I see the paper on which I'd written WHORE in large block letters the night before, the same word Ma hurled at me in my dreams. The paper is also covered with blotches, which on closer inspection turn out to be roughly scrawled words. They are tiny and scarcely legible. I don't remember writing them, although I must have, for no one else has been here but me. These words must mean something, since I wrote them; perhaps they are the keys to my locked memories. Then again they might just be gibberish.

I lean in to get a closer look, but my eyes don't work as well as they used to. The words are blurry. When I lift the paper to move it closer to the light, I see there is another sheet beneath it, also covered with my scrawls. Under the light, the letters begin to form words: "Thomas." "Black lips on white." "Kindness." "Census." "Lombard." There are other words, but my eyes are tired from squinting and blinking, so I close them and spell the words out in my head, whisper them aloud, taste them on my tongue. At first, none of them have meaning except one: "Thomas." I repeat the words I can read, a little louder this time, and the repetition opens windows into my past. But only one word brings comfort. "Thomas," I whisper his name, tracing the letters with my finger. "Thomas." Still, I cannot see him in my mind's eye.

Thomas. I long to remember everything...anything about him. I write his name on a fresh sheet of paper and tack it to the wall above my little desk. Perhaps I can conjure his memory by losing myself in the shape and sound of his name until I bring him back by force of will.

I look up at the skylight. Dear God, I know I am a sinner, but is there not some good in me that could be rewarded with the gift of his memory? I will sit here all day, because time means nothing to me. Breathe, say his name, breathe, say his name. Feverish, shivering, I wrap my blanket around me. Please, God, before the memory is gone for good, and my brain is scrubbed clean by the rough cloth of isolation...

And there in the fading light, by some miracle, I see him. *Yes*, I *see* him! Thank you, God, for bringing him back to me. Now I must record this memory in my journal. Although I'm shivering from the cold, and my handwriting is hardly legible, I write and write.

•　　•　　•

It was a sunny spring afternoon. The Master must have dismissed me early, because I was wandering along the streets lined with the houses of the rich, never tiring of the fancy doorways framed by columns, marble steps, and iron railings, with fanlights that bloomed above the doors like stained-glass flowers. I stopped in front of a massive brownstone, and looking up, I dreamed about what it would be like to live there and look down at the street far below my bedroom window.

As I went on and turned the corner, a sudden breeze sent a sheaf of papers flying, seemingly out of nowhere. When they fell to the ground, I grabbed a handful, looked at the one on top, and was immediately sickened by what I saw. It was a cartoon illustration of a Black man planting grotesquely thick lips on the delicate mouth of a white woman. On another, black hands were reaching for a white bosom. They were pictures meant to inflame white people. Negro men lusting after white women. *Amalgamation*, they called it, an abomination that sparked mobs and incited riots. And now I held that hatred in my hands. It burned. Eager to be rid of it, I ripped up the pages into tiny pieces. I started picking up some others and tearing them to shreds too, when someone behind me said, "It makes you angry, doesn't it?"

I straightened and turned to face a man with dark eyes and hair the color of chestnuts. He was tall and dressed formally in a frock coat, top hat, vest, and dark trousers. He took a step toward me. "It makes me mad, too."

For as long as I could remember, boys—and later men—had made advances on me, looking for something I was not willing to give them. I would have gladly offered them lively conversation, but of course they wanted something more...tangible. Although this man was clearly of a higher class than me, he undoubtedly wanted the same as all the others. He was just using trickery to get it.

I was about to rebuff him when he took off his hat, pressed it against his chest, and bowed his head in a sign of respect. As if I too were high born.

"I believe you are mocking me, sir, and I will not have it."

"Please don't be angry with me. I believe in showing respect to the fairer sex, and I believe you share my feelings about..." He grabbed one of the papers from the ground and waved it. "...about this."

Feelings? When had a boy or man ever talked to me of feelings? Was it possible that he wasn't mocking me after all? I would know soon enough whether he was a gentleman or a scoundrel. I made an exaggerated curtsey. "Perhaps I share your feelings, sir."

"Now I am afraid *you* are mocking *me*." He smiled, revealing a dimple on his cheek.

At that moment, I thought he was the most...beautiful man I had ever met. The image of a "beautiful man"—two words so out of place together, and yet so perfect a description of him, made me blush.

"And you called me 'sir.'" He laughed. "I cannot be more than a couple of years your senior. How old are you?" His voice was deep, his language refined. I imagined him coming from a family that had lived in this country long before the Revolution.

"I am seventeen, sir."

"And I am twenty-one. May I see the picture you're holding?"

Nodding, I held it out to him. He took the paper, looked at it, and muttered, "Hmm..." before giving it back to me.

"I would like to watch you rip that one up. Just as you did the others."

Something about him made me feel giddy, like a child with a handful of sweets. "Oh, yes, sir." I looked at the image again to draw my attention away from him and how he made me feel, and to remind myself what we were talking about. "The hate on this page is burning my hand."

He gave me a look I couldn't fathom. "I would enjoy watching you obliterate that monstrosity."

As I tore the paper to shreds, he asked, "Do you know about Pennsylvania Hall?"

"I do, sir. It was built by the abolitionists to hold conventions, and burned to the ground soon after it opened—about ten years ago. My father was a volunteer policeman called in by the sheriff to help control the mobs."

He scowled. "The police. So many of them stood by, like the firemen, and did nothing as the building—"

"My father was a good man," I said sharply, and told him how Da tried to persuade the mayor to protect the building...

It was a wonderful story—if only I could remember it all now. But what I do recall about meeting Thomas is so precious I am not troubled by missing details.

"Your father sounds like a good man, indeed."

"He *was* a good man. He died during the riots of '42."

"I am so sorry, Miss...Mrs....We have shared so many thoughts during our short time together, but I don't even know your name. I am Thomas. Thomas Britton."

"Britton. The family that owns the shipping company?"

"Yes, that's my family. And you are..."

I was in the presence of Quaker royalty, if there was such a thing. The Brittons were one of the most prominent Quaker families in Philadelphia. I hesitated before answering, "I'm Elizabeth O'Meara. Lizzy."

"Irish. I would have sworn you were Quaker, like myself."

"And I would have sworn you were blind. Do the red hair and freckles not tell my story?"

"It has nothing to do with your complexion. I sense the abolitionist in you."

I didn't know whether it was pride in his compliment that caused my cheeks to burn, or shame that I hadn't lived up to what he thought he saw in me.

"Well, I have not met many Irish people who share my feelings on the subject, Lizzy."

He was right. Other than my father and my brother, I didn't know anyone else in the neighborhood who felt that way, but I was ashamed to admit that to this man. "I'm sorry you have such a low opinion of my people. There are other—"

"I apologize for the insult." Now it was his turn to blush. "I have been taught to believe that every person is loved and guided by God, and there is God in everyone."

"Such a beautiful belief. You are the first Quaker I've met, but I know about Quakers. If not for your careless statement about the Irish, I would have thought you perfect, but..." I paused, and he smiled and raised his eyebrows, waiting for me to finish my sentence. "...But now I see you are a mere mortal like myself, which is a great relief."

Thomas threw back his head and burst out in raucous laughter, not unlike the men who lingered outside the pubs and oyster houses. I thought only drunken men laughed like that.

"Lizzy, you are...words fail me."

"Don't worry. I'll make up for that failure. We Irish are never at a loss for words."

He laughed again, and I smoothed my hair, suddenly self-conscious. I had never flirted before—never wanted to encourage male attention—

but there I was, as brazen as Caitlin Byrne, who had borne a child before she was fifteen. And it came so easily!

"Lizzy, would you like to spend a little more time walking with me so you can demonstrate how the Irish are never at a loss for words?"

"I am afraid I cannot. It is late, and I am expected home for dinner."

He pulled a black notebook out of his pocket and held it up. "This is the reason I have been walking up and down these streets. If you agree to see me again, I'll tell you all about it."

"Are you offering me a bribe, sir?"

"Indeed, I am."

•　　•　　•

Such warm memories. I am sure I will sleep peacefully tonight.

My baby is crying in the midwife's arms. When I reach out for her, everything goes dark. I open my eyes. Now the midwife is not cradling my baby but holding her under her arms so she's dangling overhead like a rag doll. I try to hear my baby's voice, but Ma is shouting so loud I can't hear whether my baby is still crying. Is she crying? All I can hear is my mother's crazed tirade. Please let her be crying.

CHAPTER 15

"Census." One of the words I'd scribbled in tiny letters. I know each word is a clue to my past, and I have resurrected some of them, but this one remains a mystery. Over time, I have discovered that taking a walk outside often lifts the fog that clouds my mind; and if I repeat a word as I pace, its meaning might reveal itself to me. So today I circle the exercise yard, repeating "census" softly, like a prayer. And finally, it comes to me—the memory of my second meeting with Thomas on the streets of Philadelphia. When I return to my cell, I pick up my pen and write.

•   •   •

As he'd promised at our first meeting, he explained why he carried a notebook. The Quakers were compiling a census of the Negro community, and he was a volunteer census taker. His instructions were to record not only their names and addresses but also the stories they told. He opened the notebook and showed me some of the information he had gathered so far, and asked me if I would like to accompany him on his rounds.

I told him there was nothing I would like better, as long as we did it in a neighborhood where I was not likely to run into anyone I knew, for if I was spotted, idle gossip would make its way through the neighborhood straight to my mother. Not that I had anything to hide, but Ma seemed to find fault with everything I did, so what would be the point of telling her what I was doing and who I was doing it with? For the time being, I intended to keep my association with Thomas a secret. Despite the size and bustle of Philadelphia, it was not uncommon to encounter someone you knew, but the farther the distance from Moyamensing, the less the chance that would happen.

Despite my precautions, I was dismayed to spot a familiar figure up ahead. If only I could come up with an excuse to duck down a side street to avoid a face-to-face encounter with Timmy Doyle. Once he attached himself to me like an evil spirit, he refused to let go.

"Red!" he called out when he got within half a block of us. I tried to ignore him, but as he approached, he said, "What a coincidence, you and me on the same street at the same time."

"Oh, no," I whispered, taking Thomas' hand and squeezing it so tightly I could have sworn he winced. He looked at me and mouthed, "Who?" but I shook my head, and he said nothing more. When I was with Thomas, I could almost forget I was a poor Irish girl, daughter of immigrant parents; but Timmy was a reminder that Thomas and I came from different worlds.

I would have given anything to avoid the embarrassment of this meeting, but all I could do was straighten my shoulders and prepare to face him head on. Although he scared me, I would do my best to show anger rather than fear. Thomas had to see I differed from the likes of Timmy Doyle.

I could not understand Timmy's hunger for me, as there were so many opportunities in the city for him to take his pleasure. There were brothels everywhere—on South Street, Walnut Street, Spruce Street—so many of them that a book had been published listing each establishment to acquaint gentlemen visiting Philadelphia with all that was available to them; although it was said that native Philadelphians frequented these establishments as often as visitors did. It was called, I think, *A Guide to the Stranger.* I believe that was its name. I was told it provided descriptions of the women who worked in these houses of pleasure—like which ones had the most beautiful ladies—which places were clean, which should be avoided by "gentlemen," and which were of dubious reputation. And these women didn't confine themselves to the "disorderly houses" where they conducted their business; they strolled through the parks and business areas during the day and planted themselves outside the theaters at night. Yet despite the presence of such women everywhere, Timmy continued to hound me. And here he was yet again. For a moment, I regretted I had not told Aiden about him, but it was for the best. Aiden would have been out for blood, and the blood most likely spilled would have been his own once Timmy's cousin got involved.

With Thomas' hand in mine, I walked as fast as I could to get away from him. But Timmy was determined to have his way, despite the presence of the gentleman by my side, or perhaps, because of it. Timmy ran ahead of us and blocked our way. He planted himself inches from my face, his customary leer smearing his features. I released Thomas' hand and put my hands on my hips, but my fear and anger were such that I had trouble keeping my balance, and Thomas took my arm to steady me as Timmy let loose with his tirade.

"Ah, Red. You've broken me heart. I stayed pure for you, but you couldn't wait for me, could you?" He looked Thomas up and down disdainfully. "I don't take kindly to havin' me heart broken. Red here knows who my cousin is. Bull McMullen. And everyone knows what he can do, him and his buddies at the Moyamensing Hose Company. They don't call him 'Bull' for nothin'. And he's willing to do anything I want."

"Get. Away. From. Me. *No more!*" I raised a hand to strike him, as I had once before, but he grabbed my wrist with one hand and raised a fist with the other.

Thomas took a threatening step toward Timmy. "Get your hands off her right now!" Thomas was taller than Timmy, but Timmy was solid and muscular, and probably more used to fighting than Thomas.

"No, Thomas," I said firmly. "I'll take care of this," and he stepped back.

Timmy lowered his fist, leaned his head back, and laughed like a madman. Then he walked past us, bumping his shoulder against Thomas with such force he almost lost his footing. "So sorry," said Timmy, spitting out the words as he went on his way.

What a lowlife Thomas must think me, to be consorting with the likes of Timmy Doyle. But there he was, looking at me with admiration. "I don't think I've ever met anyone quite like you, standing up to a bully like that," he said. "Everyone knows who Bull McMullen is, and Timmy Doyle is a bully just like his cousin. You should tell the police he's harassing you."

"I may do just that," I said, knowing I wouldn't. The police would never stop Bull McMullen, one of the "rowdy boys of Moyamensing," whose name frequently showed up in the newspapers in connection with his misdeeds.

We walked in silence for a few moments. Then Thomas said, "In light of what just happened, perhaps you would like me to see you home."

Although shaken and embarrassed, I said, "I would like nothing more than to accompany you on your interviews."

"Somehow that doesn't surprise me."

Although we visited many homes that day, I can only remember our first interview. The woman we visited was not easily forgotten. She was tiny and bent with age, but her radiant, toothy smile was a bright spot in the dingy room she inhabited. She told us she had been kidnapped into slavery with her mother and brother when she was a child. Soon after, they were sold to different masters, and she never saw them again. Her master told her he would free her when she could buy her freedom. It had taken her many years, saving what she could until she had the seventy-five dollars it cost to buy herself back from her master.

"I was eighteen, nineteen, mebbe. From that day, I took every job I could get. Emptying slops, peddling potatoes, onions, apples. I worked hard, I did, bone tired every day, thankful to Jesus that I had been released. Not a day passes that I don't think of my mother and baby brother."

By the time she finished, I was in tears, and I hugged her before we left. She put her hand on my cheek then touched hers. "We cry the same tears, don't we, chile."

Outside, Thomas put his hands on my shoulders and looked at me in a way that opened my heart.

CHAPTER 16

The days are long and the heat oppressive, like it was the day I arrived. That was my first summer at Cherry Hill. Is this my second or my third summer in this cell? I do not record dates in my journal, and every day is like the last—a daily dose of misery and despair. I am losing weight. I am losing my mind. Every night in my dreams I cry for my baby while my mother calls me a whore.

I was sentenced to four years and have no idea how much time remains until my release. But what does it matter? By the time they open my cell door to set me free, there will be nothing left of me.

Lately I've been plagued by a new nightmare in which my cell shrinks as the walls slowly close in on me, and I wake up screaming as they are about to crush me. Last week I awoke with blood on my hands, my knuckles raw. But the other night, for the first time, the dream didn't terrify me. No, quite the opposite—I welcomed the walls' embrace, begging them to flatten me. But when they touched my arms and feet, I woke up and was disappointed to find myself still intact.

This morning I hear keys jangling in the lock. Could it be the burly guard who assaulted me coming back to finish what he failed to do the last time? Maybe it's Sunday and the priest is coming to pay me a visit. I have no time to dress properly, so I don a sweater over my nightdress and tuck my hair behind my ears.

The guard escorts a man into my cell. It is not my assailant, nor is it the priest. I have never seen him before. I expect the guard to hand me a hood to cover my face, but to my surprise he walks out, leaving me alone with this stranger. Unaccustomed as I am to human contact, I have forgotten how to interact with people, no less someone who looks so different from almost everyone I've ever known. He is dressed in a proper gentleman's suit and is clean-shaven, with dark curly hair that frames his face and falls to his collar. I step back, but his deep brown eyes suggest a sympathetic disposition that puts me at ease.

He smiles. "I have come to ask you a few questions. May I?"

He speaks with an accent I do not recognize. He's from somewhere far away, but definitely not Ireland. What new horrors are about to be inflicted on me?

"Y...yes." My voice cracks from disuse, so I clear my throat and repeat my response.

The man reaches out and shakes my hand. "My name is Charles. And you are...?"

"Elizabeth O'Meara, sir. Pleased to make your acquaintance." I curtsy, and he smiles.

"May I sit here?" He points to the lone chair in the cell, and I nod and seat myself on the bed facing him.

Through the slot in the door comes a voice. "Mr. Dickens, I'll be waiting outside the cell. So when you're ready to leave, just come to the door and call me."

I ponder the name Dickens as my visitor walks to the door, leans down to the food slot, and says through it, "I trust you will not be listening to our conversation, as that was one of the conditions of my visit." I do not hear the guard's answer.

Ah, Dickens. Now I remember. It's a name I saw on a list of books in the prison library.

Mr. Dickens reseats himself on the chair and opens a notebook. "I am from London, and I am touring America to write a book. I find the prison system here most fascinating."

Ah, so that's what proper English sounds like. Thomas was the only person I knew who sounded even the least bit like Mr. Dickens. As for his mission, why anyone would want to tour Eastern State Penitentiary was beyond me, but I nodded.

"Tell me, how long have you been here?" He looks around my wretched cell.

"Two years, maybe three. I'm not sure."

"Not sure," he says quietly and writes something in his notebook. "And do they treat you well?"

How to answer that? "Mmm...yes..." I say softly.

I sense he is waiting for more, and I take a deep breath. Do I tell him about my punishment for speaking up? The guards who tied me up and...touched me? Being locked inside this cage day after endless day? What will he say to the warden? Surely when they hear, they will find ways to make my life even more miserable. Or perhaps not. They are Quakers after all, and Quakers have the best of intentions, even if they do not always follow through with kindness. They believe each of us is blessed with the inner light of God...and yet...here I am, imprisoned. I must weigh the consequences if I answer truthfully. Best to be prudent.

But then he adds, "You may speak your mind. I promise I will not be reporting our conversation to any of the authorities while I am here."

While he is here. What does that mean? Do I believe his promises? "They treat me well, sir. I am given three meals every day and a bath every two weeks."

He looks at me and says nothing, so I continue.

"I am allowed to walk outside." I shift my gaze to the door at the rear of the cell.

His eyes follow my gaze, and he nods. "Yes, I have seen an exercise yard...Please go on," he smiles encouragingly.

I find it surprisingly easy to make my life sound like a pleasant one, as if I am an actress on a stage. "They give me books to read and paper to write on. I am comfortable enough here. I can see the sky and can tell day from night. They say my life would be ever so much harder in Moyamensing Prison."

Mr. Dickens writes something in his notebook and looks around the room, his attention caught by the paper with Thomas' name tacked to the wall. Mercifully, he does not question me about it. "Tell me how you spend your days."

"I...I spend most of my time thinking about what they say I did. Even when I am doing my needlework, though not when I'm reading."

"And what is it they say you did?" He leans forward. I see both curiosity and acceptance in his expression, as if he has already seen and heard the worst of humanity.

"They say I killed my baby." He does not look shocked. Instead, there is pity in his large brown eyes.

"And would you say that all your thinking has made you a better person?"

His eyes do not leave mine as he waits patiently for my response. We are surrounded by silence.

"A better person? I don't know how to answer that. How can I be a better person if I did not kill my baby?" The words spill out before I can stop them. "And I am so, so angry at the injustice. I have lost my baby and *they* are making *me* pay. Every day. Here in this cell."

As we sit there silently, I think of the agony of my nights. Dare I tell him? I cannot stop myself. "I know I am innocent, and yet there are dreams...nightmares...that tell a different story of what happened when I lost my baby. Each night more and more is revealed. And I believe those dreams are the memories of what really happened." I shudder uncontrollably and then break down sobbing.

"You poor girl."

The sympathy in his voice is a balm, and between sobs I pour my heart out to this stranger. I cannot harness my anguish. "Some days I am so confused, I think I'm going crazy. Other days I know I am crazy—a prisoner of my own mind." I bury my face in my hands and weep.

He waits until I stop crying. "You poor dear girl. How do you bear it?" He puts his hand on my arm. The same gentle touch as my father.

After wiping the tears from my eyes and collecting my thoughts, I say, "I recite prayers, read the Bible, hum the songs my father once sang to me, but softly so they don't hear."

"I cannot imagine your isolation, though I do know something about prisons. My father was sent to a prison in Southwark, a district in London. I believe there is a district in Philadelphia with the same name."

"Yes, Moyamensing, where I live...lived...is very close to Southwark. Why was your father imprisoned?"

"He owed money to a baker and couldn't pay, so he was sent to prison for the crime of being a debtor. I was twelve and had to leave school and go to work."

"It's so unfair, how they make us pay. I cannot imagine what would have happened to me if I'd had to leave school."

Mr. Dickens cocks his head, as if pondering my words. "Miss O'Meara, I sense a well of strength and compassion in you."

I am overflowing with gratitude to this man. And yet... "If my dreams reveal my guilt, then I am not who you think I am. A compassionate person does not murder her child."

"And I am certain that you did not commit that crime." The sympathy in his deep brown eyes speaks to me as profoundly as his words. "I am a good judge of character, and I believe your prolonged solitude has no doubt affected your ability to determine what is true."

"I fear for my sanity, sir." Again, my eyes fill. "But your words strengthen my belief in my innocence. And for that I thank you."

"My dear girl, I hold that this slow and daily tampering with the mysteries of the brain is immeasurably worse than any torture of the body, because its wounds are not upon the surface. And I am convinced that there is a depth of terrible endurance which none but the sufferers themselves can fathom, and which no man has a right to inflict upon his fellow creatures."

"Like what they are doing to me. And like slavery."

His eyes flash with anger. "Yes, like slavery. An abhorrent institution, slavery. Thankfully, we outlawed it in England some years back."

"And we live with it still. In Philadelphia, even free Black men are treated as if they are less than human. I was a member of the Philadelphia Female Anti-Slavery Society, and my best friend is an abolitionist. As is my...was my..." I must not think about Thomas. It is too painful.

"My dear child—do not lose hope. And please do me the honor of reading my book, *Oliver Twist*. If it's not among the offerings in the prison library, I will procure a copy for you."

"That I will do, sir." For the first time in many months, someone has treated me with respect, and my mind is surprisingly clear and focused.

"Thank you for talking to me." He rises from his chair, then bends down so his face is level with mine. I smell lavender and cinnamon. He whispers, "You are an impressive young woman, and I am confident you will accomplish much in your life if you can just keep your wits about you until you're released."

I am overwhelmed by his words, unable to stop my tears. "Oh...sir...I do not know if I can live up to..."

"I'm so sorry, Miss O'Meara, I didn't mean to upset you."

"Oh no, sir. These are tears of hope. Your words have meant so much to me. More than I can begin to tell you."

His eyes crinkle, he tips an imaginary hat, and then he's gone.

I silently thank him and wish him Godspeed on his journey.

CHAPTER 17

For days I cherish the memory of my meeting with Mr. Dickens, who spoke to me so sympathetically and with such an appreciation of my suffering in this dreadful place. He believed me to be innocent, even when I confessed my fears that my nightmares were memories of what actually happened. When he told me my prolonged solitude had no doubt affected my ability to determine what was true, his words gave me hope.

And Mr. Dickens talked to me as if I were his equal, just as Thomas had talked to me so long ago. When we discussed subjects like history and justice, my beloved was attentive to my responses and placed a high value on what I had to say. Our friendship, which had begun with a meeting of the minds, gradually blossomed into a love that bound our hearts as well. I remember and I write.

•   •   •

In time, Thomas broached the idea of marriage, and I allowed myself to dream about a life with him, a partnership of mutual love and respect. But in the harsh light of day, I feared that the differences in our backgrounds would be too wide to bridge. Though I shared the Quakers' abolitionist fervor, there was little else I shared with the Brittons.

They had come to America back in William Penn's time and fought in the Revolution. They were bankers and lawyers and shippers, with a mansion on one of those fancy streets whose name I can no longer recall. And they had an estate on the other side of the Schuylkill. Whereas I was the child of parents who had grown up poor in County Kerry and emigrated to America not so many years ago. We lived in a neighborhood where laundry was strung between windows in full view, children ran ragged in the streets, neighbors shouted at each other—some with accents thick as porridge—and you couldn't walk a block without passing a tavern. And then there was my mother with her sharp tongue, intolerant attitude, and moods as unpredictable as April skies; would he not see her as the person I would become some day? When I shared my fears with him, he told me none of that mattered because all that mattered to him was me.

But I knew it was one thing to hear something described, and another thing entirely to experience it. So I resisted introducing him to my world and told him I wasn't ready to enter his. Our only recourse was to share our mutual affection in secret, taking advantage of the hidden paths and secluded wooded areas in and around the city. But with each meeting it became harder to control what our bodies ached for. When he slipped his hands beneath my skirt and blouse and caressed me, and I pulled him on top of me and touched him and we pressed ourselves tight against each other—wanting each other desperately—it was all I could do to pull away; but as an unmarried woman I didn't want to risk the inevitable consequence of unchecked passion.

Such a handsome, accomplished, and wealthy man as Thomas could have had any woman he desired, yet he never gave up on me. And so it was that once again the subject of our future together was the topic of conversation during an excursion one sunny autumn afternoon on the banks of the Schuylkill. We walked across the new wonder of a bridge at Fairmount. Thomas called it a suspension bridge and said it was the first of its kind in the country. There were cables that stretched from the ground to the two granite pillars on each side and then draped gracefully between them. They looked too delicate to support the weight of the many people who traversed the bridge.

When we reached the west bank, we walked downstream where we could have a view of the waterworks and spread out a blanket. Across from us, its buildings shone white like the Greek temples I'd seen in picture books. Behind them were cliffs, and at the top a gazebo. Women wearing fashionable bonnets and brightly colored dresses and men in their Sunday best climbed the steep steps to get a panoramic view of the scenery below.

How we talked, just the two of us. The exact words are lost to me, but I remember the feelings, and I believe the conversation and interactions I resurrect here reflect the essence of what actually transpired.

"Oh, Thomas. Such a magical place. I could sit here forever with you."

"And I with you." He kissed me, his tongue exploring the inside of my mouth, and I did the same. The intensity of the sensation as it reached my most intimate places took my breath away, and I longed to surrender to him then and there. Reluctantly, I pulled away.

"Ah, Lizzy, we are so wonderful together. Why do you continue to resist my proposal of marriage?"

"And why do you continue to ask?"

He nodded. "I know. My family. My parents. I cannot count the number of times I have told you they are good people who are not put off by race or social class. They respect me and my life choices. So how can I make you understand they would welcome you as my wife?"

"I still find that hard to believe. But knowing what an honest man you are," I said, smiling, "I suppose I will have to take your word for it. But again, I ask you, how can I ever feel comfortable in a world of high-toned parties and social clubs and luxury? How will I know which fork to use? How can I avoid saying something that might offend your people?"

"Those things can be learned quickly, and we are not easily offended—least of all by the improper use of forks."

"Perhaps. But there is the other problem." I stared out at the boats floating lazily down the river, and the women walking along the cliff paths in dresses the vibrant color of autumn leaves. "Your family has been here for generations. My father grew potatoes in the old country before he came here and labored in a factory until he died. My mother is uneducated, she weaves straw hats to make ends meet, she can be coarse and sharp-tongued and..."

"None of that matters in America, Lizzy. There are no kings here. No titles passed from father to son. The Declaration of Independence says that all men are created equal. That's why we fought a Revolution. Although that sadly doesn't hold true for Black people, I believe it will come to pass if we continue to fight for equality. And for women, too."

"The Declaration is just a piece of paper. We know that's not how things truly are," I said.

"Unfortunately you are right about how things are. But the Declaration is a powerful document, declaring that God has granted us certain rights that no one can take away. These are the rights we are fighting for. It's not an easy fight, but it's one we'll win in the end. I feel it even more strongly when I'm with you, Lizzy."

We kissed again, then I gently pulled away.

"Still you hesitate to give yourself fully to me," said Thomas. "You may remember the story I told you about my brother's trip to the West Indies two years ago for the family business. How he fell in love with a smart and beautiful woman from the islands. Let me remind you that the color of her skin didn't matter a whit to my parents when they met her. All that mattered was her kind heart and fierce love for my brother. They had a ceremony in Jamaica and another here in Philadelphia in the Quaker church. My parents will see your kind soul and will embrace you as they embraced her. As I embrace you now."

Many minutes passed before Thomas whispered, "Elizabeth O'Meara, will you marry me?"

And there on the banks of the Schuylkill, I could finally imagine myself as this man's wife. With Thomas, I knew I would not be limited to a life of domestic chores, but instead would have the freedom to follow in the footsteps of women like Lucretia Mott and Angelina Grimké, who had managed to continue the fight against slavery while bringing up children. And yes, I wanted children. Thomas's children.

"There are two things I must do before I say yes. First, I will tell my brother. Then I must talk to Ma and tell her about you."

"But—"

I pressed two fingers against his mouth. "This is not to ask for her blessing, although it would be wonderful if she did bestow it upon us. I just want her to know I will accept your proposal whether or not she approves. I know this makes no sense, but..."

"It makes sense to you, and that's all that matters. You are a good daughter, Lizzy."

And we kissed as if I had already said yes. Soon we would be joined body and soul. And soon I would know the joy of making love to this man.

How could Ma not approve of Thomas? He was such a fine gentleman. Why would she care if he was Protestant, or that he was so far above us in station, or that he believed that Blacks and whites were equal? On that afternoon of high hopes, I could believe the impossible.

• • •

Mr. Dickens gives me a book he has written, and as soon as he leaves, I open it to an illustration of Thomas and me in a formal parlor receiving visitors. I look beautiful in my satin dress, matching bonnet, and jeweled necklace, smiling as I extend my hand to welcome a guest. Thomas is dressed in his finest suit, looking at me with love and pride. There are cakes and pies on the tables, fine china, crystal goblets. As I lean in closer to the page to see the details, the illustration fades away. I turn the pages and all of them are blank. As I weep, a guard rips the book from my hands. "Whore!" he yells, then laughs as he tosses it into the Schuylkill where it disappears beneath the murky waters. "Murderer!"

I am sick and feverish, lying on blood-stained sheets. I think I have been asleep for a long time. When I wake up, the midwife is dangling the baby over my head. This time my little girl isn't moving or crying. "Look what you've done. You've killed your bastard child. You'll go to prison for this."

CHAPTER 18

This morning my courses flow, so I know another month has passed. Which month it is I neither know nor care. I have no present and no future, and my memories of the past will soon be gone as well. Except for the memory-dreams of what happened the night I gave birth. I know they are true, and last night I saw my baby's corpse. That doesn't mean I killed her. How could I possibly forget that I killed her? There must be some other explanation for the dead baby. I will not dwell on that now or I will start screaming and never stop.

As I secure the rags beneath my undergarments, I try to think back to the time when I was still a virgin, unspoiled, in love, and bursting with hope. Perhaps I'll remember my season of happiness if I write.

•   •   •

"Can you help me when I tell Ma about Thomas?" Aiden was whittling a block of wood while we talked, a bowl at his feet to collect the shavings.

"Of course I'll help you, but you know you don't really need me. You're a big girl now, Lizbet."

I smiled at the use of the name I called myself when I was too young to say Elizabeth. "It doesn't matter how grown up I am. You know as well as I do that she's more likely to listen to you than to me."

"True. It shouldn't be that way, but it's true."

I nodded and for a moment, memories of my troubled past with Ma blotted out the joyous thoughts of Thomas and the words, *Elizabeth O'Meara, will you marry me?*

"I suppose you'll be wantin' me to meet him before I help ye plead yer case with Ma, wouldn't ye now?" Aidan added with a sly smile.

I laughed at his just-off-the-boat accent, which sounded exactly like Meg's. Meg Donavan had attached herself to Aiden when she first moved into the neighborhood, fresh from Ireland. Throughout their childhood the two were rarely apart, and there was no doubt they would soon be man and wife.

"I suppose I would be wantin' ye to meet him," I said, staying in the moment. Although I had already told my brother all about Thomas, he knew I was waiting until the time was right to introduce him and formally announce our engagement to him and Meg. And that time had come.

A week later Aiden, Meg, and I met Thomas for dinner at the City Tavern. The tavern had been frequented by George Washington, John Adams, and other members of the Continental Congress back when our country was being born. It was not quite the fine dining establishment it once had been—a fire had damaged it a few years back—but it was still quite impressive.

Aiden and Meg had already arrived, and Thomas was waiting for me outside when I got there. He led me through a maze of rooms, stopping frequently to greet acquaintances. He seemed to know everyone. Although I was not the kind of girl who took note of what I wore at any given time, I remember what I wore that night: a fitted cotton afternoon dress the color of copper. I had fancied myself quite the stylish woman when I left home, but there amidst the wealthy and fashionable I felt shabby, more like one of their servants than one of them.

When men turned to follow me with their eyes as we passed, I recognized "the look," which was surprisingly undiminished by my inferior dress. I felt out of place, like someone who was "passing" as Lucy called it. I asked Thomas to point me toward our table, telling him I was feeling a little dizzy, and I needed to sit down. I would never admit the real reason: to avoid any further introductions to his various acquaintances, whose manner of speech was so much more refined than mine—a demoralizing experience.

Aiden and Meg were sitting at the table when I arrived, and Thomas soon followed. Meg had barely changed since the first time we'd laid eyes on her. The little slip of a girl with dark curly hair, green eyes, and a smile that radiated pure sunshine, had grown into a woman, still small in stature, with a smile that was as luminous as ever.

We chatted until the server came, spent some time discussing the menu, finally ordering a sumptuous dinner. I don't remember the particulars, but I'm sure it included oysters and turkey pot pie. As we waited for the first course, I rested my hand on the table and Thomas covered it with his.

"I think you already know I have asked for Lizzy's hand, and once she talks to your mother, she will do me the honor of becoming my wife." He turned toward me and touched his lips lightly to mine.

"If I hadn't been told, I'd have known it as soon as you walked into the room," said Meg. "Something told me that the faeries had visited each of you at birth, too." There was a twinkle in her eye.

"I didn't know the faeries visited Quakers," said Thomas, "but I'll allow you may know something I don't."

We all laughed.

Aiden whispered something to Meg, and she nodded.

"Meg and I are planning to wed," he said as he took her hand and squeezed it. "And you two are the first to know."

"Congratulations," I said, "that's wonderful news. But I can't say I'm surprised."

"Sure and you wouldn't be," said Meg, who had never lost the accent or the reverence for magic that came with being born in Ireland. "The faeries decided our fates when we were born, and ours was to be together." She tilted her head toward Aiden. "Did you not know that from the first, love?"

"Well..."

"If you didn't," I said, "then you were blind, Aiden O'Meara. She's been following you around since the day she first set eyes on you."

"And one day I turned around and realized she'd been there all along. The love of my life." Aiden squeezed her hand, then turned to Thomas.

"Lizzy told me you work in your family's importing business," said Aiden.

"Yes, I work with my father."

"What's that like?"

"Except for a few minor disagreements, I must admit it is a joy."

Aiden looked wistful. "If I could've followed in my father's footsteps, I'd be building train cars at Baldwin by his side, but..."

"Lizzy told me what happened to him. Such a good man."

Aiden's face brightened. "Yes, he was. I guess I'm honoring his memory by building tracks for the Reading—tracks that carry the trains my father built."

Meg reached into her purse and pulled out a tiny wooden replica of a steam engine. "My love is a fine whittler, he is. Whittled this engine for me as a birthday present. See how he carved my name along the side?" she said, handing it over to Thomas, who indicated he'd wanted a closer look.

Thomas cradled the wooden train in his hands, smiling broadly. "Seems like our worlds are more alike than anyone thought. I have been whittling since I was a young boy. I find it eases the mind and brings me great pleasure."

"Yes," said Aiden, nodding. "Exactly."

The men talked enthusiastically about their mutual hobby, and Meg and I beamed at our husbands-to-be.

Before we parted company, Meg exclaimed, "Oh, it's a grand time we'll be having, the four of us." And for a moment I believed the faeries had indeed joined all of us at birth.

CHAPTER 19

Today I will try to write about the end of my season of happiness. It is a painful chapter, but one I must write.

· · ·

The day after our meeting at City Tavern, before Aiden and I had a chance to talk to Ma, the Master forced himself on me. Even as I was suffering his assault upon my body, I knew I would now be unfit to be anyone's wife, much less Thomas', a fine gentleman who deserved a fine, unspoiled partner.

How could I tell him I could never see him again? He was already a part of me, and cutting him out of my life would be no less painful than chopping off a limb. But I had to break both of our hearts—for his sake—and I would tell him tonight at a private celebratory dinner we had planned at City Tavern.

When he met me outside the entrance, we embraced. I don't know how long we stood there with our bodies entwined, while the sounds of the city faded, and the world was reduced to the velvety touch of his lips on mine and the beating of our hearts. When we broke apart, my heart grew heavy, knowing this meeting was the beginning of the end of our future together.

As Thomas led me to our table, the play of the candlelight reflecting off the shiny silver and glass was disorienting. Seated across from him, feeling lightheaded, I considered keeping silent about what had happened to me. He wouldn't have to know. In his eyes I'd be the same girl I'd been two days before. But he would know. Men know those things.

I told him I wasn't hungry, but he said he would order oysters for us anyway, and I could eat as much or as little as I wished.

"Why so quiet?" he asked as we waited for the server to arrive. "Are you feeling poorly? We could postpone our celebration and I could take you home."

What if I told him the truth? Loving me as he did, he might have accepted me, impure as I was.

"What's the matter, Lizzy?"

I could offer no words, just tears. He reached across the table and brushed away my tears with his thumbs. Then he framed my face with his hands, and I was nearly undone.

No. I could not tell him the truth. Thomas did not deserve a deceitful, damaged girl like me. So, I did my best to shut down my heart. "I cannot marry you."

"You are toying with me," he said. "This is not you," he protested, with a look of disbelief.

"I'm so sorry, Thomas, but I'm serious. I cannot marry you." I kept my eyes averted from his so he couldn't see even a flicker of untruth there.

Oh, the look on his face! Incomprehension? Incredulity? I lack the words to describe it. He shook his head despairingly. "I don't understand."

I said the words I had rehearsed. "I have thought long and hard about this and concluded that I would always be an outsider in your world..."

"But we already talked about—"

I had to get the words out. "—your world of wealthy high-class people."

He gestured with his hand for me to stop, but the words kept coming. "We come from—"

"Stop!" he said with a vehemence that shocked me and turned heads nearby. His face was red. "Is this about not knowing what fork to use?" Then as quickly as his anger had come, it fizzled out. "I'm sorry, Lizzy. I just—" he couldn't finish as he choked back tears.

That was all I remember of the last time I saw Thomas in the flesh, though he often visited me in my dreams.

CHAPTER 20

A month after our farewell, my courses didn't come, and then again the next month. After the third month, I could no longer ignore what was happening to me. And yet, my stomach was still flat and I had not suffered the morning sickness, so maybe I was wrong. But then came a feathery flutter in my belly. The quickening. Proof that a new life was growing inside me from a seed planted against my will.

I hated the Master for forcing himself on me. I hated myself for continuing to work for him, but did I have a choice? He threatened to slander my name far and wide if I dared to quit, so I would never find other employment.

Every day was a torture. The mere sight of him enraged and sickened me so, I had to clamp my mouth shut to keep from gagging. And I hated *this* Lizzy O'Meara, who had once dreamed of fighting slavery and was now voluntarily enslaving herself. A Lizzy O'Meara who could have fought mightily against the baseless lies the Master would spread about my whorish ways, but chose not to for fear of losing that fight. But most of all (and God forgive me) I hated this...*thing* growing inside me. This thing that would one day be a baby and would bring shame and misery to me and my family. I wanted it *out.*

I put down my pen as I remember that unspeakable thought and pound my chest. Could someone who wanted more than anything to be rid of her unborn child, be capable...even eager...to do away with her newborn? Painful as this next chapter is, I will continue to write. For it brings my salvation.

•   •   •

I stood naked in my bedroom, clawing at my belly, watching streaks of blood blossom on the white flesh. As if that would rid me of this thing, although I knew there were ways to really make that happen. One couldn't miss the advertisements in all the newspapers for Female Monthly Pills, Lady Pills, and French Pills to "stop blockages" of the menstrual cycle. Although they were delicately worded, everyone knew what they were for.

Most apothecaries sold these "remedies," and I chose one far from my house where no one was likely to recognize me. I waited until all the customers were gone, then I approached the proprietor and asked to purchase a packet of Madame Restell's Female Monthly Pills. I remember how his eyes passed judgment on me, but I was determined to get what I wanted.

"I see that you have packets under the counter. Could you please fetch me one?" I took out my purse, but he just stood there. "Is something the matter? If so, I can certainly take my business elsewhere."

"Oh, no, miss." He handed me a box of Madame Restell's pills. "A mild, safe, and efficacious remedy for married ladies whose health forbids a too rapid increase of family."

"And it's *Mrs.*, by the way. Mrs. George O'Malley."

I walked home with a confident stride. For a few blocks I was, indeed, Mrs. George O'Malley, preparing to take what was described as "the very best medicine that ladies laboring under a suppression of their natural illness can take and they very seldom fail to relieve when taken according to the directions."

At home, I closed my bedroom door, removed the required number of pills from the box, and washed them down with a cup of cider. I looked forward to "suppressing my natural illness," and waited throughout that day and the next for the pills to have the desired effect, but nothing happened. I took a second dose and felt a cramping, but nothing more. Maybe he had sold me sugar pills. Or maybe the pills that "very seldom fail to relieve when taken according to the directions" had indeed failed?

If I didn't act quickly, it would be too late. There was only one other remedy, one that terrified me, but I had no choice.

Madame Restell's office was located on the same block as the milliner who bought Ma's straw hats. I'd delivered those hats many times but had never noticed her establishment until I overheard a conversation between two women outside the milliner's shop, long before I had need of her services. When the young woman confessed her fear that she was pregnant, the older woman recounted the story of a married friend of hers in New York who had become pregnant with her fifth child. This friend had visited Madame Restell's office on Fifth Avenue. Madame had given her pills and said if they didn't work, she could perform a procedure that would take care of the problem, which is exactly what happened. After the procedure her friend left the office feeling just fine. The older woman added that Madame's practice was so successful she'd recently opened an office in Philadelphia, just up the street.

And that's how I found my way to Madame Restell, whose assistant assured me they would "take care of my problem" the following week.

The day of the procedure, I approached my mother and volunteered to deliver some hats to the milliner so she wouldn't be suspicious. I bundled myself up in a cloak and scarf that covered half my face and kept my head down as I entered Madame's office.

There were no other "visitors" there at the time, and to my surprise, Madame herself greeted me. I had envisioned a hardened, sharp-featured woman with a permanent scowl, but as I recall, she was surprisingly attractive with a sympathetic countenance. I told her my husband beat me and I did not want to bear him another child. Then I showed her the empty pill box. She said she was sorry the pills had not worked, but was confident that the operation would be performed without pain or inconvenience, and I'd be able to walk out afterward "relieved of my natural illness."

She led me behind a curtain to a darkened room, helped me remove my clothes, and gave me a sheet to cover myself. I hated this baby. I hated its father. I desperately wanted to be done with both of them.

Moments later, a man parted the curtain and stood silhouetted against the light that filtered through the glass window of the door to the office. He was holding an instrument of some sort in his hand, something he would insert into my most private self just as another man had done months before with a different "instrument." I shuddered at the thought. He approached, and I could see him more clearly, an oily smile on his face as he held up the instrument and told me to spread my legs wider. "This won't hurt a bit. Over in a minute," he said impassively.

Just like the Master—two men intent on violating me. "Get away from me. I don't want this. Let me go!"

He backed away, with that phony insinuating smile still pasted to his face. "All right, sweetheart," he said, "but just so you know, we won't give you back your money."

He was so like the Master I wanted to scream...and I did: "Let me out of here! Let me out of here!" I didn't stop screaming until he left the room.

Still covered with the sheet, I sat up on the table, hugged my belly, and rocked. I felt an almost imperceptible tap against my palm and stopped swaying. *Tap. Tap.* Then nothing until I started rocking again. *Tap. Tap. Tap.* Gentle and steady, like the beat of my pulse against my thumb. It was the baby announcing itself—*her*self. Was she kicking me, sending a message that she was glad to be alive? Was she telling me to keep rocking? I could feel my heart beating the same rhythm as her kicking. Perhaps her heart was keeping time as well.

I don't remember getting dressed and walking home, but somehow I managed to do that. And somehow I managed to tell my mother I had a fever and needed to rest. Then I went to my room and closed the door.

After fleeing Madame Restell's establishment, I allowed myself two days in bed, my listlessness convincing my mother and brother that I was truly ill. But I was not alone. My baby reminded me that she was there, and I would never be alone.

Sometimes I cried when I remembered how close I had come to losing her. I had nightmares about that man with the sickening smile—knife in hand—threatening to cut my throat, my belly, telling me to spread my legs. I would wake up covered in sweat. Then I'd trace circles on my belly with my fingers, relieved when my baby responded.

I was tempted to tell my mother I was pregnant and get it over with, but decided to wait until I could no longer hide my condition. I had to prepare myself for her wrath. At the very least, she would say it was my fault for becoming pregnant and bringing shame to the family. And I wouldn't have been surprised if she kicked me out of the house. If that happened, I didn't know where I would live, but Aiden would surely help me.

●   ●   ●

I put down my pen and trace the tracks of the marks I had clawed with my fingernails when my baby was an "it" not a "she." As I lie on my bed looking at the Eye of God, I whisper, "Am I guilty? Did I do it, oh, righteous Judge?"

Why should I expect an answer? God is my judge, but He doesn't hear me. His only response is silence.

I shall now pronounce judgment," says the judge, seated high above me in the courtroom.

"I do not remember doing what they say I did, Your Honor."

"Two eyewitnesses testified that you beat and smothered your baby. This proves beyond a reasonable doubt that you are guilty."

Guilty...guilty...guilty.

CHAPTER 21

This morning I am awakened by someone banging at my door and yelling "book" through the food slot. I hurry over and hold out my hands as the book is passed through to me. It is one I selected from the prison library list shortly after meeting with Mr. Dickens—the first volume of *Oliver Twist.* I run my finger over the faded gold letters on the spine that spell out the title and the name of the author, Charles Dickens. A famous man who offered me sympathy, called me impressive, and asked me to "do him the honor" of reading his book.

On the first page is a likeness of Mr. Dickens, looking a bit younger, but recognizable, nonetheless. I page through the book, stopping at the illustrations. One illustration shows a young man—probably Oliver— asking an evil-looking man for more food; another depicts the same young man about to be beaten by an angry woman. There are many more images that make me eager to read the story.

But excitement turns to frustration when I open to the first page, and I'm reminded that the strain of reading and sewing in dim light for such a long time has weakened my eyes. Even with light streaming through the skylight on a sunny day, I find myself leaning in closer and closer to the page to make out the words. I consider taking the book out into the exercise yard where the brighter light will make reading easier as I've done before. But once outside I invariably find myself unwilling to sacrifice the precious little time I have to move about freely, so I end up walking rather than reading.

I lean in, and when my eyes are mere inches from the page, I read the first paragraph of Mr. Charles Dickens' book:

Among other public buildings in a certain town, which for many reasons it will be prudent to refrain from mentioning, and to which I will assign no fictitious name, there is one anciently common to most towns, great or small: to wit, a workhouse; and in this workhouse was born; on a day and date which I need not trouble myself to repeat, inasmuch as it can be of no possible consequence to the reader, in this stage of the business at all events; the item of mortality whose name is prefixed to the head of this chapter.

I can barely make sense of the text and slam the book down in frustration. I had read so many books in the past with ease; why did I find it so difficult to decipher the meaning of what was in front of me. I was losing the ability to comprehend. I reopen the book to the image of Mr. Dickens and promise him I will persist and live up to the high expectations he had of me. Reading this will require all my concentration, as well as frequent use of the dictionary they have allowed me to borrow. If I had the energy, I would unlock the meaning of this first paragraph and then, chapter by chapter, I would absorb Mr. Dickens' prose. But my time in prison has killed all ambition, and I already lack the motivation to press on.

What if they keep me here forever? What if they decide four years isn't enough to restore my "inner light"? The more I dwell on that possibility, the more convinced I am I will never be released. Every day I lose a piece of the woman I once was, the woman Thomas described as defiant and fearless. No, I will likely die in prison by someone else's hand or by my own, if I am not betrayed by my mind first. They have taken away my freedom, they are robbing me of everything that has made me who I am. Soon there will be nothing left, not even that inner light they are so eager for me to uncover. That will be extinguished too.

Mr. Dickens' book is still open to the first page, and my eyes linger on the oversized "A" that begins the paragraph. There is something familiar about the ornate script, something just out of reach. I pick up my pen and draw the first two letters of the alphabet in large strokes. Then I draw lines that run parallel to the original strokes, creating thick, double-line characters. I can go no further. The meaning of those letters is lost to me. Unless I can find a clue in my journal. Perhaps I wrote something about them and have forgotten.

As I leaf through the pages, I see how much my writing has deteriorated over time. I can barely decipher my later entries. As luck would have it, the entry I am looking for was written a while ago. How long I do not know, for I stopped trying to date my entries after the first few pages. But it was early on when my mind (and my writing) was clearer and I could still recall events that have long since been lost to me.

The letters I had drawn on the page are ornate, decorated with diamonds and circles. Beneath them I had written: "These are the letters that appear on the first two pages of the *Anti-Slavery Alphabet.*" What did that even mean? It was a chapter of my life that would have completely disappeared if I had not recorded it in my journal. I read on and learn (or re-learn) that the poems that accompanied each of the letters in the *Anti-Slavery Alphabet* taught children about the evils of slavery, just as the *McGuffey's* had taught me how to read. Each letter described a different horror visited upon slaves. How they were whipped, chained, kidnapped, and starved.

"**A** is an Abolitionist—
A man who wants to free
The wretched slave—and give to all
An equal liberty."

"**B** is a brother with skin
Of somewhat darker hue,
But in our Heavenly Father's sight,
He is as dear as you."

We sold this book, along with homemade clothing, baked goods, and ornaments emblazoned with anti-slavery symbols at the Female Anti-Slavery Fair to raise money to aid fugitive slaves. Was it only four years ago that I was stitching needlepoint pillows at Lucretia and James Mott's house to sell at the fair?

"It's very important," said Lucy, "that we do not sell goods made by slave hands. That is why we are stitching pillows of linen, not cotton."

(I wonder who will wear the shirts I make here in my cell.)

As Mrs. Mott circulated among the volunteers, Lucy whispered stories about her. "Did you know some of those stodgy Quakers disapprove of her including engravings of her likeness on the products she sells? But she sells them anyway."

"Shh," I said to Lucy, "she's coming over here."

I looked up at the slender woman with the sharp nose and dark hair covered by a bonnet in the Quaker custom.

"Thank you so much for coming, Lucy. And for bringing your friend." She held out her hand and shook mine. "I'm Lucretia. And you are...

"Elizabeth O'Meara, ma'am."

"Oh, yes. The Purvises have mentioned your name to me. We are very grateful there are young people like you who choose to join us." Then, addressing the volunteers in her parlor, she said, "Do your best work, young ladies. We are hoping to raise a lot of money this year." Then she moved on.

"It's a fact that only rich people can afford to buy clothing made by free people," Lucy said softly. "And it's also true that the money we raise to fight slavery comes from the rich. But you don't have to be rich to do your part."

"I am well aware of that, Lucy. You and I are certainly not rich, but if we are lucky, the things we make will fetch a pretty penny."

There must have been twenty women, both Black and white, seated on the elaborately carved wood chairs, the tufted sofas, and matching loveseats scattered around the parlor. They talked in hushed voices as they stitched and ironed, while others baked and cooked in the kitchen.

"You and I do not live far from each other," I said to Lucy," but do we ever see Black and white people doing anything together in our neighborhood?"

"You and I are probably the only ones. And that's why Mrs. Mott joined with my Auntie Harriet and a few other women to start the Women's Anti-Slavery Society. Other organizations don't allow colored people to belong. And most of them are restricted to men only. Mrs. Mott believes women should never be in an inferior position."

Lucy examined the needlework she had just completed, an intricate design that was showing up on posters, dishes, and any other object onto which it could be affixed. It was the figure of a Black slave woman on one knee holding up her chained hands, over which was written the slogan: "Am I Not a Woman and a Sister?" The design had been adapted from the original which showed an enslaved man and read: "Am I Not a Man and a Brother?" Satisfied with her work, Lucy put it down and picked up another cloth to embroider.

•   •   •

I close my journal. How hard it is to recognize the girl in that entry as me.

CHAPTER 22

The heat is stifling, so it must be summer. And although much of my past is lost, some memories have stayed with me through the long days I've spent locked within these walls. With a shaky hand, I write and I remember.

•   •   •

Despite how tempted I was to leave the Master, I knew we couldn't do without the money I brought in. Ma could no longer make hats because her fingers had stiffened, and her mind tended to wander. And Aiden had lost several weeks of work because of a broken arm. Thankfully, the Master was away on business a lot and fretting about financial matters when he was home, so most of the time he left me alone. But he still fancied me from time to time. And when he took me, I concentrated on the scar that remained on his face from the wicked gash I'd inflicted months before.

For a long time he was too busy taking his own pleasure, or too distracted to notice the condition of the vessel he used. But one day his hands lingered over my belly, and although I was still small at six months, he knew. "Whore," he hissed when he felt the swelling. "Filthy Irish trash. Be gone from this house." So I fled, feeling a great burden had been lifted from me, at the same time worrying about how I would continue to provide for my family and keep my secret from them as long as possible.

Who knew what my mother with her unstable mind would have done to me if she knew? Beat me? Kick me out onto the street? Blame me for the rape? Lucy was the only person I could trust. And she proved herself worthy of that trust, enfolding me in a blanket of sympathy as she echoed my anger with the Master and a society that would punish me for being a victim. She promised to find someone willing to employ me. Eventually, she found a woman—Mrs. Cates—who agreed to take me on, with the understanding that my employment with her would be short-lived.

Mrs. Cates matter-of-factly assured me that she didn't care a whit about my condition and told me I could continue to work for her as long as I wished. So I bound myself up as tightly as I could to flatten my belly and wore loose garments. I was able to keep my secret for a couple of months, bringing home my weekly pay as I had when I worked for the Master. But the day finally came when I was almost eight months gone and the binding and loose-fitting clothing no longer hid my pregnancy. So late one evening, I asked my brother to meet me out back near the privy, and it was then that I told him what had happened.

"I'm going to Northam's house," he yelled, "and confront the fecking bastard. I'll fecking kill him!" His face was red with rage; I don't think I'd ever seen him so angry.

Suddenly, one of our neighbors called out of an open window nearby, "Quit the racket out there! A working man needs his sleep."

"Shhh," I put my finger to my lips, then to Aiden's. "Please, you need to be quiet about this."

Aiden took a couple of deep breaths, then whispered fiercely, "I mean it, Lizzy. I'm gonna kill the bastard."

"Please don't fight him, Aiden. It will be my word against his, and who would take my word against such a rich and powerful man. Please, I don't want you to end up in prison."

"That doesn't matter to me," he said. "How can I rest knowing what that bastard did to you?" He balled his hands into fists. "I'll take a knife to him, carve him up."

"Sweet Jesus. I'm in enough trouble as it is, and I'll need your protection. Especially from Ma when she finds out. How can you help me if you end up in prison for murder?"

I had planned to tell Ma with Aiden by my side, but one evening she walked into my room before I could cover myself.

"Shame. Shame," she cried. "Whore!" she screamed over and over, slapping my cheek with each repetition.

And God help me, I believed her. There must have been something in my manner or how I dressed that had drawn the Master to me, even though I'd always kept my eyes lowered and tried to stay out of his way. Something wicked about me that caused Timmy Doyle and all those other boys and men to look at me that way. Still, I wanted to believe I was wrong to blame myself. After all, *they* were the ones with the wicked thoughts, not me. But I could not dismiss the belief that somehow I had been complicit in my undoing.

"How far gone are you?" Ma ran her hand roughly over my belly. "Seven months?"

"Almost eight," I said so softly she made me repeat it.

Her eyes widened. "You thought you could hide it from me?" she shrieked. "Just go off somewhere and have it, then come back like it never happened?"

"No, ma'am. The priest says all life is sacred."

"You should have thought about that when you lay with that man," she said scornfully.

"I did not...lay with him. He took me—" I protested.

"Enough!" Ma said as she covered her ears. "I don't want to be hearing about what you did under the blankets." She squeezed my belly, gave it a pinch, and the baby kicked her. Then she made a face and left the room.

I rubbed the spot Ma had pinched. "You are a fighter, little one," I whispered, "and I will be a fighter again, as soon as I leave this house with you in my arms." I lay back down and stroked my belly. "I am so proud of you, my baby girl. I will not let anything happen to you."

When Ma told me how much she hated me, she was telling the baby she hated her, too, because the baby and I were one. Could my little one feel that hate? I vowed she would not suffer the same fate as me. I would give her all the love I never got from my mother. And no man would ever touch her like the Master touched me.

As my baby changed positions, I watched the ebb and flow of her movements across my belly. I felt a tidal wave of love wash over me.

CHAPTER 23

Hate! What was it about me that made my mother hate me so? Or was it something in her? I fall asleep with those questions and wake up with answers. I write quickly before I forget. I cross out as much as I write, and soon the page looks like a child's scribbling. But it is the best I can do.

•   •   •

When I was growing up, Ma would sometimes take to her bed and not leave her room for a day, two days, even longer. Before she disappeared, she would often go quiet, refusing to eat, losing interest in everything—us included. At other times, she would lose her temper over every little thing, shouting at Aiden and me about how we needed to show her more respect, before telling us she needed to be alone and not bother her.

I could not fathom what she did up there all alone during the day, but whenever I peeked in, the blinds were drawn and all I could see of her was a lump under the covers. She said nothing, not one word of explanation, when she rejoined us. It was as if those days had been wiped from history.

Finally, Aiden and I decided we wanted to understand why Ma behaved as she did. So one night when she was up in her room, and I had cooked sweet apple pudding—Da's favorite dessert—we refused to let him up from the dinner table until he explained what was going on.

"Why doesn't Ma love me and Aiden?" I asked him.

His eyes widened. "And why would you be thinking she doesn't?"

"Because she goes to her room and leaves us," Aiden answered.

"'Tis true, she leaves me, too, but sometimes she feels too sad to be around us."

"Why?" asked Aiden.

"Yes, Da. What did we do to make her sad?"

"'Tis not because of anything you did. It's something inside her. Her mother had it, too. And *her* mother before that. They call it melancholia. Your ma was probably born with it."

"Will Aiden and I get it, too?"

"No, lass. If you had it, you would know."

"But there are times I feel so sad, too."

"And do ye take to your bed?" he asked.

"No. Never."

"Then you've nothing to worry about," Da said reassuringly.

Reflecting on that memory led me to recall other puzzling aspects of my mother's behavior. It was then I began to understand why she got so angry when I didn't want to play with dolls and went wild with anger over my unladylike behavior; all the times she told me that being married and having babies was the most important thing a woman could do, and that the fate of an unmarried woman was a lifetime of grief and misfortune. It was Aiden who told me the story Da had told him about what had happened back in Ireland.

When Ma was still living with her family, her unmarried older sister, Siobhan, became pregnant. The family tried to keep it secret, but once the news got out it inevitably spread throughout the small village. Ultimately, they blamed Ma's parents for her sister's loose morals. The village children would even taunt my mother, calling her a whore like her sister, as if something like that were catching.

One tragic day, Ma discovered her sister's body hanging in the barn, her belly swollen with child. I don't think Ma every got over the horror of what happened that day and the shame that stuck to the family like tar.

CHAPTER 24

Earlier today I was taken to the bathing room for the bath we are allowed every two weeks. A woman helped me disrobe. Then I stepped into a small tub of warm water, just large enough for me to sit in if I bent my legs almost to my chest. I scrubbed myself clean with water that was already cool.

Tonight, as I lie here in bed, I remember how good it felt to bathe today, even though I could barely fit into the tub. Tonight, I imagine immersing myself in a deep pool of warm water, scrubbing away the past, and emerging reborn. The water is as comforting as a lullaby, so I will rest here a little longer. I close my eyes and...

Scalding! The water. I must get out but can't because it's not the water that's burning, it's my body. It burns with a fever that pulses with my every breath. The fever has no beginning and no end. It just is. And then the pain, coiling like a snake, building and building till the world is reduced to a ball of pain in my belly. And still it grows. A gruff voice. The midwife.

"Hold her down. Baby's coming fast. It wants to be born."

Please—please make it stop! Suddenly the pain is gone, and all is black. Then it comes again, worse than before.

My mother's voice: "Better it was born dead."

There is no end to the pain. Please let me die. Again, all is black as death until an explosion of pain tears my insides. "Push. PUSH." More pain. "PUSH, dammit!" The midwife is holding my baby just out of reach. It's a girl and she's crying.

"Let me hold her," I implored.

"No, I have to take care of her," barks the midwife. "She is sickly."

Fever. Chills. Then nothing.

I awaken in a pool of blood. The midwife is holding the baby under the arms, dangling her body just out of my reach. But this time—oh, dear Lord!—this time my baby's head is hanging oddly as if it doesn't belong to her body, and she is not crying. There are bruises on her face, on her arms.

"Look! Look what you've done!"

"No! No!" I want to turn away, but my body has turned to stone.

"Look." She shakes the silent child. The corpse...

Awake now, I walk the floor and bang my fists against the wall to dissipate the image of the dead baby that haunted me in my dream and continues to haunt me during my waking hours. I do not remember killing her, and even though evidence of my guilt is clear, it is not proven. I will try to hold on to that sliver of doubt for the rest of my confinement, however long that might be.

Confinement. I remember another confinement—the one imposed by my mother—the one that ultimately led me to this place.

CHAPTER 25

When Ma learned I was with child, she insisted I leave the house at once with only the clothes on my back. But no sooner had I crossed the threshold than she pulled me back inside—no doubt worried my condition would become public knowledge and shame her, as it had shamed and killed her sister Siobhan. She insisted that I remain in the house with no visitors, as if she could hide my situation from our gossipy neighbors.

Although Ma confined me to the house, she made it clear she couldn't stand the sight of me. I could see it on her face and the way she turned her back on me more often than not. As a result, I stayed in my room, emerging only to get food from the kitchen when she was not around. But it was inevitable our paths would cross in such close quarters. When I encountered her occasionally in the kitchen, she rarely acknowledged my presence; except one time she called me Siobhan, and another time she lectured me about loose morals. When her bouts of melancholia flared and she took to her bed, I could fetch food from the kitchen whenever I wanted, and use the privy outside instead of the chamber pot.

Without Aiden's support, I would not have survived my confinement. He was my guardian angel. He worked seven days a week, tirelessly laying track to pay our rent, at the same time putting aside a little for a place of his own with Meg. His visits at the end of each day brought light into my dreary days. Despite being exhausted from his job, he brought me food that he often prepared with his own hands when Ma had made only enough for one. When I begged him to find a way to get me out of there, he counseled me to be patient.

"You will soon be done with all this," he told me.

"Not soon enough. Sometimes I've half a mind to hang myself before the time comes."

Aiden looked stricken, but before he could reply, I put my hand on his forearm and squeezed.

"I'm sorry I shocked you. Only half a mind means that the other half wants me to live. But it's so unfair that you spend your days doing backbreaking work, then come home, bring me food and...take care of my other needs." I looked over at the chamber pot he emptied every night when I was asleep.

"There are worse things in this world. I'll survive, and so will you."

I was not so sure.

•   •   •

I had been homebound for about a month, when Aiden told me he had accepted an out-of-town work assignment and he'd be away for four weeks.

"You're leaving me for four weeks? I don't know what I'll do without you—alone with Ma." I started trembling at the thought.

"Ah, try not to worry, Lizbet. I won't deny it'll be hard on you, but you've always been the stronger one. I know you can make it through to my return. Such good money—double what I'm making now. And I calculated that in four weeks, I'll have enough money to marry Meg and rent our own place."

"When are you leaving?"

"Couple days."

"A couple...I have a bad feeling about this, Aiden. You *must* be here when the baby comes in July. Can you swear to it?"

"I swear on Da's grave that I'll be back when you have the baby. Nothing can stop me."

When Aiden left, the endless days stretched even longer. I knew every inch of this tiny room: the dark wood floors with the worn red carpet, the nightstand with the chipped blue-and-white chamber pot, the scratched pine dresser. And reflected in the mirror above the dresser was the face of a pale, worn-out girl with tangled red hair, sad eyes, and a huge belly. She looked so much older than her years I could have wept. But I didn't, because my belly was hard and strong, and I believed all the strength and vitality that had drained from the rest of my body was nurturing my baby.

•   •   •

It might have been the cramps that woke me in the middle of the night. Or the baby's fierce kicking that turned my belly into a battlefield. I hadn't felt well all evening, and when I fell so ill, my first thought was that Ma had poisoned me. But when I heard her being sick in the next room, I realized the more likely cause of my distress was the sausage both of us had eaten for dinner.

I awoke the next morning with fever and chills, which continued for several days. Although I slept most of that time, I remember a few things. Like how the baby kicked and pressed against my organs. She was strong, my little girl, fighting to be free, but my mother who was now forced to attend to me, didn't see it that way. "It's a sign," she said. "It wants to kill you. Normal babies don't kick like that." I also remember my mother talking to someone downstairs, their voices so loud they awakened me.

"Why, if it isn't Timmy Doyle? I haven't seen you in ages. You've grown so tall, yet I still recognize you. And what might you be doing on our doorstep?"

"Ah, and it's a sorry tale I'm here to tell you, but me conscience forces me."

Timmy Doyle! How could it be that he was still stalking me after all these years? And speaking as if he was fresh off the boat, to charm my mother. I shuddered in anticipation of the "sorry tale" he was about to tell.

"Surely you know about the man your daughter has been cavorting with."

"What man?"

"I don't know his name, Mrs. O'Meara, but he comes from a hifalutin family, and he must of found it amusing to consort with a girl of a lower class. Excuse me, Mrs. O'Meara, I don't mean to call you or meself lower class, but that's what men like that think of us good, hard-working Irish."

"'Tis the truth. But I don't know anything about my Lizzy associating with a man above her station."

"I saw it with me own eyes. Sneakin' down dark alleys together. Why once I saw her pressed against a wall, her legs wrapped round his waist, as he...ah, forgive me, Mrs. O'Meara, I didn't mean to be telling a lady like you all that."

Timmy Doyle! Why do you haunt me after all these years? The baby kicked in sympathy with my anguish. I heard my mother cry out, but I couldn't make out the words.

Later, she came into my room. "I've a whore for a daughter. And a liar." She spat out the words. "You told me you were raped by Master Northam, but now I know the truth. You were whoring, just like I thought, and it's your own damn fault you're carrying that bastard child."

I prayed for Aiden to return soon and once again be my guardian angel.

CHAPTER 26

Thomas and I sit by the river, its water murky and opaque. Behind us, a forest arises thick and impenetrable, its thirsty black leaves sucking the sunlight from the sky. Strange, this, since I bid Thomas a final goodbye so long ago, but here we are. I lean in to kiss him. But his lips are gone, and his face has hardened into a white disk that rolls off his shoulders and into the river. I open my mouth to scream, but hear instead the voice of a woman coming from behind me. "Am I not a woman and a sister? Help me."

"Yes," I say." I'm coming." I turn to see a woman dark as coal emerging from the forest behind her. The rattling of the chains is so loud, I can no longer hear her voice. "I'm coming," I yell. "Hold on." Just as my hand touches hers, a pair of arms encircles my waist and drags me to the river. Now I'm the one weighted down by chains.

"Gotcha, Red," he says. "You've got one last chance to give me what I want," he smirks, grabbing me between my legs. I spit blood at him. "In you go, Red," he says, but the Master has taken his place, tossing me into the icy, crimson waters of the Schuylkill. My mother yells, "Whore, murderous whore," as the bloody water claims me.

·   ·   ·

Sometimes in my dreams I glimpse images of myself taking pleasure in the Master's touch. On those mornings, I awaken with a certainty of my own sinful nature. I could never commit to paper the shameful details of my encounters with the Master. Yet they stay with me, so they must be true. One morning I rip up the paper with "Whore" written on it. But then I rewrite the word on another sheet of paper as a reminder of what I am beginning to believe I might have been.

CHAPTER 27

My fevered dreams bring my memories closer and closer to the truth of what happened that night. I am afraid I will remember killing my baby. I do not want to relive that moment, but I am a prisoner of my mind, and the mind will have its way. If I am guilty, only one thing will free me: death.

This morning I awaken on my knees in bed, pressing down on my pillow. I have done this before. And I remember.

• • •

I have given birth and I am lying on the bloody sheet. The midwife holds my child. It's a girl and she's crying. "Let me hold her." "No, I have to take care of her. She is sickly." I am feverish and so tired I cannot keep my eyes open.

When I wake up I am on my knees, pressing down on a pillow.

Ma is screaming, "Look what you've done," as she pulls my baby out from under the pillow. She hands the baby to the midwife, who dangles her over me. Her head is hanging at an odd angle, and she is covered with bruises.

"You killed your bastard child," yells Ma.

"No! No!" I try to turn away.

"Look," says Ma. Then, "Get dressed quick. They're coming."

"Who's coming?"

"You'll see." She sounds happy.

"I shall now pronounce judgment," said the judge sitting high above me in the courtroom.

"But I do not remember doing what they say I did, your honor."

"You saw the body, did you not?"

"I don't remember, your honor."

"Be that as it may, two eyewitnesses testified that you beat and smothered your baby. And the coroner identified the corpse."

I hung my head as the judge found me guilty and sentenced me to four years at Eastern State Penitentiary.

I stood before him, trying to cover the stains on my dress from the milk that leaked from my breasts. I was numb. I felt nothing.

At the time I protested that I was innocent. But now that I remember smothering her, I know I received the sentence I deserved.

CHAPTER 28

I will hang myself like Aunt Siobhan, swinging from the barnyard rafter. Grabbing articles of clothing from the drawer, I knot them together to fashion a noose and tie them tight, before I remember there is nowhere to hang it. No rafters. Nothing but the skylight, which is too high to reach, even from a chair atop a table.

Dinner arrives, but I don't eat it. They punish me by withholding my food, but it is of no consequence. Everything tastes like straw. The guard tells me I must eat, and I tell him I don't care. Hunger is my friend. Day after day I eat small portions of the food they serve me, then I throw it up. I look down at my legs, grown skeletal, preparing my body for death. Starvation is slower than hanging, but it will take me to the same place.

One morning I am too weak to get out of bed. A guard comes in to take me to the doctor. He commands me to cover my face with the hood. I am too weak to walk, and struggle for breath, so he carries me down the hall. I no longer try to peek out from underneath the sack to see my surroundings, as I once did. Instead, I welcome the darkness as I am carried.

"She has no fever," says the doctor. "Take her back and make her eat. You know how they watch us. They make reports. A death from neglect would be a stain on our reputation. We cannot afford to let anyone die of starvation on our watch."

They deposit me in my cell, seat me at the table, and threaten to punish me if I don't eat. They tell me they will bind my hands and make me wear the hood all day. Although I long for death, the hood is something I cannot abide, so I swallow the straw food as the guard watches me eat. After he leaves, I press my fingers against the back of my throat and vomit in the toilet. Eventually they catch on to what I am doing and promise to punish me if they detect the smell of vomit in my cell.

They say I am not sick. That is because I have a sickness no one can see.

CHAPTER 29

Oh, joy! I see a little girl with red hair walking away from me into a misty forest. I have had occasional glimpses of her in the past—just before sinking into slumber—but this is the first time I recognize her, though I have never met her. My daughter, Sarah. Such elation. I did not murder her after all. I race to catch her before she disappears, but just as I reach out and my fingers grasp her dress, she dissolves, and I am swept away into the void. She is gone forever, killed by my hand.

CHAPTER 30

It is morning. I am in my cell and my loins ache as if I have given birth. I smell the blood. I see the tiny broken body. The pillow. Oh, God, that vision is so real, so true. Hard as I pound my head with my fists, I cannot rid myself of the memory. I look up at the Eye of God that watches me even as I sleep.

"Jesus, you say the truth shall make me free. But I shall never be free. You say the wages of sin are death, so why does my heart still beat? Oh, God, kill me now...Please, Lord, I beg You to relieve me of this life. I wait for your answer, but your Eye never blinks and as always you offer me only silence. So, it is I who must do it. I cannot hang myself or starve myself. Let me leave this world in blood just as I came into it. Just as my baby came into it four years ago."

I grab a fork and drag it heavily across my belly, carving bloody tracks over the ones I'd clawed while I was pregnant. But it is not enough. Holding the sides of the sink, I bang my head against the wall. I do it again, and blood flows into the sink. Let them hear me. What more can they do? Again, again, harder, until a river of blood flows. The room spins. I welcome the darkness.

Now I am in bed, my head covered with something. A hood? No. Only the top of my head is covered, since the world is not dark. I touch the top of my head, which appears to be wrapped in a bandage. I do not remember them taking me out of my cell, or wrapping up my head, or berating me, which they undoubtedly did. The last thing I remember is the river of blood in the sink before descending into death. Or so I thought.

My wounded head conjures an odd memory of the doll Ma gave me. I had hated it so much I wounded it by marking it with a spot of blood I pricked from my finger before I gave it to Lucy. What little girl wants to wound a doll? One who grows up to murder her child. Every memory leads to that murder.

From that day on, I do not eat the meals they serve or drink the water. I do not go outside to exercise. I do not care.

CHAPTER 31

I stay in bed. No longer crying. No longer hoping. Although I have not taken food in days, they do not punish me. They let me starve because they know I am not worth saving. I do not change my clothes or wash my face. I leave the bed only to relieve myself, because I refuse to die in my own filth. I no longer hunger for the sound of a human voice. The silence has won. I will spend my remaining time in bed repenting, as they wanted me to do all along. They have won.

CHAPTER 32

Your solitude has affected your ability to determine what is true," says
Dickens, feeding me porridge. *"This slow and daily tampering with the
mysteries of the brain is worse than any torture of the body, because its
wounds are not upon the surface."*

"Do not listen to the man," says the priest in the confessional. *"It is
not your imprisonment that is the cause, but your mother's madness that
you have inherited. You must do penance for your sin or you will burn
in hell."*

"There is no hell," says the Quaker matron. *"There is just your inner
light. But all this time in solitude, and you still have not uncovered your
inner light or repented. You are no different now, B358, than you were
when you came in."* Her face dissolves, but she continues to speak. *"So,
you will remain B358...*

"B358." Someone shakes me.

"Go away, let me sleep," I murmur.

"B358, I have news. Wake up, B358..."

CHAPTER 33

"B358." It is the kind guard with the harelip, and he will not stop shaking me. "I have news."

"What are you doing in my dreams?" I ask, bewildered.

"Your dreams?" he lisps. "No, I am real. If you open your eyes and sit up, I will tell you."

I struggle to sit up, so he leans over and gently assists me. "In two weeks, you will have served your four-year sentence, and you will be released."

"I do not understand what you are saying."

"In two weeks' time you will be free."

I close my eyes and open them. He is still there. He is, indeed, real.

Has it been four years since they locked me into this cell? Empty years that could just as easily have been centuries.

"And where will I go?" I mutter more to myself than him.

"That, I cannot say. But I can tell you that your brother is coming to get you in two weeks," he says smiling.

"How do you know that?" *He was not with me at the birth. He did not come to my trial. Why would he deliver me from this prison now, after he has forsaken me?*

"Here." He hands me an envelope. "From your brother. I will leave now."

The envelope bears my name, written in my brother's hand.

Dear Lizzy,

I cannot tell you how many letters I have written to you, knowing they would never be delivered. They allowed the delivery of this letter, since you are so close to the end of your sentence. Just two weeks!

How cruel you must think me for being absent from your bedside when you gave birth and my absence from the trial, which I didn't learn about until my return. I will explain everything when I see you. Not a day has gone by when I haven't thought of you. Much has changed since you left, and I have so much to tell you. I write this letter in haste as I want to get it into your hands as soon as possible. Please believe me when I say these absences were caused by events beyond my control.

I truly believe you are innocent. The Elizabeth O'Meara I have known all my life would never commit such a crime. I have done everything I could to clear your name. I went to the judge and spoke to him of your fine character. I begged him to reconsider his sentence and he refused. But I will not stop until I have proven your innocence. I am trying to locate the midwife who delivered your baby, and I know she will confirm you didn't murder your child. I am getting closer to finding her, so please do not lose hope.

Two weeks from now when the doors open and you step out into freedom, I will be waiting outside for you with open arms. Two weeks seem like a lifetime. But in the blink of an eye, we will be together.

Your loving brother,

Aiden

My brother has not abandoned me after all, and he will be here in two weeks to take me home. But what good is freedom if I leave here as a convicted criminal. Aiden is so sure I am innocent. I wish I could share that belief, but those nightmares—the pillow, the dead baby dangling from the hands of that woman—they are the memories of a guilty woman.

I may have arrived here believing I was an innocent woman, but I leave here as a guilty one. I had been right in thinking that I lacked the maternal instinct every woman seemed to be born with. Like the doll I hated and gave to Lucy, who loved it instinctively although she was only a child. All those girls who pretended they were mothers while I read my books. How I tried to murder my unborn baby.

For better or worse, I am to be released in two weeks, yet lack the strength to even walk down the hall. So I'll need to eat every meal from now on and walk as much as possible in my cell and in the yard. I must prepare myself to walk out the front door and into the world.

CHAPTER 34

The kind guard comes in the morning to take me to the warden's office; from there I will be released into the world. He tells me his name is George and calls me Elizabeth, the first time I have been addressed by my given name in four years.

"Thank you for giving me back my name."

He smiles his crooked, mustached smile. "You have served your four years and survived them in your right mind."

"There is still a lot that is not right," I said.

He smiled. "But it will be. You have earned your freedom."

"I earned nothing." My cheeks burn.

He lets my last remark linger in the air and says, "Before we leave this cell, is there anything you'd like to bring with you?"

"I leave with nothing, just the same as I entered." Then I spot my journal on the worktable. "Except for this." I pick it up, but it drops from my shaky grasp and falls open on the floor. I reach down to pick it up, but lose my footing, and George catches me. I sit down on the bed, and he brings me the journal, which is still open. I read the words on the page: "One thing I know to be true is this: My brother Aiden was my best friend. This I also know to be true: My brother would never lie. It's against his nature."

But is it? People change. Has he really done everything he could to clear me? Maybe he couldn't. Maybe he discovered something that proves my guilt?

George hands me the hood. "I'm sorry, but you must put this on."

I am unsteady beneath it, but George holds me firmly as he guides me out into the hall and down the corridor to another; and then, surprisingly, outside into the morning air. *Is this how I am to be freed?* But he leads me onward, through a door and into a warm space that smells of tobacco and woodsmoke.

"You may remove your hood, Miss O'Meara." The voice is low and gravelly.

George supports me as he removes the sack, staying close until he sees that I can stand steady on my own. "Godspeed," he whispers before slipping away.

The warden sits behind a mahogany desk that smells freshly polished. Although it is a large desk, the warden's bulk makes it appear small.

"It is our hope that you have benefitted from your time of solitude and reflection, Miss O'Meara, and have truly repented for your crime."

"I killed my baby," I murmur. With him seated and me standing, it's easy to avoid each other's gaze.

"Yes. That's why you spent four years here."

"Thought I was innocent...then I...murdered..." My voice trailed off, and I looked down.

"You leave here a changed woman. We are confident you will henceforth lead an exemplary and righteous life."

Changed? Exemplary? Righteous? How, if I leave here a criminal and cannot prove my innocence? If I am a criminal.

"You will go now with the matron." He beckons to a woman who was standing behind me, unnoticed by me till that moment. "She will exchange the clothes you are wearing with the ones you arrived in, and then you will be released."

I clutch my journal tightly and nod.

The matron helps me dress in my old clothes, as I am too weak and muddled to perform even the simplest of tasks. My dress hangs loose on me. I cannot believe I once wore this garment. They have washed out the milk stains, the reminder of my lost years of motherhood.

This was to be a joyful day, a day I looked forward to for four long years, but all I feel now is numb.

The matron hands me my journal, and I follow her down the hall.

CHAPTER 35

They open the heavy oak front door of the penitentiary and raise the iron grate, and I step outside into my freedom. Although it is July, I shiver in my cotton dress. The early afternoon light is blinding, and I shield my eyes. I realize that what I saw from the exercise yard was just a pale slice of the real sky. Peering between my fingers I glimpse a dream world. Before me is a meadow with a grove of the few cherry trees that remain, the trees that gave the penitentiary its name. Beyond that, the city.

The sight of the bright green leaves of the trees against the glorious blue of the sky lift my spirits. Dare I imagine that Aiden found the midwife and Sarah, and he will bring her to me? My eyes adjust to the light, and I look around for my brother, but I am alone. My hope quickly turns to despair. I am a fool. Why should I be surprised that he chose not to come? Why should I believe what he wrote in his letter about believing in my innocence? I know better—his four-year silence said it all.

I wait in front of the prison, leaning against the low stone wall that borders the grounds, but there's still no sign of Aiden. Where will I go now that my brother has deserted me? I wish I had died in my cell. *How will I find my way in all the noise and confusion that lies before me?*

Beyond the meadow lies the city, smoke rising from its many factories—the city I am a stranger to now. My heart races, nearly exploding. The world spins...

After I brace myself against the wall and struggle to regain my balance, I turn and look behind me at the gray stone towers of the fortress that has held me captive for the past four years. How ironic that the building meant to convey misery to the unfortunate being about to enter it, now beckons to me as a place of safety.

"Lizzy!"

I turn around and there he is, my brother—taller, broader, and more handsome than I remember—running toward me with open arms. He is alone. As I step toward him, my knees buckle, and I collapse to the ground.

PART II: The Doll

CHAPTER 36

Aiden reaches around me to help me up, and at first I recoil at the touch of a man's hands on my body. He senses my distress and slips his hands out from under me. I look into his eyes. Green, like mine. My brother. I wrap my arms around him, and he raises me to a sitting position on the low stone wall. Still clinging to him, I close my eyes and surrender to the unaccustomed joy of his loving touch. As he lifts me to my feet, I inhale the familiar scent of his soap. He holds me for a long time, and once again I am overwhelmed by the unfamiliar sensation of being embraced by someone who loves me. But my joy is short-lived.

He steps back and shakes his head. "Ah, Lizzy, what have they done to you? You are so..." There are tears in his eyes. I know he is seeing a hollowed-out version of the sister he knew, and my tears echo his. How can I begin to tell him all I have suffered these past four years? But those concerns evaporate in the wake of what Aiden says next.

"Your baby is alive, Lizzy."

"Why are you lying to me, Aiden? I know I murdered her," I say.

"That is *not* true." His eyes, once beacons of truth, bore into mine.

"If she is alive, where is she?" My voice is so weak he must lean in to hear me. I take a deep breath and try again. "Where is my little girl?"

"I don't know."

"Then...how can you tell me she's alive?" I look at him pleadingly, afraid to believe the impossible.

"I swear by all that's holy. We don't know where she is, but we're very close to finding her."

I pull away. "I don't understand." I had been wrong to give in to the delusion of false hope. "You're lying. I know you're lying. She's dead and I killed her. Let me go."

I get up and stumble back toward the prison doors, but my legs do not obey and once again I'm on the ground. This time, Aiden lifts me in his arms. "No," I protest, but I'm too weak to resist.

"My poor Lizzy," he says as he carries me down the hill. "You're but skin and bones."

Too feeble to respond, I think: Yes, this is what Ma and the Master and the four years in prison have reduced me to. And I have paid for their callousness with my body and my soul.

As we approach the street, the city announces itself with clattering hooves, wheels on cobblestones, clanging fire engines, cries, and laughter. My head aches.

Aiden brings his mouth close to my ear. "We are very close to finding her, Lizzy, but it's a complicated story." He goes on about Baldwin, and Ma, and a midwife, and many other things, but I can make no sense of it. After four years, all he can tell me about my daughter is that he's close to finding her. If he hasn't been able to find her after all this time, why should I believe he will now?

"Ah, Lizzy. I can see this is too much for you. Let me get you home and get some food into you. Then I'll tell you everything." He summons a carriage and the driver helps him lift me on to the seat before he climbs up next to me.

Everywhere I look, smokestacks belch into the clear blue sky, staining it a dark and dirty gray. As the carriage bumps and shakes, I close my eyes. It is a frightening world.

•   •   •

I awaken with a pounding heart in a strange room. Somehow I have escaped my cell, and now I must brace myself for punishment. I stumble out of bed and feel a smooth floor under my feet. Wood. How can this be? I must be dreaming. Holding on to the furniture, I guide myself to a door that opens out on to a hallway. I make no noise until I twist my ankle and cry out in pain. What have I done? Now they will beat me. A door opens and a man hurries toward me. I cover my chest with my arms to protect myself from the assault that is sure to follow. The man comes closer and I tremble. *Please, no.*

A voice says, "Lean on me."

It's not a guard after all. My brother. Ah, now I remember. The release from prison. The carriage ride. This is not a dream.

"Lean on me," Aiden says again, "and I'll guide you back to your room."

My brother. My room.

"Now sleep," he commands.

"Yes, sleep," I murmur.

CHAPTER 37

It is early morning, and in the dim light I see a pitcher, a glass, and a plate on the table next to my bed. The guard must have delivered my breakfast. Why didn't he pass it through the slot for me to take? How did he get into my cell?...I can't keep my eyes open...

A burst of light startles me awake. The curtains are open, and someone is standing silhouetted against the light from the window.

"I'm so sorry I disturbed you, love," a woman says, "although you did sleep well. All yesterday and last night."

"We're not allowed to sleep a whole day."

"What do you mean, you're not allowed?"

I sit up panic stricken before realizing I'm not in a cell. And I see it's Meg standing at the foot of the bed. "I'm sorry...I get confused. Whose room is this?"

"'Tis yours, love."

"I don't remember this room."

Meg laughs. "Oh, you're thinking it's your childhood bedroom. Well, someone else lives in that house now. We're living in a much grander place. Three stories. Isn't that something? Aiden has done well these last few years. He'll tell ye all about it."

I look around at the nightstand, the dresser, the bookcase, and a cheery picture of an English country garden.

"Would ye like to come downstairs?" Meg says. "Or would that make ye too uncomfortable?"

Everything makes me uncomfortable: the strange room, the door I can open, even Meg's cheery voice. There is nothing cheery about my life. "I want to stay here."

"I understand. I'll be collecting these dishes and bringing ye something fresh to eat."

I close my eyes. I don't want anything to eat. I don't want anything.

Later someone comes into the room, treading lightly. I keep my eyes shut. Let her think I'm sleeping. She puts something on the table next to my bed, and I wait until the door shuts before I open my eyes. She has brought bread and boiled eggs. I don't remember when I ate last, but the thought of eating sickens me.

When I open my eyes, the sun is no longer shining directly through the window. I look out and can see a tiny sliver of sky, like I saw in the exercise yard. Is that where I am now? I close my eyes again and dream that Aiden has once again abandoned me.

I am awakened by the touch of a hand on my shoulder and someone whispering in my ear. Aiden. He wants to tell me why he wasn't able to return in time for the birth. Say what he will, I believe he could have made it back if he had wanted to. The brother I remember could do anything he set his mind to. He just didn't try hard enough. He talks and I hear only bits and pieces of what he says.

"Nearly killed me that I couldn't be with you...gave you my word...laying track out near Altoona...good money...pay for you...baby...house...wedding. Cholera swept through camp...death's door...calomel and opium...survived...too late to return in time. When I came home, Ma told me you'd murdered the baby."

Now I pay attention.

"I called her a liar," he says, "but she insisted you'd done it. I told her she could prove she wasn't lying by giving me the name of the midwife, but she refused. I went to the judge and told him what a good person you are, someone who wouldn't harm a fly. I begged him to reconsider his sentence. But he told me his hands were tied. The police had seen the dead baby, and Ma had told them she'd seen the murder with her own two eyes. By then, you were already in prison."

The dead baby. "Please go away, I need to sleep now," was all I could manage.

Aiden murmured something, but I was already slipping away.

CHAPTER 38

Sometimes I am back in my cell, sometimes in this room. More and more in this room. I have eaten a little, and I can now walk around it. Meg and Aiden talk to me, bring me food, encourage me to eat. One morning I am already out of bed when Meg comes in.

"Ye have strength in ye. Would ye be ready to come downstairs soon?"

"Maybe tomorrow."

Time passes. Days? Hours? I think it's tomorrow now, and when she asks me if I'm ready to go downstairs, I say yes.

"Aiden has good news," she says. "*Very* good news. Why don't ye get dressed? He'll tell ye about it downstairs."

Meg opens the dresser drawers to show me the clothes she bought for me. I thank her and tell her I will meet her downstairs.

I take my time getting dressed in the chemise, drawers, and blue-print cotton day dress Meg has chosen. I am unaccustomed to the feel of clean, soft fabric against my skin. The dress is loose fitting, the brown booties are comfortable. I look in the mirror and see a drawn face, tangled hair, and sad eyes. It is me and it is not me.

I hug the banister and take a step down the staircase as Aiden climbs up to meet me. When I stumble he catches me, and I lean on him as he leads me to the dining-room table.

"Let me get ye some tea," says Meg once I'm sitting.

Aiden takes my hand and runs a thumb over my broken nails and cracked skin. "My poor Lizbet."

Meg sets a cup on the table and pours me tea. I lift the cup with trembling hands and somehow manage not to spill a drop as I take a sip and set it down. There is something familiar about the cup. Tracing the outlines of the English tea roses with my finger, it comes to me. This is something I used to do as a child, and Ma would warn me to be careful not to break the cup because it was part of a set given to her as a wedding present. I loved the pattern of pink and white roses nestled in a tangle of vines that seemed to climb up and over the sides of the cup.

Meg watches me. "You'll be recognizing bits and pieces from your old house. We brought them here after your Ma died."

"Ma is dead?" I feel a twinge of sadness, which passes quickly and gives way to relief that the woman who wished I'd been born a boy, blamed me for Da's death, and called me a whore, can no longer hurt me.

"How? When?"

"She went totally daft in the end, so I moved her into the asylum at Blockley," says Aiden. "Her heart gave out a year ago."

I take a sip of tea.

"I was afraid she'd go to her grave with the truth about you and the baby locked inside her. But in a bout of delirium right before she died, she revealed the name of the midwife—Mrs. Woods."

Mrs. Woods. The name calls up an image of a scowling, big-boned woman.

"It took some time, but we finally located Mrs. Woods, and she is coming here next week."

My teacup drops to the floor and shatters, splashing tea everywhere. Brown like dried blood.

Blood on the pillow, on my hands. Blood everywhere. The world turns crimson as I press down. Murderer!

I feel my brother's hands on my shoulders.

My hands on the pillow. My baby is gone.

"Lizzy, where did you go just now?"

I cannot answer. My heart is pounding so hard I fear it will escape its chamber. I would do anything to wipe that bloody image from my mind, but it is not done with me.

"Shall I go on?" says Aiden, but he does not wait for my answer. "At first she refused to talk to me, saying she'd never heard of the O'Mearas. But when I offered to pay her a good sum of money for her cooperation, she agreed to come and talk to us."

"What's this woman going to tell me? I know what happened. I remember. You can talk to her if you want but I won't," I said defiantly.

"If anyone can tell you where you little girl is, she can. In fact, she said she'd tell us the baby's location. For an additional fee, of course. I agreed, and she said she'd have positive confirmation of that location by the time she met with us. I told her I'd pay her then."

"And if my baby is in the grave, Mrs. Woods will tell me that as well. There was a corpse, and I went to jail, Aiden. I know what happened."

"I cannot make you talk to her, but I hope you will at least listen to her."

"All right, I will if that's what you want." I look down at the remains of the teacup. *Broken like me.* "I'm going to my room now."

CHAPTER 39

When Mrs. Woods walks in the door, I recognize her from my nightmares and grip the arms of the chair to keep myself from running out of the room. I agreed to be here, so I will keep my promise. She is big, six feet at least, with a prominent jaw, large nose, and heavy brows. Her gray-streaked brown hair is pulled back into a severe bun. There is nothing sympathetic or nurturing in her appearance—nothing to mark her as someone who would choose a profession that brings life into this world. I shudder to think of her rough, meaty hands between my legs.

"What do you want to know?" she asks once she is seated. She addresses herself to Aiden, although I am sitting right next to him on the sofa, but that's just as well.

"The truth," says Aiden.

"All right, then. I'll start at the beginning. When the girl's ma hired me, the first thing she tells me is the girl's a whore."

Aiden leans forward. "You will treat my sister with respect and address her by name."

She turns to me. "*Lizzy*," she says flatly, "your ma called you a whore."

I do not need to answer this woman. I know that's what Ma called me.

"Anyways, soon's I saw you, I could tell how sick you was, so I figured your kid wouldn't last too long."

It was time to end this. "You were right," I say. "The kid didn't last long because I killed her. I suffocated her with a pillow. You can't deny that."

Mrs. Woods scoffs.

"Why are you mocking me?"

She chuckles. "I *can* deny it, because you didn't suffocate your baby."

"I don't understand."

"It was your ma's idea."

"What was my ma's idea?" My heart is racing.

"That I should take your little bastard as soon as it was born—them was her words, not mine. Give it away, she says, leave it outside somewhere, all the same to her. I says I have no problem doing that."

I close my eyes and hear this woman's voice as I heard it that night. *She's bleeding. Baby's coming fast. It wants to be born.* "I remember Ma saying, 'Bastard child. Better it was born dead. Then we wouldn't have to...' something I can't remember. Is that what she said?"

"Probably. Don't remember 'zactly."

I lean forward, grabbing her thick wrist and squeezing it. "Tell me. I remember my baby was crying when I woke up, wasn't she? And I wanted to hold her."

"Yeah, you was begging to hold your Sarah."

Sarah! This is the first time anyone besides me has uttered her name. Something deep inside me opens wide. "How do you know her name?"

"That's what you called her right after she was born."

"My Sarah," I whisper, letting go of her wrist. Then, louder, "Yes, I remember now. I begged Ma to let me hold her, but she wouldn't let me."

"And I told you I needed to take care of the baby before you could hold her because the child was sickly. You was feverish and then you passed out. You was out a long time. Almost a whole day. That gave me time to take the baby and give her to my cousin who wanted one."

"Your cousin?" says Aiden, but I hush him.

"I remember waking up...oh, this is the part that breaks my heart. I remember my mother screaming, 'Look what you've done!' And I was...I was on my knees, pressing a pillow down on...smothering my baby. Ma pulled the baby out from under the pillow and dangled her over my head. 'Look what you've done to your little bastard. You killed her. You're a monster.'"

"Yeah, that's what happened."

I'm on my feet. "How can that be? In one breath you tell me my child is alive, and in the next you tell me I killed her!"

"Bit of a riddle, ain't it?" She smiles, clearly amused by her story. "Yes, the child under the pillow was dead. But she weren't your child, and you didn't kill her because she were dead before we put her under that pillow."

"That makes no sense."

"Your ma wanted you to think you killed your own child. That woman was more than a mite soft in the head if you ask me, but it ain't for me to look a gift horse in the mouth—if you catch my meaning. When she hired me, she asked if I could find a stillborn baby to take the place of your child if it was born alive. No one's never asked me to do that before, but like I said, she was paying me good, so I told her I thought I could find one if I had to. And I did. I got a brother who's a gravedigger, and a cousin who's a coroner is how.

I shake my head in disbelief. "But I woke up on my knees with a pillow in my hands. That's not possible."

"You're wrong about that." She sniggers, as if this is all a big joke. "We was so clever. While you was half asleep, we propped you up on your knees with the pillow underneath your hands, and the dead baby underneath the pillow. I held you like that, and then we woke you up."

"She was a sick woman, our Ma," muttered Aiden. "If I'd known how sick, I'd never have left you."

I close my eyes and remember the rest. "Ma said something I'll never forget: 'You'll go to prison for this.'"

I open my eyes and look at the midwife. "After you carried the dead baby out of the room, Ma said to me, 'Good, you stopped bleeding. Let's get you dressed.' I told her I was too tired to get dressed then, but she started putting clothes on me, although I was covered with blood. She said, 'They're coming.' When I asked her who was coming, she didn't answer. Then the police came to the door."

"All true. And I showed them cops the dead baby and told them you killed it. Your ma said the same thing."

A weight heavier than the iron bars of a prison cell is lifted from my shoulders, and I feel I will float away if I don't hold on. The Bible says the truth will set you free. And it has. "You said you gave her to your cousin."

"Yeah. My cousin Charlotte and me made a deal. Her baby just died, she wanted another, and I had a baby to give her. Her husband worked, so they could afford to feed another mouth, dress her nice and all. But Charlotte was spending money as fast as it came in. And she didn't stop spending after her husband left her for another woman, so no surprise the money disappeared. Then one day, Charlotte disappeared too, and I lost track of her."

"So you don't know where she is," I say. "My little girl could be dead or discarded somewhere like trash."

"But I do know where she is. Got a letter from her 'bout five, six months ago. Said her and the kid been staying at the Bucks County Almshouse."

I squeeze my brother's hand.

"Said they was wearing rags and didn't have enough to eat. Asked me to send money. Twenty dollars would do just fine. And if I didn't send it, she would tell everyone how I stolled the kid. Can you believe that bitch blackmailed me? My own flesh and blood."

Cut from the same cloth. "So you sent her the money?" I ask.

"'Course I did. And another twenty when she wrote a couple months later. Ain't heard from her since."

I squeeze my brother's arm. "Aiden, they're starving my baby. Dressing her in rags. We have to get her."

"I think we've heard enough," says Aiden, rising from his seat. "Let me see you to the door and pay you what I promised."

"And enough to pay my cousin Charlotte before she opens her mouth—"

At the door, Aiden hands her a packet. "This is more than enough."

When Mrs. Woods leaves, it's as if an evil spirit has been driven from the house.

"Doesn't sound like *dear* Cousin Charlotte has feelings for her *dear* little girl," says Meg.

"No," says Aiden. "It appears that Mrs. Woods and dear Cousin Charlotte have feelings for little else than money."

"Horrid women," I said. "What a sad life my poor Sarah has had from the very minute she was born." I hold back tears." "Do you think we can get her back?"

"I honestly believe we can," says Aiden. "You are the rightful mother, and if we ever had to prove it in court, I would get Mrs. Woods to write an account of what happened when Sarah was born. Not the part about the dead baby, just the birth. I already told her we might need her services in the future, and we'd pay her for her account. And like *dear Cousin Charlotte*, I said we'd tell the court how she stole the child if she refuses."

"We must go to the almshouse," I tell Aiden.

"I'll get word to the steward there to arrange a meeting."

"How long a journey is it?"

"Eight hours or so by stagecoach to get to Doylestown, but I'll find out for sure. And I'll inquire about the arrival and departure times."

"Eight hours! That means we'll have to stay at an inn the night before the visit and the night after. Oh, Aiden, such a costly trip. Can you even afford it? Why don't I make the journey alone?"

"Lizzy, love," says Meg, "you'll be moving heaven and earth to get her back, won't ye? But sometimes, heaven and earth need an extra push. That's why Aiden and I will go with ye. That is what family does. Right, Aiden? And once we have Sarah, our family will be complete."

I lie in bed unable to sleep. Am I ready for this reunion? What kind of mother will I be to a four-year-old child if I have been a stranger to motherhood until now? Will my daughter accept a mother she has never known? We have both been through so much, are either of us capable of love? I have to believe the answer is yes. And with that, I am ready to sleep.

CHAPTER 40

We are to leave for Doylestown the following week, and I hardly know what to do with myself as I count the hours. I welcome Meg's chatter as she works at the loom she drags into the center of the parlor during the day.

"You wouldn't believe how many mills have sprung up while ye were gone," she says. "They're everywhere. A lot of the owners put out yarn to weavers like myself, and we get paid for the cloth we weave for their factories."

We sit in comfortable silence, and I watch her hands as she slides the shuttle through the warp threads. The movement is hypnotic in its repetition, and I find it soothing and comforting, like Meg's voice.

"Four years." Meg breaks the silence. "There's so much ye missed while ye were gone, I hardly know where to begin."

"You can begin anywhere, because I had no communication with the outside world. No newspapers, no correspondence."

"Ye probably don't even know the name of our president."

"President? No, I don't. There were no elections, or holidays, or calendars...or tomorrows, where I lived."

"So cruel they were," Meg says under her breath, then continues. "When ye went away, James Polk was the president. In '49, they elected

Zachary Taylor, but he died in '50 on the Fourth of July. You'll never guess how." She giggles. "Cherries." The giggle grows into a laugh, and her amusement forces her to put down the shuttle to continue talking.

"He died from eating a big bowl of *cherries*, washed down with a whole jug of milk. They told him he shouldn't be eating that much, but he was stubborn and paid dearly for his gluttony. The doctors gave it some highfalutin Latin name, but everyone knows he died from cherries. His vice-president, Millard Fillmore, is now our president because of...you know."

Her amusement is contagious, and I join in. Not so long ago, I had despaired of ever laughing again.

She takes up the loom shuttle. "You know, some people have to work day and night to survive, but I'm lucky. I can work when I feel the need to earn a few extra pennies for some luxury or another, since Aiden got the job at Baldwin."

"Building locomotives like our da?"

"No, he's a bookkeeper now, and he works closely with Mr. Baldwin. Every day he dresses all proper in a suit. Few Irishmen can say the same. Most need to wash up when they get home."

"A bookkeeper?"

"Aye. He was always good with the numbers."

"Yes, he had the gift. Top of his class. But to get a plum job like that, working with Mr. Baldwin. How did he do that?"

She tells me it all started when Aiden was laying track on a section of the railway called Horseshoe Curve near Altoona. His foreman had brought his eight-year-old son on a visit to the work site, but the foreman got distracted and lost sight of the boy for a few moments.

"Aiden was the first one to notice the boy was missing and raced off to find him struggling to stay afloat in a nearby reservoir. The boy wasn't breathing, but Aiden pressed on his chest, breathed into his mouth, and saved his life. 'How can I repay you?' the foreman asked him. Aiden knew the foreman was a close friend of Matthias Baldwin, so he asked if there might be a bookkeeping job at the locomotive works for someone good with numbers like himself. 'Well, prove it then,' said the foreman, handing him the books for the Horseshoe Curve project. 'I suspect there's been some funny business and there's money missing. If you can find the proof, I'll recommend you for the job.'

"You know how Aiden can add numbers in his head. Well, he took one look at the ledger and knew the totals of the receipts were off. Sure enough, when he checked the totals, they were too high. Some of the receipts were going into someone's pocket. And not only that. He noticed they were paying a lot more money to some suppliers than to others for the same goods. Special favors. He said someone needed to look at that. Oh, he's a smart man, my Aiden is. I think that's why Mr. Baldwin has a special fondness for him. He saved them a lot of money, he did."

I rejoice in my brother's good fortune momentarily, until I'm overcome once again by my anxiety over my impending reunion with my daughter, Sarah.

CHAPTER 41

Two days before we set off for Doylestown, Lucy appears on our doorstep. We cling to each other in the open doorway like long-lost sisters. When we step back, I see how much she has changed. She is taller than I am, slim, her face framed by an abundance of light brown hair, her skin the color of almonds. And her eyes! Green as emeralds. How had I not noticed those remarkable eyes before? A woman this beautiful must surely have a beau. As if anticipating my inquiry, a man in a dark suit climbs the front steps and stations himself next to her. Her eyes sparkle as he takes her hand.

"Lizzy, I would like you to meet my husband, Benjamin."

Husband! I can hardly believe it, but there he stands, a handsome man, an inch or two taller than Lucy and several shades darker, with closely cropped hair, even features, and a gaze that is somehow both serious and good-humored. He extends a hand.

"Benjamin Jacobs."

"Lizzy O'Meara." I shake his hand eagerly, then take a step back. "Oh Lucy, I'm so happy for you. What I would give to have been there at your wedding to share your joy."

"Your absence diminished my joy." Her eyes glisten.

"I missed so much...so much...oh, where are my manners? Please come in. I'll make us some tea."

"Not for me, I'm afraid," says Benjamin. "I have something I must attend to. But Lucy has told me so much about you. She calls you her Irish sister." He chuckles. "That's why I insisted on stopping by now to make your acquaintance."

"Please come in and sit, if only for a few minutes," I suggest. He agrees and we all step inside.

"I'm delighted for the both of you," I say, as I prepare the tea. "And you, Lucy, your parents must be overjoyed to see you happily married."

Lucy's smile fades. "Sadly, our joy was further muted by the absence of my parents. They were struck down by a runaway carriage as they were crossing the street only a month before our wedding."

"Oh, Lucy, how dreadful!" I say as my eyes suddenly fill with tears. "Your mother was a remarkable woman. I will never forget how she talked to me—how kindly she treated me—that day she took me into your house."

"It didn't seem remarkable to me at the time...it was because I was so young, I guess."

"Well, it was a truly special moment for me. She entrusted me—a stranger, and a little white girl at that—with the story of your ancestors." I pause momentarily to collect my thoughts and calm my emotions. "You know, when I was in prison, I would sometimes conjure up the image of that quilt bird, and I could soar with him in my imagination."

"We have so much to talk about, Lizzy," says Lucy nodding, as a church bell chimed the hour. "Benjamin, you'll be late if you don't leave now."

"You're right, my love. It would not do for the teacher to be tardy. My students would never let me forget it."

We say our goodbyes as Benjamin leaves.

"Where does your husband teach?" I ask Lucy. The word "husband" feels strange on my tongue. Only yesterday Lucy was a shy little girl, clutching the cast-off rag doll I had given her.

"He's a teacher at the Institute for Colored Youth, a new school that opened last year, just a few blocks away. Seventh and Lombard. It's a wonder, Lizzy. They teach Greek, Latin, physiology, philosophy, advanced mathematics. All the teachers are colored, and only the smartest young men and women can get in. But it's *your* stories I want to hear. I can extol the virtues of education at a later time."

As we slowly drink our tea, savoring our moments together, I share all that has happened to me in the past few days. I tell her I'm counting the minutes until Sunday, when I will meet my daughter. She does not press me about my experience in prison, and for that I am grateful. I am not ready to speak about those awful years that hollowed me out.

"It's going to take time for you to return to this world in spirit and body," Lucy says. "It's not unlike former slaves I know who have had to learn how to be free after so many years of slavery. But it didn't take long for them to adapt, and it won't take you long either."

"I hope you are right."

"I know I'm right." She takes my hands and squeezes them. "Walk with me. It will do you good."

"I don't know..."

"Just a few blocks."

"Meg took me out yesterday. We walked a little, but the noise, the shouting was..."

"I understand. We can turn back if it's too much for you. Why don't I hold your hand like you used to hold mine when I was afraid?"

"Oh, Lucy." My eyes fill. "I forgot how dear you are to me."

"Come. I'll tell you where we're going as we walk."

Outside, I link arms with her, and we walk to the end of the block. We are halfway across the street when a horse and cart misses us by inches, and the driver hurls curses at us.

"Lucy, I don't think I can..." She slips her arm around my waist to support me, and I let her lead me on. Rounding a corner, I see something that stops me short.

"What's the matter, Lizzy?"

"Th...that poster. Outside the saloon over there. Isn't that a picture of Bull McMullen?"

She scowls. "Yes, that's his saloon. And he's making a name for himself in local politics. He's about to be elected alderman, though he's still the thug and bully he always was. But I'm guessing it isn't McMullen who disturbs you as much as his cousin, Timmy."

Someday when you're least expecting it—next week, next year, who knows—I'll hurt you so bad, you'll curse the day you did this to me. That's what he said after I blackened his eye in front of his friends. *Us Doyles we never forget.* I shiver at the memory.

"He wouldn't leave me alone, Lucy. Every time he laid eyes on me, he—"

"I hear he's married now. With a wife to take care of his...needs...I don't think you have to worry about Timmy Doyle anymore."

We stop at a corner and wait for a line of carts and carriages to pass.

"You're probably right. I'd best set my mind on more immediate concerns." I try not to think about the possibility that he might not be done with me yet. "I think I would like to go home now, Lucy, if you don't mind."

CHAPTER 42

Meg, Aiden, and I depart for Doylestown at 8:00 a.m. from the Buck Hotel at Second and Race streets. We are crowded together in the stagecoach with three other passengers, sitting face to face on two padded leather seats. Once we leave the city, we travel rutted dirt roads and are bumped and jostled as the driver speeds the horses' gait from trot to gallop. Still, it is not fast enough for me. I pass the time imagining my first glimpse of Sarah, the first time I hold her, the feel of her arms around…I am suddenly thrown against the side of the cab, and everything fades to gray. Someone is holding me, saying something I can't make out. Slowly the fog clears.

"Are you hurt?" says Aiden. "Meg, give me a handkerchief, will you."

"What happened?" My voice is so weak, I need to repeat the question.

"The carriage hit a rut. I'm afraid you got the worst of it," Aiden said sympathetically.

"Carriage?" I close my eyes as Aiden wipes my head. "Oh, I remember now."

"It's only a bruise," he says. "No blood, maybe a little bump."

The other passengers ask if I'm all right, and I nod. But I am not all right. Those thoughts of an idyllic reunion with Sarah have been knocked out of me, and now all I feel is dread. *What if they don't let me take her? What if she's not there?* My mind is a jumble of what-ifs. My head aches, and I am having trouble catching my breath.

"Lizzy," says Aiden. "Everything's going to be okay."

"But it's not." Tears fill my eyes.

"Meg, why don't we switch seats. I think Lizzy needs a woman's touch."

Meg takes my hand but says nothing for a while. Then she begins to speak, quietly narrating our ride.

"Ye have never traveled outside Philadelphia, have ye? Just countryside and a few farmhouses. When we stop, ye'll inhale the fresh country air. Not as fresh as Irish air, but it will revive ye." Her sweet voice with its familiar Irish lilt gradually soothes me. By the time we stop at the village of Jenkintown, the ache in my head has subsided. And she is right about the healing properties of the fresh country air.

Our next stop is Abington, where we get off the coach and walk about while the horses are changed. Then we're off again, passing a few shops, a post office, and a large stone church, till we're out of the town and back in the countryside. There are no stops for the next couple of hours, save for the occasional tollgate. I sleep off and on until we stop at Hartsville, where the rest of the passengers get off. Aiden moves to the seat across from us, and we begin the last leg of our journey to Doylestown. Once again I am consumed by worry about what lies ahead. *Will she rush into my arms when she sees me for the first time—when she learns I am her mother? Will her hair be red, her skin fair like mine, or will she be dark complexioned like the man who planted his seed? Will I love her less if she bears his features?*

Aiden's voice breaks into my thoughts. "Thomas came to see me at work the other day."

I blush.

"He asked about you. And that wasn't the first time, Lizzy. Would you like to know what I said to him?"

Although I am filled with trepidation about tomorrow, there is something in me that awakens at the sound of his name. I nod.

"I told him what happened to you."

"You told him? I insisted you were not to say anything about me. And you went and told him—"

"You think he wouldn't have found out? Word gets out, you know."

"Ah, yes. I should have known there are no secrets in Philadelphia."

"That's probably not far from the truth. But I swear to you that the first time he came to me asking about you, I told him nothing. That was shortly after I returned from Altoona, and I'd just started working at Baldwin. He found out where I worked and came to see me. I have to tell you, Lizzy, it wasn't easy keeping quiet. The poor man wore his sadness on him like a suit of clothes."

Oh Thomas, I'm so sorry I hurt you.

"He couldn't understand why you'd broken off your relationship just when you were about to announce your engagement. 'How could she have left me like that?' he said again and again. It was as obvious as the nose on his face that he still loved you."

I feel the pain of our last time together and remember how I lied to him about why I was ending our relationship. I lied because he deserved a wife who was whole and unspoiled, which I was not. Now my thoughts spiral off into memories of my despoilment, and I am once again plunged into depression.

"Lizzy, did I just lose you?"

"No. I'm...here."

"He visited me two weeks before your release."

That gets my attention. Although it shouldn't matter to me now, I listen.

"He knew you'd been imprisoned, and why. As you said, there are no secrets in this town. He said he could never believe you had murdered your own child and couldn't understand how you came to be imprisoned for that crime."

"And you told him..."

"I told him of course you hadn't done it, although at the time I didn't have actual proof of your innocence. He asked about the circumstances of the birth. I told him that information would have to come from your lips."

And that was never going to happen. My history with Thomas was just that: history.

The conversation ends just as we arrive in Doylestown.

Although my head no longer throbs, I grow faint when we descend from the carriage. Aiden says he will try to find transportation for me or carry me to the inn himself.

"You said the inn isn't far," I say, "so I will walk on my own two feet from here on." The weather has turned cool for September, and we are not wearing warm coats, but the cold breeze is a blessing in disguise, as it's keeping me moving.

It's not long before we see the sign for the Cross Keys Inn, where we will spend the night. We find ourselves in a large room dominated by an enormous fireplace with a crackling fire that spreads a warm glow throughout the room. Aiden had explained that the inn is frequented by farmers, and the patrons seated at tables and standing by the bar are a rough, noisy lot who appear more interested in consuming alcohol than food. It appears that we are the only guests who are not farmers, and Meg and I are the only women, which garners us much attention when we enter. The innkeeper takes us upstairs to our rooms, where we deposit our bags. The room I occupy with Meg is sparsely but adequately furnished with a bed, chair, washstand, and chamber pot.

Downstairs, the welcoming fire and aroma of roasting meats lift my spirits. My moods are a bumpy road, tossing me up and down from certainty to uncertainty, hope to despair. After a hearty repast of meats, cheeses, and fruit, we retire for the night.

•   •   •

The morning dawns bright and clear, and my mood is surprisingly bright and clear as well. Meg and Aiden each hold one of my arms, although I tell them I am perfectly capable of walking on my own. We walk for about an hour, then climb a hill from which we can see the almshouse.

I was expecting a dilapidated, depressing institution, but the four-story fieldstone building is well cared for and the grounds neatly groomed. To my surprise, the men and women we pass on the way are both Black and white. Such mingling of races is rare, even amongst the poor. And I am relieved these people do not have the look of destitution I see on the faces of those who wander the streets of Philadelphia. I expected them to be clad in ragged clothing, something Charlotte had complained about in her letter to Mrs. Woods. Instead, they are wearing simple, practical garments—plain cotton trousers and shirts for the men, simple shifts for the women. Maybe Sarah's life was not as harsh as I thought.

After we enter the building, a young man introduces himself as the steward's assistant and leads us down a long corridor to the steward's office. Aiden knocks, and a booming voice from inside bids us enter. We find ourselves in a well-appointed room with paneled walls and fine, polished furniture. I had not been expecting such an expensive setting in an institution that houses the poor. An oversized man with a protruding belly stands behind a massive desk that echoes his proportions. His round face is framed by a fringe of dark brown hair that outlines his cheeks and jaw. The assistant introduces the steward as William Richter. Then he crosses the room to an adjoining office and closes the door behind him.

I tremble in anticipation of what this man will say and do, since he holds the key to my life.

"Now, who is it you are seeking here?" the steward asks, once we are seated.

His question is addressed to Aiden, but I answer before my brother can open his mouth.

"We are looking for a woman named Charlotte McCrory. She's here with a little girl named Sarah, who is around four years of age."

"Charlotte? Sarah? I am not familiar with those names. But you see, I have only recently taken up my position here as steward. Let me check the records. When did you say they arrived?"

"We don't know, sir. We received a letter dated two months ago stating they were living here, so we assume they are still here," I said evenly, straining to hide my impatience.

He nods. "Give me a moment." He pulls a ledger from a shelf behind him and dons a pair of reading glasses. "These are our records for the past three years. Let me see what I can find."

We watch in silence as he slowly shuffles through pages, running his finger down columns of writing, mumbling to himself. It is all I can do to keep from grabbing the book away from him and finding the information myself.

"Ah, here it is. They arrived on the tenth of November, 1848. A woman thirty-five years of age and her daughter Sarah, four months."

"Not *her* daughter—Charlotte McCrory is *not* the mother of that child. *I* am."

He scowls. "That is not my affair, miss. You'll have to sort that out amongst yourselves."

Aiden leans over and whispers, "Don't worry, Lizzy, we'll fix this. Let me do the talking. You know as well as I do that men listen to other men and expect women to be silent."

Silent women. Although I am no longer in jail, I am still not free to speak. But Aiden is right that I'll do more harm than good if I do, so I'll restrain my impulses.

Aiden looks directly at the steward. "Do your records show that they're still here?"

He sniffs. "If you stop interrupting me, I'll find that information for you."

What an offensive man, scolding my brother as if disciplining a recalcitrant pupil. The sooner I get my daughter away from here, the better.

He turns the pages more slowly and deliberately than before— punishment, no doubt, for our impertinence. His finger stops at an entry, and he looks up at me. "Ah ha, here it is. It says here they left two months ago."

I cover my mouth with my fist. First, he says she's here, then he says she's gone. For God's sake. How long until I find her? "Left?" I manage to squeeze the word out. "Where?"

"There's a note here. Let me see. Hmm. It says that we discovered Mrs. McCrory had been lying about being a Bucks County resident." He leans back in his chair. "You see, it's the county's responsibility to pay for the indigents who stay with us. We have a very limited budget and rely on taxes to pay our expenses. Apparently, someone was paying for Mrs. McCrory and her...er...the child she brought with her. Then that person stopped paying. Mrs. McCrory admitted she was actually a resident of Philadelphia. So the Directors of the Poor of this jurisdiction sought an order of removal and..." He takes out a handkerchief and blows his nose.

Are you taking your time because you enjoy watching me suffer? That would not surprise me. But I must hold my tongue or I might never get the answers I need. I press my lips together to keep angry words from spilling out.

"Where was I? Oh, yes. So, the Directors of the Poor here in Doylestown initiated legal proceedings against the Guardians of the Poor in the district of Southwark, where McCrory was a resident, in order to seek compensation for our expenditures in caring for her and the child. The City of Philadelphia refused to reimburse us. And even if they had, we would have had no choice but to let McCrory and the child go. You understand."

"All my sister wants to know is where they went," Aiden said patiently.

"And how would we know that?" he said with a shrug. "Once they leave these premises, they are no longer our concern. All it says here is that transportation was arranged—which we paid for, I might add."

"Oh, Aiden, they could be anywhere," I said, blinking back tears. "What am I going to do?"

Mr. Richter hands me a handkerchief. "There, there, dear. You ladies are so sensitive."

I accept it, even though I want to shove it down the man's throat.

Aiden stands and leans forward with his hands on the steward's desk until his face is inches away from Richter's. "Look here, Mr. Richter, you must know something."

I had not noticed until now how Aiden's physique had changed during my absence, how muscular he had grown as a result of his years of hard labor. The implied threat of Aiden's proximity in combination with his bulging biceps clearly visible through his shirt is not lost on Richter, who slides his chair back from the desk.

"S...sorry, I can't help you," he says meekly. "But I may know someone who can." He rings a bell, and the assistant emerges from his tiny room. "Gregory, could you fetch the matron, please."

"Yes, sir."

The matron enters the room, and she is as round as the steward.

"Let me introduce my wife, Anna Richter," he says with a weak smile.

"Which of you's looking for Charlotte McCrory?" Her voice is as rough as gravel.

"I am," I announce hastily.

"Follow me, please."

We all stand.

"No, just you, Miss..."

"O'Meara."

"You understand, Miss O'Meara, that we don't want just anyone wandering the halls."

She glares at Aiden and Meg as if they were criminals, and the two of them look over at me for affirmation. I nod, and they sit back down. I follow the matron out the door and down the hall.

"I am going to introduce you to a friend of Charlotte McCrory. She might know something," Mrs. Richter says, leading me up a set of steps to the second floor, which is far more dilapidated than the first. "Wait in that room across the hall, and I'll fetch Molly from the sewing room."

The little room where I wait is piled high with broken chairs and tables. With some effort, I am able to locate and extract two intact chairs. A moment later, the matron brings Molly into the room and says she'll wait outside until we're finished.

Molly is somewhere in her forties with abundant chestnut hair swept off her face and a tiny cleft chin. She would have been attractive were it not for the pursed lips and downward turn of her mouth that realign her features into a tableau of bitterness. When I tell her who I'm seeking, her face lights up.

"Yeah, we was close. We stuck together, me and her. Things weren't so bad here till the Richter family took over. They line their pockets and eat high on the hog, leaving the slops for us, if you know what I mean. Her and me we got a lot in common. We both grew up poor in the city. Both had husbands who done us wrong. When the baby she had with her husband died, she thought she wanted another, so she got one from her cousin. But she weren't no mother. You could tell. Her face got a look like she'd sucked on a lemon whenever she had to do anything with the kid."

Oh, my heart.

"That were one thing I didn't like about Charlotte. I told her that little one was a beautiful kid and she should treat her good, but—"

"Did she tell you why she didn't abandon the baby?"

"Not exactly. Maybe 'cause she promised her cousin she'd keep it. She said she'd of ended up on the streets like me if some relative of hers who lives up here hadn't told her to come to the almshouse."

"Molly. Please. Do you know where they went? Charlotte and the child?"

Molly scowls and scratches her head. "Hmm. She talked about going to...to...some place in Philadelphia that starts with B. Block-something. Don't remember if she were going to the Block place, too, or if she were just dropping the kid off there. That's all I know."

I thank her and follow the matron downstairs. Here I was thinking we were so close, only to discover we've been chasing a shadow.

•   •   •

"She told me they'd gone back to Philadelphia," I said as we walked back to the inn. "To a place called Block-something."

"Blockley," Aiden and Meg say simultaneously.

"Isn't that where you took Ma when she went mad? Sarah is in an *insane asylum*?"

"Lizzy," Meg says softly, taking my arm to steady me. "The asylum is just one part of Blockley. 'Tis also a hospital and an almshouse, and they have an orphanage."

"Where exactly is this Blockley place?"

"On the other side of the Schuylkill," says Aiden.

"How soon can we go there?"

Aiden looks thoughtful before answering. "I'll set up an appointment when we get home. If I have to, I'll try to get Mr. Baldwin to put in a few good words for me to make sure the matter is given the attention it deserves. I expect it will take a few days."

That's a few days too many.

CHAPTER 43

My poor baby is in peril. I know it. I lie in bed and worry about everything that could go wrong. What if Aiden can't get an appointment at Blockley? What if they refuse to hand my child over to me because I've been in prison? What if Sarah isn't at Blockley after all? Sometimes it's hard for me to believe that my daughter even exists. At times I am convinced she is nothing more than an illusion. Uncertainty gnaws at the hope that has sustained me since Mrs. Woods confirmed Sarah was alive. I run my fingers over the scars on my belly, reminding myself what "hopeless" feels like. I have to believe she is alive. I *must.*

Aiden gets us an appointment for next Tuesday, three days from now. It feels like an eternity. I pace the floor and chew my fingernails, as I did when I was in prison, and would surely have bitten every nail to the quick again if Lucy hadn't stopped by. She asks me to accompany her somewhere, but won't disclose the destination until we're outside.

"Listen," she says, leaning in. "I have to say this quietly. I'm taking you to an underground railroad station."

"A railroad station? Underground?"

"Not literally. It's a term some people use for those of us who help fugitive slaves make their way north to freedom. Remember the trapdoor at Uncle Robert's house, where they hid runaway slaves?"

I nod.

"Their house was an underground railroad station—although we weren't calling it that back then—and my aunt and uncle were 'conductors.' The house I'm taking you to is not far from here on Delhi Street. It belongs to William Still. You met him once, a long time ago, when he was working at the Anti-Slavery Society office."

"I think I remember him. But...why you are taking me to this station now, when all that's important to me is finding my daughter?"

"That is the very reason. I want to remind you that you were once passionate about the fight against slavery, and you are still that same person. I am trying to reconnect you with yourself."

I button up my coat and lower my head against the wind as we walk down the familiar neighborhood streets. I feel a flicker of gratitude toward Lucy for encouraging me to look past my own struggles—not an easy task, but I would try. Although September has just given way to October, there is an unseasonable chill in the air. Trees are already losing hold of their summer finery, and dry brown leaves twirl in the wind like tiny streamers. We weave our way through the usual tangle of vendors hawking their wares, children running everywhere, dogs rummaging through garbage, and the occasional amorous young couple on a stroll, oblivious to the world around them, paying heed to no one but each other. I envy them all.

While we walk, Lucy tells me how much worse things have gotten during my absence. "Two years ago, they passed an abominable law called the Fugitive Slave Act. It says that runaway slaves must be returned to their masters, even if they are living in a free state. And citizens must assist in the capture of runaways or face punishment. They're snatching Black people off the streets willy-nilly. They assume every Black person is an escaped slave, although so many of us were born free in Philadelphia."

We stop at a corner, and she points to a spot across the street. "A slavecatcher snatched a Black woman who was holding her baby. It happened right there, not long ago. The slavecatcher planned to return the woman to her master in Maryland in exchange for a generous bounty.

Before he shoved the poor woman into the carriage, he grabbed the baby out of her arms. He told her she could leave the baby with her father, a free man, so the child would be free as well. But the woman refused to be separated from her only child, even if it meant taking him back with her into slavery."

Lucy continues the story, but I no longer hear her words. I am back in my bedroom, newly delivered of my daughter, and covered with blood. *She is taking my baby and I am too weak to fight. I am begging to hold her, but the woman's rough hands continue to encircle my baby like chains. I beg, but she turns away and I am left with nothing but tears and blood.*

"What is it, Lizzy? I thought you were going to faint. Thank heavens I caught you."

"I'm sorry, Lucy. Sometimes frightful memories come on so suddenly, they're as real to me as when they happened."

Right there in the street, Lucy cradles me like a child. A couple of women pause to stare, commenting on the unseemliness of whites and Blacks embracing. One of them mutters, "If that was a man and woman, there would be violence."

When the last traces of my living nightmare have dissipated, we continue to the Still house, which looks no different from the other narrow, brick rowhouses on the block. Perhaps the steps of 625 Delhi Street are a little more worn than those of the surrounding houses, which would hardly be surprising, considering the number of "passengers" who have used them to enter and exit the "station." The neighbors must be aware of the unusual activity at 625, so why do they not denounce Mr. Still, especially now that the harboring of fugitive slaves is illegal? Could it be that the white people of Philadelphia, despite their hatred of Black people, lack the fervor of their neighbors to the south to pursue escaped slaves?

These thoughts flee as soon as Mr. Still opens the door. He is a tall man, formally dressed in a dark jacket, white shirt and red cravat, with close-cropped hair, full lips, and dark eyes that blaze with intensity.

"You must excuse me, ladies, but I am currently working on living arrangements for some guests who are visiting my home. It should require no more than fifteen minutes of my time. Lucy, why don't you show Miss O'Meara—I'm assuming that is who you are—around?"

We enter a large room, more office than parlor, with a tall writing desk in the corner, chairs scattered about, and shelves piled high with books and flyers. The curtains are closed, and it takes a moment for my eyes to adjust to the low light. As Mr. Still takes up a pen and writes in a ledger on his desk, I walk about the room with Lucy. A poster on the nearest shelf draws my attention. I pick it up and bring it close to my face to read the details in the dim light.

$200 Reward
Five Negro Slaves

To-wit: one Negro man and his wife, and three children. The man, who goes by the name Cooper is a black negro, full height, very erect, thin face, about forty years of age. Several of his teeth are gone. Mary, his wife is a mulatto woman, quite stout and strong. The oldest child, a boy of twelve, is a dark mulatto with heavy eyelids. Matilda, the second child, six years of age, is a dark mulatto, bright and smart looking. Malcolm, the youngest is a boy four years old, a lighter mulatto.

I put the poster back and pick up a couple of newspaper clippings from one of the shelves.

Twenty Dollars Reward

Runaway from the subscriber on Tuesday the 30th, a bright colored Negro man named Abner, bought by me of William Brown. Said Negro is about 21 years old, 5 feet 7 inches high or thereabouts. Very slim and straight. The above reward and all reasonable charges will be paid for apprehending and lodging said Negro in jail or returning him to the subscriber WHO HAS FOR SALE two first-rate HORSES, a DRAY, and a Negro WOMAN, cook, washer, etc.

A dray horse and a Negro woman. No difference. Both animals.

Ten Dollars Reward

Absconded from the subscriber's dwelling on August 5, the Negro girl FANNY, aged about 30, has lost her front teeth, very dark skin, branded on left breast. With her daughter, a mulatto aged about 7.

Branded like an animal! I am about to rip the clipping to shreds, when I am interrupted by a soft voice behind me.

"My mother was a fugitive slave like those, with a price on her head."

I turn to face Mr. Still. His gaze flickers briefly to the clipping, which is now crumpled in my hand. Before I can apologize for damaging his property, he fixes his gaze on me, his dark eyes reflecting a deep-rooted sadness. I do my best to smooth the paper as I listen to his words.

"Twice she escaped from her bondage to join my father, who had saved enough money to purchase his freedom."

Although he speaks with the voice and diction of an orator, there is something intimate in his communication, something that directs his words straight to my heart.

"The first time my mother escaped, she took all her children with her. But they were apprehended and returned to Maryland to once again take up the yoke. The second time she took only her two little girls, leaving her two young sons behind. Although she and my father were reunited in freedom in New Jersey and had many more children together—one of whom was me—my mother spent the next forty years grieving over the children she left behind. Her heart never knew what it was to be free from anxiety about her lost boys. And then a miracle."

He paused, and I held my breath. *A miracle.*

"One of those sons, nearly fifty years of age, turned up in Philadelphia seeking his long-lost parents. He was directed to the Anti-Slavery Office where I was working at the time, and when he told me his story it struck a chord, since I, too, was searching for my lost family. I remarked on the unmistakable similarity of his features to those of my mother, and we discovered we were brothers. So it was here in

Philadelphia that I made the acquaintance of my brother Peter for the first time. And soon after, he was reunited with our mother."

"A miracle," I whispered, my cheeks wet with tears.

He nodded, handing me a handkerchief. "Lucy tells me you are all too familiar with the pain of separation. She told me you are about to be reunited with your child."

"By the grace of God." Although God was no longer a part of my life, it was somehow comforting to say those words. "And that is what you are doing as well."

"Indeed, reuniting my brothers and sisters and saving their lives."

"Lucy told me you have to transport people all the way north to Canada, since it's no longer safe for them in this country."

"We do what we must. There is already a small community of former slaves in Canada."

As late afternoon gives way to evening, a woman emerges from the shadows to light the lamps. Mr. Still introduces her as his wife, Leticia, and she shakes my hand. Mrs. Still is tall, with a fair complexion, a pleasing countenance, and a large belly on which she rests her hands after she shakes mine. It's clear she's expecting.

"Lucy has spoken often about you, and it is a pleasure to make your acquaintance. Someday soon we will have time for a proper conversation, but right now there are pressing matters to attend to." She turns to her husband. "Transport for our guests will arrive within the half hour, and we are expecting new visitors later tonight. So we must prepare."

The flickering gaslight illuminates a couple quietly descending the stairs. They must be the "guests" Mrs. Still just mentioned. They reach the bottom of the stairs and hold hands, their eyes downcast. The woman nervously clutches and unclutches the skirt of her striped calico frock. Her unruly hair is tamed with combs. The man, dressed in a red checked vest, faded white shirt, and brown homespun pantaloons carries a small bundle.

Mr. and Mrs. Still hurry over to them and tell them when they will be picked up and where they will be stopping next. Mr. Still excuses himself and goes outside to wait for the carriage.

"There's a chill in the air," Mrs. Still tells them. "You have a long journey ahead, and you'll be needing more suitable clothing. Come with me." She takes them into the next room. When they emerge, the man is wearing a dark frock coat and a hat with a deep crown and narrow brim. The woman is wrapped in a woolen shawl and carries a bonnet.

"Here, let me help you put that on." Mrs. Still arranges the bonnet on the woman's head, then points to her reflection in the mirror. The woman registers her pleasure with a wide smile. "Thank you, Miss Still. You is truly an angel of mercy."

"Mercy is something you deserve in abundance, my dear, and I wish you Godspeed on your journey." Once the couple leaves, Mrs. Still turns to Lucy and me.

"I'm so glad you had a chance to talk to Mr. Still," Lucy says to me. "He's a remarkable man."

"Indeed he is!" Mrs. Still chimes in.

"Mrs. Still," I say, "I know all these people have names. Lives. If only your husband could record all their names before they pass through. So each of them would be remembered." I vividly recall a time when they called me B358, and Elizabeth O'Meara ceased to exist. But, unlike the names of slaves, my name was returned to me once I was released from prison.

Mrs. Still doesn't answer, just smiles thoughtfully, so I wondered if her husband was, in fact, keeping a record of all those he helped, despite the danger of doing so. Addressing Lucy, she says, "I am reluctant to impose upon you, but I wonder if you would consider spending the night with us. We just learned that several guests will arrive late this evening, and my husband and I will need extra hands. Of course, our little Caroline will be here, and she is always eager to help, but since she's only five..."

"Hmm...Lizzy and I came here together, and..."

"You go ahead, Lucy. I'll be fine walking home by myself."

On my way home, I reflect on how Lucy has given me a gift by restoring my connection to a world that is much larger than mine. And I promise myself that whatever the outcome of my search for Sarah, I will volunteer to work for Mr. Still's underground railroad station.

CHAPTER 44

Even before the carriage takes my brother and me across the Market Street bridge over the Schuylkill, the massive brick and stone buildings rise before us. Blockley stands atop a hill, dominating the woodlands surrounding it.

"Such an imposing and forbidding structure," I observe.

"As it was meant to be," says Aiden, "to discourage people from accepting charity and coming here. Who would want to end up in a place like this?"

Surely not my child, yet that is where she is.

As we approach the building, Aiden tells me that Old Blockley, as some call it, was built as far away from the city as possible to prevent people from escaping, as they did when the almshouses were located in the midst of the city. Which makes me recall a time when people wandered the streets after running away from an almshouse a few blocks from our house.

I tell myself that Blockley is an almshouse, a hospital, an orphanage, and even an insane asylum—not a prison. But those heavy doors and high walls lock people inside just the same. At this moment they are locking my daughter inside, but thankfully not for long.

Oh, Sarah, I promise I will save you. I have been there, too. I'm the one who put you there. No! I should not blame myself for something over which I had no control. Still, I am battered by regrets. *If only I could have been a mother to you from the start, when my body was ready to nurture you. But the milk that should have been my first gift to you served only to stain the garments I wore in court and in prison. The day my milk came in full, and my breasts ached, they were locking me in a cell. I promise you with all my heart that I will make it up to you.*

We step down from the carriage and walk past the main building to a second one that houses the orphanage, where we are directed to the steward's office. A tall, bespectacled gentleman greets us at the door. Once we are seated, I let Aiden ask the questions. We are so close to finding her, and I don't want to alienate the man before us who can make that happen.

"My sister is here to be reunited with her daughter and take her home."

The steward looks down at an oversized ledger that lies open on his desk. "I'm afraid that is something she cannot do."

"What do you mean?" Aiden says incredulous. "She's her *mother!*"

"That is not our understanding. When Charlotte McCrory came to reside here with the child, she told us she had cared for the child from the beginning and that her birth mother had abandoned her."

"Abandoned her? *Abandoned her? She was taken from me.*" I was unable to restrain myself, feeling the heat in my body rise to my cheeks.

"It would be best if you calmed down, young lady."

Have I ruined everything? I grip the edge of the chair to keep myself from pounding his desk, or his face. I look at Aiden, silently pleading for him to speak for me.

"My sister will calm down when you acknowledge that she's the girl's mother, and Mrs. McCrory has no right to keep her."

"At this point, Mr. O'Meara, it doesn't matter. Mrs. McCrory is no longer here. She was offered employment in the city, and once she was no longer a ward of the state, we let her go."

"Without the little girl?"

"Yes."

"In that case, my sister wants to take her daughter home."

"That is not possible," he says sharply.

How can he deny me my child? "You are saying that my daughter is here, but I can't take her home? I'm sorry, but I don't understand," I say evenly, despite my sense of outrage.

"You cannot take your daughter home because she is *not* here," he says with a patronizing smile.

I cannot be hearing him right. I look at Aiden, who shakes his head in bewilderment.

The steward points to a line of the ledger. "It says here that the little girl was bound out to a family."

"Bound out?"

"Indentured."

Enslaved! Someone has taken my daughter and put her in chains? I leap from my seat. Aiden rises with me and puts his hand on my shoulder to calm me. "That's impossible," he says. "There must be some mistake. She's barely four years old."

"Obviously you aren't aware of how things are done here. Impoverished children can be indentured at any age," he says with a distinct note of condescension in his voice.

My legs buckle. Aiden catches me and eases me back into the chair. "And what possible use can a four-year-old be to a family?" he asks.

"Well, they start them at an early age. Train them to do domestic work. Housewifery. The girls will stay till they're of marrying age. The boys are bound out to do farm work. They often—"

I can't hold back a second more. "You have no right to make her a slave. I insist that you get her back."

The steward, red faced, removes his glasses. "Let me remind you, young lady, that an indentured servant is not a slave. We do indeed have the right to bind her to a family if the birth mother is absent. And as for getting her back—dissolving the contract—that can only be done in court."

"What can I do?" I say, sobbing. "I gave birth to this child, and now I have to fight for her in court? Where is the justice for me and my daughter?" I try to brush the tears away with the back of my hand.

The steward's face softens. "Let me give you some advice, Miss O'Meara. It won't be easy to win custody of the child. First, you'll need to prove that you are the birth mother. You'll also need to prove that you have the means to care for the child."

"She'll have no problem with either of those requirements," says Aiden.

"Good. The court will decide which party serves the best interests of the child. The child's welfare is always paramount in custody cases."

"Who better than a mother to serve the best interests of a child?" I say.

"Again, that will be up to the court to decide. And one other thing. To proceed with a court case, you'll need to know the name of the family to which she is bound."

"And what is that name?" I ask.

"Mr. and Mrs. Timothy Doyle."

The world turns red as I am battered by images of Timmy Doyle as a boy and as a man, always tormenting me, threatening to come back to hurt me. I clench my fists, preparing to do battle with him again.

"We'll take the Doyles to court," says Aiden during the ride home. "Don't worry. You'll get custody of Sarah."

"After all these disappointments, I just don't know anymore."

"Like you said to the steward, you're the mother. And the judge *must* award you custody, since it's in the best interests of the child."

"Does he? Timmy Doyle has a powerful ally in his cousin. Whenever he came after me, he would use the threat of Bull McMullen as a weapon...I wonder how Timmy even knew about my child and where she was living?"

"It's possible he didn't know. Perhaps he was seeking to indenture a young girl, and just happened to end up with Sarah. But if he knew the child was yours, we'll never know exactly how he found out. His cousin has eyes and ears all over this city, so he could have learned about this from any number of sources. McMullen might have been there in the courtroom when they decided where Charlotte McCrory would reside after she was kicked out of the Bucks County almshouse. It's possible your name was mentioned during the proceedings. Perhaps McMullen remembered his cousin's 'special' interest in you and told him. Or he saw something in the newspaper, since they often publish court proceedings and hearings. No matter. I'll talk to my mates at Baldwin, or to Mr. Baldwin himself if I must, to find out how to start legal proceedings."

•　　•　　•

We hire Arthur C. Baker, Esq. to represent me, and we meet to discuss how we will prove Sarah is my daughter. Mrs. Woods is the only living witness to Sarah's birth, besides me, and Mr. Baker tells us she cannot testify, because under questioning she'd have to disclose all the criminal things she and Ma had done. She would perjure herself if she withheld that information, and she'd end up in jail. Instead, Mrs. Woods could sign a notarized affidavit attesting to the legitimacy of Sarah's birth. It would be the equivalent of her appearing as a witness, and she could not be questioned about anything else that happened concerning the birth. Aiden said he'd have no trouble getting written testimony from Mrs. Woods, so I would have the proof I needed that I was the mother.

Mr. Baker files a writ of habeas corpus on Timothy Doyle to surrender Sarah's custody to me and schedules a court date.

CHAPTER 45

Old City Hall looms large as we approach the entrance. Mr. Baker reminds us that this building was used by the Supreme Court of the United States when Philadelphia was temporarily the nation's capital, but at this moment I don't care a whit about history. My sole focus is winning the battle that lies ahead. I stand tall as I make my way to the entrance, accompanied by Mr. Baker, Aiden, Meg, and Lucy.

"*Red.* I told you we'd meet again."

That voice. I turn to face Timmy...no, Timothy Doyle, only inches from me. His massive torso strains the confines of his fine gray suit. His body may have changed, but his face is the same smirking obscenity it always was. He still has the sinister, predatory look of a wild animal about to devour its prey. Standing next to him is a hard-looking woman with sharp features. Even though her ample hips and prodigious bosom are covered in modest garb, she has the look of a prostitute. Mrs. Doyle, no doubt.

"I told you I'd repay you some day for what you did to me." His spittle showers my face. "Well, that day's come. We're going to win this case. Your so-called 'daughter' is ours, and we'll show the judge that you're a whore. Unfit to have custody. See you in court," he sneers.

And with that, the two of them push by us and enter the courthouse. They move too quickly for me to respond, which is just as well, since I am now shaking so hard I can barely stand. I wipe his spittle off my face and tell myself I must maintain an air of confidence at all times in that courtroom, or all could be lost.

"We're going to get that fecking bastard," Aiden whispers in my ear as he takes my arm and leads me inside. "We will be walking out this door with Sarah."

We take our places at the table that stands a few yards from the platform where the judge will preside. Mr. Baker seats himself next to me and leans close to assure me that justice is on my side. He is about to tell me more when the judge enters, a tall, commanding figure with a fringe of gray hair and a face lined by experience.

We rise as commanded. Then we sit and the trial begins. Mr. Baker has already explained to me what is going to happen, but my nerves have wiped much of that information from memory. Still, I remember enough to know the challenges we face and what each of us must do.

The judge calls on Mr. Baker to make his opening statement. He stands next to the table and faces the judge.

"Your Honor, today I am going to prove to the court that it is in the best interests of young Sarah, to grant custody of her to her mother.

"To do this, we will establish that Miss O'Meara is, indeed, the mother of the child in question—a child who has until now been called Sarah McCrory but is legally Sarah O'Meara. We will prove that Miss O'Meara is a respectable and responsible woman who sees her child's welfare as her highest priority.

"The defense asserts that Mrs. O'Meara is of dubious character. They further claim that her time in prison renders her unfit to be a mother. We will argue that someone who has been unjustly incarcerated should not be doubly punished by being denied the custody of her child. We will show that Elizabeth O'Meara has always been an upstanding young woman, despite the assertions to the contrary. And we will show that Mr. and Mrs. Doyle are unsuited to be the parents of the child in question. And finally, we will prove that Miss O'Meara has the means to support the child and will provide a nurturing home environment. Barring any compelling reasons to the contrary, a child belongs with its mother, and we will show you that *this* child belongs with *this* mother."

The counsel for the defense, Clarence Peterson, is a tall, lanky young man whose face and body seem composed entirely of angles. He makes his opening statement, placing great emphasis on my having been convicted of murdering a child and spending four years in prison. He says that regardless of my guilt or innocence, those four years amongst the worst elements of society have rendered me unfit to take on the responsibility of motherhood.

"Mrs. O'Meara bore a child out of wedlock," he says, "which speaks to her character and dubious reputation. When my client, Mr. Doyle, encountered little Sarah, she was a resident of the orphanage at the Blockley Almshouse..." Brief hesitation for emphasis. "Until recently, the woman who had been caring for Sarah since birth, Charlotte McCrory, was also in residence at Blockley. But when she was offered employment in the city, the institution let her go, as she was no longer a ward of the state. That is when Mr. and Mrs. Doyle," he glances at the two of them and smiles, "took the child into their own home. And you will note that they received no financial compensation. This was a genuine act of kindness, which speaks to their character and motivation. The Doyles have provided her a good home and treated her well. It is our opinion that awarding custody to the Doyles is in the best interests of the child."

Our counsel rises to offer proof that I am Sarah's birth mother. He holds up Mrs. Woods' affidavit.

"Each of us has a copy of Mrs. Dorothy Woods' affidavit, which has been duly signed and notarized. Mrs. Woods is the midwife who ushered Miss O'Meara's child into the world on July 8, 1848." He reads the affidavit, which describes my baby's birth and points out a significant detail. "According to Mrs. Woods, Miss O'Meara called out the name 'Sarah' when she first laid eyes on the child, proving that it was Miss O'Meara, the birth mother, who gave her daughter the name the child carries today."

Mr. Baker is about to call Meg as the first character witness, when Mr. Peterson voices an objection. "Your honor, I submit that this affidavit is invalid and should be withdrawn as evidence. Mrs. Woods states that the child was born on July 8th, but the police report states that Miss O'Meara was arrested on July 10th, the night she gave birth. Since this affidavit is a sworn statement of fact, and the midwife has gotten the facts wrong, it throws into question the accuracy of the entire document. It also includes nothing about what happened to the baby after she was born, or how the body of a dead baby ended up in the hands of the police."

"Your honor," says Mr. Baker. "If I may."

The judge nods.

"The veracity of the affidavit should not be based on what is missing from the document, only on what is written. And Mrs. Woods swore under oath that what she reported here was true and correct to the best of her knowledge. As for the mistaken date, Mrs. Woods has many births to attend to, and it is understandable that she might not have remembered the exact date of a particular delivery. But I contend that she answered to the best of her knowledge."

The judge calls the two attorneys up to the bench. After a heated discussion, the two lawyers return to their seats, and the judge announces that he is ruling for the defense, and the affidavit is withdrawn as evidence. I am about to protest, but Mr. Baker puts a hand on my shoulder and whispers that the judge's ruling is final. "Don't worry," he whispers. "We can still win this case. And we will."

Our attorney calls Meg to the stand, and then Lucy, each of whom speaks so beautifully about my caring and compassionate nature that I am brought to tears. My brother talks about how determined I was to track down my daughter, and he explains how our domestic and financial situation will enable us to support my daughter.

Finally, Mr. Baker calls me to the stand and asks why I think I should be granted custody, in light of the fact that I spent the last four years in the company of convicts and that I bore a child out of wedlock.

I intend to speak as loud and clearly as I can, to be sure the judge can hear every word, because in the end I am the one who must ultimately prove myself worthy.

"Your Honor." Despite my intentions, my voice is soft and childlike. That will not do. I take a deep breath, straighten my spine, and summon the strength to speak out forcefully. "Your Honor, in the matter of my being tainted by my time in prison, I want to make it clear that surviving four years in that place with my wits intact shows that I am a strong and determined woman."

I am aware that I am not telling the *whole* truth, for there was a time in prison when I had taken leave of my senses, but that is a truth I will keep to myself.

"I was incarcerated for murdering my child, an accusation that has been proven wrong, considering that the alleged victim is not only alive, but is, in fact, the basis for this trial. And it is true that I bore this child out of wedlock, which carries a stain, but why should I continue to be punished for something over which I had no control? I was the victim of an assault. It is the perpetrator who should suffer society's punishment, not I. That would be true justice. But I know that the responsibility of men in these matters is not what this trial is about, so I will say no more about this."

I pause a moment to reflect upon what is at stake, as tears fill my eyes. "Your Honor, I just want to add one thing more. What kept me alive those four long years was my desire to right the wrong of my unjust imprisonment. When I realized that Sarah was not dead, I was determined to show her I was her mother, and that I would walk the ends of the earth to get her back."

Tears blur my vision, and the clerk helps me to my seat, where I will now have to endure the arguments for the defense.

The first witness to take the stand is Timmy...Timothy Doyle.

"I have known this woman since she was a young girl, and I can tell you she had loose morals even then. She'd strut all around and then act all innocent. I caught her one time in the alley with her legs all up around—"

I tell Mr. Baker that is a lie, and he springs to his feet.

"Objection, Your Honor. Mrs. O'Meara will swear under oath that she was never in an alley under those circumstances."

"Objection sustained. Since the alleged incident cannot be substantiated, Mr. Doyle's last statement shall be stricken from the record."

His attorney asks him what motivated him to take the child.

"When I heard from my cousin," he nods to Bull McMullen, who had entered the courtroom sometime during the proceedings, "that this poor child been abandoned at the Blockley Almshouse, my heart went out to the poor thing. Such a sad life she's had. A bastard child, all alone. So out of the kindness of our hearts, my wife Mary and myself arranged to have her bound out to us."

It's inconceivable that Timothy Doyle would do anything out of the kindness of his heart.

"And it's a good life she's been having in our home. She has her own bedroom, which we fixed up nice with wallpaper and all. Mary and her cook together in the kitchen. We bought her lots of fine clothes."

Have they actually done all that for her? I cannot imagine they have. But he sounds so convincing, it's possible.

Mary Doyle is called to the stand, and their lawyer establishes that she is of good character and well qualified to be a loving mother.

When Mr. Baker cross-examines her, he holds up a book. "This book has been entered as evidence. Are you familiar with this, Mrs. Doyle?"

She looks at the title and says emphatically, "No, sir."

"Well, you should be." He looks up at the judge. "The title of this book is *Guide to the Stranger: A List of the Gay Houses and Ladies of Pleasure in the City of Brotherly Love...and Sisterly Affection.*"

There is laughter from the courtroom visitors, and the judge calls for silence.

"Most of you are undoubtedly not familiar with this little pocket guide, so I will explain that it is a list of every gay house in the city including descriptions of the quality of each. In the introduction, the author states that he visited each of the 'establishments' described in the book and interviewed all relevant personnel. I call your attention to the entry for Elsie Hewitt at Fifth and Pine. According to the *Guide*, and I quote: 'This house is the resort of very common people.' I interviewed Miss Hewitt, who confirmed that Mary Doyle had been employed in her establishment."

Mr. Peterson is on his feet. "Objection, Your Honor. Hearsay. Mrs. Hewitt died before she could sign an affidavit."

"Overruled. Since the author wrote that he visited each of the 'establishments' described in the book and interviewed all relevant personnel, no affidavit is necessary. The book remains included as evidence."

"But, Your Honor, I..."

"*Overruled*, Mr. Peterson. Does the defense have additional witnesses?

Mr. Peterson says he does and calls Bull McMullen to the stand. McMullen testifies that Timothy Doyle is an upstanding citizen, belongs to a fire company, saved many homes, etc.

I want to shout out that this is a pack of lies and ask what happened to the truth, the whole truth, and nothing but the truth. But of course I say nothing, because during my testimony, I, too, omitted truthful information about my mental state in prison.

McMullen talks about his extensive personal and political experience in Moyamensing. He says he has met more incarcerated individuals than he can count, and in his opinion, at least ninety percent of them come out of prison in worse shape than when they entered. "Now, I am not a betting man, Your Honor. But if I was, I'd bet that based on those odds, Elizabeth O'Meara would be one of the damaged ones."

McMullen is such a powerful force in the city, I fear the judge will be inclined to rule in his cousin's favor.

Once everyone had been heard and cross-examined, the judge calls us to order again.

"Now that I have heard all the testimony, I find there is only one missing piece of evidence that will help me render judgment. And it is the proof that Miss O'Meara is the mother of the child in question. The child's birth was not registered, which is often the case with children born out of wedlock. And although we may never have definitive proof that Miss O'Meara is the mother of this child, there may, perhaps, be a resemblance between mother and daughter that would provide a clue to familial connection. To that end, I will have Sarah brought into the courtroom before I determine who should be granted custody of the child."

My heart pounds wildly. Although I would like more than anything to see my child, I am afraid she might not look at all like me. What if she resembles the Master? Or even bears a passing resemblance to Timmy Doyle, although they are not related. Why should custody go to the person the child most resembles? That is unfair.

My sentiment is echoed by Mr. Peterson. "Your honor, physical resemblance proves nothing. A child can look exactly like one parent and not the other. Or he can bear the physical characteristics of an ancestor who looks nothing like the parents."

The judge responds that in the absence of any other proof of birth, a physical resemblance to a parent could be helpful. He instructs the clerk to fetch Sarah, and I tremble as he exits. We wait. Minutes pass. I've anticipated this moment for so long, and now that it is about to arrive, I tremble with fear. I don't know what to do with myself and my unruly heart.

The door opens and the clerk enters, followed by a woman holding the hand of a little girl clutching a doll to her chest. Everything stops. Sarah's skin is as fresh and bright as daylight, her hair the color of the setting sun. I am in love. There is nothing of the Master in her countenance. No one in this room could deny she is my child.

I stand and hold my hands out to her, but Mr. Baker, apologetically, insists that I sit.

I hear the judge's voice, but it is hazy as if he were speaking from far away. "Although we lack documented proof, there is no doubt in my mind that Elizabeth O'Meara is the mother of this child. And from what I have heard today about Miss O'Meara's character, circumstances, and love for this little girl who was snatched from her at birth, I believe it is in the best interests of the child to award custody to the mother."

Cheers ring out at our table, and even the strangers in the audience applaud. The judge bangs the gavel, and I leap from the chair and run to my daughter.

"Sarah, dear," says the woman who fetched her and is kneeling by her side. "This is your mama. She has come to take you home."

I hold out my hand, so eager to touch her for the first time, but she refuses to let go of the woman's hand. In my dreams Sarah comes to me, whispering "Mama" as she wraps her little arms around my neck, and I am reborn. I hold my breath, waiting for my dream to come true. But when Sarah looks up at me, her lip quivers, her face reddens, and tears spill from her eyes.

"I don't want to go with you."

CHAPTER 46

"I don't want to go with you," Sarah repeats, breaking my heart again. She adds, "You're not my mama."

Her words render me speechless. But as I watch her tears flow, I am ashamed that my first thought was of my own feelings, and not those of the little girl weeping before me, this child who never had a home or a mother. I kneel in front of my daughter, careful to keep some distance between us so as not to frighten her, and I speak softly. My words come easily, for they are the words I'd always longed to hear from my own mother.

"My darling Sarah, you will always have a home with me, no one will take you away again, I will keep you safe—and I will always, *always* love you."

Her face expressionless, she says nothing, but something in my voice and my words apparently touch her, for she releases her guardian's hand and takes mine. In the background I hear Doyle shouting, and the judge adjourning the court, but neither I nor Sarah turn around. We leave the courthouse with Aiden, Meg, and Lucy.

Once home, Sarah remains silent, but accepts my offer of fruit and bread and allows me to walk her through the house. I show her my bedroom and the one next door, which we had outfitted for her. When

I tell her this can be her very own room, she shakes her head and points to my bedroom. I am heartened by her decision, and we move the second bed into my room.

That first night, I sing to her, tell her stories, assure her I'll stay with her all night, so she needn't be afraid. Her expression remains neutral. Is she relieved, exhausted, apprehensive, confounded? I am hopeful she will reveal her feelings in her own time. So I tuck her in and kiss her on the cheek. She closes her eyes, and just when it appears she has drifted off to sleep, she sits bolt upright, raises her hand with her index finger extended in my direction, and asks with innocent childlike trepidation, "What is your name?"

What to answer? "My name is Mama, Sarah. I am your mama."

"I mean, what is your *lady* name?"

"I am Lizzy."

"Lizzy." She says my name slowly as if tasting the sound of it on her tongue. "Good night, Lizzy."

•　　•　　•

Sarah's past life is a mystery to me. She alone knows what she endured, and because she is too young to put it into words, I must look for clues in her actions and reactions, try to make sense of them, and do what any mother would do to protect her child.

What does it mean when she glimpses a woman in the street and dissolves into tears? Does that woman remind her of someone who hurt her? What does it mean when I try to hold her and she pulls away, or at best tolerates my embrace? Is she afraid of getting too close to people for fear of losing them? So many people must have come and gone in her short life. So she clings most steadfastly to the little rag doll she calls Cora, a sad-looking playmate with painted-on eyes, nose, mouth, and dark hair. The doll is dressed in a lace-trimmed white petticoat, which is stained and torn. Her left eye and most of her red, bow-shaped mouth have been loved off of her. Cora sleeps with Sarah, accompanies her to the privy, and shares her meals with her. Sometimes after I put Sarah to bed, I hear her talking to the doll, although I can't make out the words. There are times I wish I were Cora.

Until now, my quest to find my child had consumed my life, and I hadn't thought about anything beyond the moment of our reunion. A part of me naively expected us to live happily ever after, for what child doesn't thrive on maternal love, something I harbored in abundance? More than enough to nurture a multitude of Sarahs.

Two weeks pass and very little changes. Once or twice, there is a break in the clouds, glimpses of a sunny smile, hints of the little girl she might have been and hopefully will be someday. But not yet. In repose she looks like a fine china doll—porcelain skin, button of a nose, red bow of a mouth, and bright red hair that curls around her face. Her beauty takes my breath away.

Nothing of Northam shows itself in her, thank God. I pray that any Northam blood that flowed through her veins has been washed away by mine. From the moment I brought Sarah home, I stopped thinking of Northam as the Master, a title that acknowledged the power he had over me. No more. Northam is nothing more than a man to me now. No— *less* than a man, since he lacks the inner light the Quakers believe resides within each of us. I cannot believe God kindled a spark in him or in others who turn my blood cold with their cruelty.

Sarah is already beautiful and will likely become more so over time. But beauty can be a blessing and a burden as I know too well, having struggled mightily to protect myself from the unbridled lust of so many men. I will teach Sarah to fight if I must, but if she is anything like me, she'll possess the instinct to fight back on her own.

Some mornings when I wake up, Sarah's bed is empty. Although her bed is only inches from mine, it could be miles away. One morning I find her sleeping in the closet, another morning outside in the hall. Does she walk in her sleep, or consciously seek a place where she feels safer than in the bed next to mine? Some mornings I discover she has wet her bed. Her evident unhappiness pains me so.

The other day, an explosion—a gunshot perhaps, or a firecracker— not far from the house sends Sarah screaming from the kitchen where we are eating breakfast. I follow her up the stairs, as her screams become sobs. I know her anguish. It wasn't too long ago that I had been shaken by the sound of a passing fire truck. But my hysteria had passed quickly. Hers continues as I follow her into our bedroom, where she curls herself up in a corner, hugging herself. She doesn't welcome my touch, and I remain helpless as she continues to sob uncontrollably. What can I do to comfort her? Nothing seems to help. Then I remember Cora and run downstairs to fetch her doll. When I hand it to her, she doesn't look up, just clutches her doll baby to her and rocks her gently.

As I sit next to her in silence, her weeping gradually subsides, and she talks softly to her doll. I am grateful to have found the means to comfort her, even if she prefers the doll to me. For the essence of motherhood is to comfort and protect your child. And I am slowly learning to be a mother.

CHAPTER 47

This morning I open the parlor window to let in some fresh air, and with it the laughter of the neighborhood children playing outside, undeterred by the chill of winter. Perhaps today Sarah will be tempted to venture outside and join them instead of spending her days in the house, amusing herself with her doll and the little wooden animals Aiden has carved for her.

"It sounds like the children are having fun," I say to Sarah. "Would you like to take Cora outside to play?"

Sarah shakes her head, but I persist. "I think Cora might enjoy meeting the other dollies."

"No! Cora wants to stay in the house and play with me," she says softly, hugging her doll and putting her thumb in her mouth to punctuate the finality of her decision.

I tell myself I must not push her. Meg assures me she will come around in her own time.

"Have faith," she says.

Meg and Aiden are unable to have children of their own and plan to adopt. "There is no shortage of babies in need of love in this town. We might even be adopting more than one, but only after Sarah is settled."

The two of them will be wonderful parents. I see how the neighborhood girls gather around Meg for a hug and an occasional sweet when she goes out. And I see how the little boys squeal with delight when Aiden lifts them in the air and flies them like birds, and how the older boys sit at his feet as he teaches them to whittle. I sometimes think Meg and Aiden know more about being parents than the one adult in the house who actually is one.

I will try to heed Meg's advice to have faith that Sarah will blossom in her own time. And I will watch for cracks in the shell that protects my little chick, each crack bringing her closer to bursting out and coming into her own. Although I'll never know all the horrors she has endured in her short life, she sometimes gives us clues. Like the day Meg and I were in the kitchen chopping vegetables for soup and she was playing with her doll in the living room. Her voice rose above the kitchen sounds.

"Cora, you have been naughty, so I'll have to spank you. Stop crying or I'll spank you again. Don't you run away from me, naughty girl." In a higher register, "Please. I'll be good. I'll be good."

It broke my heart. But I reminded myself that it's important for her to act out her past and for me to get a glimpse of what she's been through. Because it's only when we know her pain that we can hope to heal it. I am not sure how I know that. I just do.

Today I am alone in the house with Sarah. Meg is out delivering her finished pieces to the agent for the textile mill, and I am preparing to make an Indian pound cake for dessert. Earlier I lit a fire in the firebox, and now the coals are red hot. As I gather ingredients from the larder—eggs, sugar, Indian meal, butter—Sarah comes into the kitchen so quietly I'm unaware of her presence until she says, "Cora loves Indian pound cake, and she wants me to help you."

Sarah is standing by the table, the top half of her head visible above the tabletop.

"Oh, she does, now. And do *you* want to help, too?"

She nods, so I pull up a chair. "Here. Let me get you up here so you can see everything. Up you go. Maybe we should put Cora in another chair. We don't want her to get all floury and sugary, do we?"

She shakes her head and smiles. "No. If she gets all sugary and floury, I might want to eat her, and I want her to be my friend, not my cake."

I laugh, and she laughs with me. She has made a joke, revealing a hint of her true nature, which has been cruelly suppressed.

"So how would you like to help, Sarah?"

"I can mash the butter and sugar."

My eyes widen. "Where did you learn about mashing butter and sugar?"

"Mrs. Doyle showed me. My room had curtains with flowers on them and Mrs. Doyle said that if I was a good girl, she would teach me to make curtains like that. But I was a bad girl. I spilled flour all over the floor. And I broke a teacup. And some other things. She said I was stupid, and she would like to get rid of me. But Mr. Doyle said I was going to stay with them."

I grip the sides of the table to staunch my anger. *For the love of God, she was barely four years old. What did those monsters expect from her?* I suspect it didn't matter what Sarah did. Timmy would torture her, and in so doing torture me. I relax the edges of my mouth to hide my rage, hoping my expression will bear some resemblance to a smile.

"Here, let me put some butter and sugar in a smaller bowl for you. Then I'll give you a fork and you can mash to your heart's content. And don't worry about spilling anything. See all the flour I've already gotten on the floor?"

I watch her tight-mouthed determination as she mashes the butter and sugar into a cream, and I imagine a reservoir of strength tucked deep inside her that will ultimately be her salvation. I put more butter and sugar in her little bowl until she has creamed it all. She tells me she doesn't want to help me with the rest of the ingredients, but she would like Cora to see what I do. So I hand the doll to her, and the two of them watch me add the eggs, flour, nutmeg, cinnamon, and wine, and put the pan in the oven. She stays on the chair, whispering to her doll as the cake bakes. When I ask her about her favorite foods, favorite colors, other personal preferences, she shrugs. But she chooses to stay in the kitchen, which heartens me, though she shows no interest in talking to me. Thus, we continue in silence until I take the cake out to cool and "sneak" slices for ourselves before serving the rest to the family as dessert.

CHAPTER 48

Today is my twenty-second birthday. It is not the happiest of birthdays, since Sarah is still unhappy, and I've discovered that my happiness as a mother is dependent on hers. But it is a special birthday nonetheless, since Lucy, Benjamin, Aidan, and Meg have arranged a most wonderful birthday present for me. Tonight, Meg, Aiden, and I will attend the Walnut Street Theater where Charles Dickens will read from his works.

I had almost forgotten about Dickens' visit to my cell. But a notice in the *Public Ledger* announcing his second American tour unlocked memories of it. I remember the sympathy he showed me and his certainty that I could not have committed the crime—a certainty even I did not share at the time. And I remember the strength and compassion he sensed in me, his words animating my shriveled soul when he declared that tampering with the brain was worse than torturing the body. Those words resonated with me then as they do now.

When I show Lucy the article in the *Ledger* and tell her about my personal connection to the great author, she is impressed. "Why Lizzy O'Meara, you are a celebrity! Did you know Dickens wrote a book about his visit to America? It's called *American Notes.*"

"No, I know nothing of the book. I've been too preoccupied with...other matters."

"Well, I think you would be interested in his impressions of life in the penitentiary. He included stories about the prisoners he interviewed and expressed shock at what he encountered. I remember one interview with a young woman..." She looks at me. "Could that have been you he was writing about?"

"It might have been. There were very few women at Cherry Hill when I was there. Did he identify the woman by name?"

"No, you were not identified."

I offer up silent thanks for that propriety.

"But I recall the great sympathy he had for your plight," Lucy continues. "And I remember the shock and horror he expressed about the institution of slavery."

"Lucy! You're a celebrity, too. I remember telling him about my best friend who was an abolitionist."

Lucy smiles. "I suppose that makes me a celebrity by association. Is such a thing even possible?"

"And there's something else I remember. Something he said right before he left me." I blush at the memory. "He said he expected me to accomplish great things. And he said it with such conviction I could almost believe him. Can you imagine that? From Charles Dickens. I regret I've not been able to live up to his expectations."

"Surely he would consider it an accomplishment that you managed to survive the penitentiary with your mind intact. That, by itself, is a great thing. But you have your whole life ahead of you to live up to his prediction."

Aiden is thrilled when I tell him I met Charles Dickens. My brother has not read any of his books, but he is impressed when I tell him I read *Oliver Twist* in prison. "It wasn't easy," I admitted. "When I tried to read the first page, I was not sure I was reading English—it was such a struggle at the beginning. But about midway through, my understanding of his prose came easier to me, and by the end I rarely stumbled over any words."

"How'd you like to attend one of his performances at the Walnut? Say yes and I'll purchase tickets for the three of us."

"Oh, Aiden. That would be much too expensive."

"Let me worry about that. After all, it's your twenty-second birthday, and what better gift than a night at the theater. I'm sure Mr. Baldwin will help me secure tickets."

"But I am not sure I want to leave Sarah. And who will mind her if the three of us go out for the evening?"

"You could ask Lucy. Sarah seems about as comfortable with Lucy and Benjamin as she is with us."

"That's true. She doesn't seem to care who she is with."

"A sign of independence, don't you think? Like mother, like child."

"Yes, I suppose so. Yet I still feel guilty at the thought of leaving her, even for a few hours. But..." The possibility of a night out tempts me, like the promise of a rich dessert after a diet of soup and bread.

"Perhaps you'll be able to meet Mr. Dickens afterward," Aiden suggests.

"Oh no, that's not likely to happen. And even if it did, I doubt he would remember me."

"Don't be too sure, Lizzy. You're not easily forgotten."

We decide Sarah will spend the evening with her "Aunt Lucy" and "Uncle Benjamin" at their house. When I tell her what we have arranged, she does not object. Nor does she show any emotion, which is not surprising, since she is most animated when interacting with her doll.

The tickets to Dickens' reading tour are not the only birthday gift I receive. Unbeknownst to me, Meg has made me a magnificent frock. Although she spends most of her time doing piecework for the textile mill, which brings in steady money, she has also made a few custom dresses for friends, and on rare occasions for other women who have seen her work and sought her out. When she tells me she is working on a dress for a paying customer, I have no reason to believe otherwise.

So on the morning of our theater date, when Meg calls me into her room and presents me with the dress, the beauty of her creation robs me of speech. She has made me a garment as fine as any worn by the rich women one sees on the streets of Philadelphia. No, that observation alone does not do this dress justice. She has made me a gown fit for a fairy-tale princess.

Meg lays the gown out on the bed and bids me to try it on. It is so perfect, I tell her, I am afraid to touch it. She laughs and tells me there are lots of things to be afraid of in this world, but a dress should not be one of them.

The material is a brilliant shade of royal blue silk. It shimmers in the light that filters through the trees outside our window. How my sister-in-law could afford so much costly silk material is a mystery to me, but when I ask her, she shushes me, saying it is not polite to inquire about the price of a gift.

Meg helps me into the dress, as the fitted bodice requires a tightly laced corset to be worn underneath, and the flounced skirt requires several crinolines, all of which she has provided. I am unused to such a tightly laced corset, which is most uncomfortable. But once I see myself in it, my discomfort is forgotten. I hardly recognize the woman reflected in the mirror. The fitted off-the-shoulder bodice that extends below my waist flatters my body in a way that is most unexpected. The long, flounced skirt puffed out by the crinolines, is elegant. I am not aware until now that since leaving the penitentiary I am no longer scrawny, and the color has returned to my face. Still, I wonder if I'm worthy of such a dress.

As if reading my mind, Meg tells me that I deserve to wear a dress as fine as this, and I should enjoy being a princess for the night. "Those are magic words," I tell her as I twirl around in delight.

That night Meg arranges my hair. She leaves ringlets on either side of my face and pulls the rest back into a braided bun. When I put on the gown, I gasp, hardly recognizing myself. The blue sets off my red curls, which have a golden glow in the gaslight. For a moment I am no longer Lizzy O'Meara, unwed mother, recent resident of Cherry Hill. It is as if the dress has lifted that burden off my shoulders, and if I am not careful, I will float away. *What would Thomas think of me tonight?* I quickly banish the thought and look away from the mirror. My life is not a fairy tale, and a prince charming is no longer a part of my story.

When I descend the steps, Sarah looks up and her eyes widen. She runs her hand lightly along the shimmering silk and whispers, "Oooh...so pretty."

Lucy and Benjamin stop by to pick up Sarah and are equally impressed by my appearance. They hand me a copy of *American Notes* as a birthday present. I thank them for giving me a most wonderful gift.

"I think Mr. Dickens will sign it," says Lucy. "After all, the two of you are acquainted."

"I don't think so," I say skeptically.

"Don't be so sure of that," says Aiden. "Mr. Baldwin says he's going to be meeting with Mr. Dickens after the performance. He told me we should seek him out and accompany him when he visits Mr. Dickens."

Although it's December, this week has been unusually mild, so we have no need for coats, only light cloaks, which we don before heading out into the night.

The Walnut Street Theater is an impressive building, especially at night when its elegant columns and regal façade are bathed in lamplight. Elegantly dressed people congregate outside, while carriage after carriage pulls up to discharge passengers. It is as if the rest of the city has fallen away—the sounds and smells muted, the ugliness erased—and this magnificent building stands at the center of the world. I am suddenly reminded of my classmates' frequent taunt: "Who do you think you are? The Queen of England?"

Yes, I can finally answer them. That is *exactly* who I am. At least for tonight. "And here is Princess Meg, my lady-in-waiting, dressed in a magnificent red silk frock, accompanied by her princely escort."

"Hello, Aiden," says someone behind us. We turn to face a man with a receding hairline and bushy gray collar-length hair that stands out on either side of his head.

"Mr. Baldwin," says Aiden, shaking his hand. "Let me introduce my family."

Matthias Baldwin carries himself with an air of authority. Not quite as tall as Aiden, he is nonetheless impressive in his elegant black greatcoat, vest, and trousers.

Aiden introduces us, and Mr. Baldwin smiles at me. "Your brother has spoken so highly of you...shared many things. He told me you've even had the pleasure of making Mr. Dickens' acquaintance in the past."

I nod, flushing with embarrassment as I recall the circumstances of that meeting, knowing that Mr. Baldwin is also aware of them.

"I told Aiden I would be delighted if you accompanied me when I meet with the great man directly after the performance." He checks his pocket watch. "Excuse me, but I must hurry off to meet with a colleague before the show begins. Why don't we meet in the lobby after the show, in front of the staircase on the left, and we'll all go in together to meet Mr. Dickens."

The three of us make our way slowly into the theater, threading ourselves around groups of splendidly attired men and women engaged in animated conversation. The rings and bracelets of the women twinkle like stars in the gaslight, and I hold on to Aiden's arm, afraid of getting lost in this sea of wealthy strangers.

It is warm inside, and I remove my cape and drape it over my arm as we begin climbing the stairs to the upper balcony. Someone taps me on the shoulder, and I turn.

"Excuse me," says a woman dressed in a brilliant scarlet gown, "but I cannot help but admire your gown. I can see that the front is even more splendid. Such a unique and well-executed application of the Bertha collar. Splendid workmanship. Might I inquire as to the name of your seamstress, or did you import it from Europe?"

I pinch my wrist to keep from laughing. Although Meg is an excellent seamstress, she does not make dresses for the general public.

"I am sorry, but I do not know the name of the seamstress. The dress was a gift from a dear friend, and I was taught not to question the giver, but to accept graciously."

"I must say, the color certainly suits you perfectly. You are fortunate to have a friend with such exquisite taste."

"Indeed. I thank you for the compliments, and I will convey them to my friend." I must pinch even harder as I can hardly contain my laughter.

I allow the lady and her companion to pass and go some distance before I dare to look at Meg, and we dissolve in laughter.

We enter the auditorium and climb to our seats in the last row of the second balcony. From that height we can enjoy all the lavish interior with its many gilded surfaces and the plush maroon curtains that frame the boxes. We are so high up that I can almost touch the ornately painted ceiling. The stage is set simply with a large maroon backdrop and a desk in the center.

The houselights dim, and a row of gas footlights illuminate the stage. Mr. Dickens walks onstage to great applause and cheers. I can barely see him from such a distance, but I don't mind, since it now appears almost certain we will meet with him later. He leans on the waist-high desk, opens a book, and announces what he is about to read. Being so far from the stage, I am afraid we won't be unable to hear him, but his voice is loud and clear, and I do not miss a word. He reads from *Nicholas Nickleby* and *The Pickwick Papers*, neither of which are familiar to me.

After ninety minutes he stops for a brief intermission, then recommences for another half hour. I am hoping for a reading from *Oliver Twist,* the one book I know, but that does not happen. However, my disappointment is short-lived because he does his final reading from *A Christmas Carol.* When he quotes Scrooge, "I will live in the Past, the Present, and the Future. The spirits of all three shall strive within me," I imagine he is speaking to me. He ends the performance with Tiny Tim's pronouncement: "God bless us, every one."

We try to hurry downstairs to meet Mr. Baldwin, but with so many people blocking our way, I am sure he will have moved on. But there he is, just as he promised. He escorts us backstage, where we stand in a line of people waiting to greet the author. When we get close, I see Mr. Dickens has aged since I last saw him. The lines around his eyes and mouth have deepened, and his beard is flecked with gray. Aiden and Meg are standing behind me, and I ask my brother to hand me the book he has been carrying for me. Mr. Baldwin is now the only person between me and Mr. Dickens. They greet each other, and he whispers something to the author, who casts his eyes in my direction. My hands are shaking.

Finally, Mr. Baldwin steps aside, and Mr. Dickens beckons me to approach him.

"My dear young woman." He takes my hand. "Matthias has told me who you are. Although much time has passed since we met, I remember you well. Of all the prisoners I interviewed, you were the most articulate. Your story touched me."

"Indeed, sir. You were convinced of my innocence when even I had doubts."

"And I have been proven right. I cannot imagine how you survived all those years in those hellish conditions and...rose from the ashes, like a phoenix. You are a marvel."

"Oh sir, you flatter me. I am an ordinary woman, nothing more." I hold out my copy of *American Notes* to distract his gaze from my undoubtedly beet-red face. "Would you do me the honor of signing your name? I received your book this morning as a birthday gift, so I have not yet had the opportunity to read it."

He wishes me a happy birthday before opening the book and writing something on the first page. Then he hands it back to me. After I thank him, he says, "I ask you to do *me* the honor of writing to me and letting me know how you are doing...and what you are doing. When I visited you, I recall you said you were involved in the anti-slavery movement, as are most Quakers, I'm told. The Quakers may have erred in their belief that a penitentiary is a more humane form of incarceration than a prison, but I admire their conviction that there is something of God in each of us, which means that we are all equal."

"Although I am not a Quaker, I subscribe to that philosophy. Thank you again for...for everything. I will do my best to write."

"Send your letters to my publisher and I will receive them."

I turn to leave and see that every eye is on me.

Out in the lobby, waiting for Aiden and Meg, I read what he has written: "I expect great things of you, Miss O'Meara." He signed with an elaborate flourish beneath his name, so that his name appears to float on a cloud. I float through the lobby on my own cloud until we step outside.

CHAPTER 49

Clanging bells, shouting men, and blaring horns announce the arrival of a fire engine. It rounds the corner and comes into view just as we reach the theater steps. A team of men holding ropes pull the engine past the theater, scattering everyone and everything in its path. That first engine is followed by another, and another. It seems that every fire company in the area is part of the wild parade. They pass us and head south on Eighth Street, toward the flames and smoke rising in the distance.

It's happening again—the riots—and I fear this time will be no different than before. The violence is too far away for me to see or hear, but I can feel it in the air. Some people across the street are cheering the fire companies, calling out the names emblazoned on the ladders, as if it's a game. Weccacoe! Northern Liberties! Fairmount! Don't they care that people might be dying only a few blocks from here?

I am momentarily stunned by the memory of Da's death in the fire that engulfed the city so many years ago. In the midst of the chaos that surrounds me, I am transported back to that terrible time. I am a little girl again...a little girl...*Sarah!* She's somewhere in the middle of the mayhem that is the destination of the fire companies. No, I tell myself, the fire isn't anywhere near our neighborhood. It's definitely farther west. And maybe it's just a fire, not a riot.

"What's happening?" Aiden asks someone in the crowd.

"Who knows?" he says, shrugging. "We're as much in the dark as you are."

He asks several more people. Same answer, and now I detect a faint smell of smoke.

Aiden yells. "Anyone know what's happening?"

"They say it's a hotel that's burning."

"What hotel?" I ask, "Some of them are near our—"

"Lizzy," says Aiden. "There are so many hotels in Philadelphia, it's probably not in our neighborhood."

A man wielding a bat runs toward us, and I can no longer pretend it's not a riot. I remember the many times people filled the streets, armed with bats, bricks, paving stones, and hatred, hunting down Black people. *Lucy. Benjamin.*

"You there," Aiden calls out, "Where are you going?"

"St. Mary's Street. They set fire to the California House. The one where Blacks go. Owner's a mulatto, wife's white. Damned amalgamation. It should be against the law."

Benjamin is Black and Lucy could pass for white.

"That's why they lit the place up." He raises his bat. "I'm on my way to make sure it burns all the way down." He hurries past.

"The California is a block away from Lucy's. What if...We have to go." I turn and run into the street, dodging everything with legs and wheels that gets in my way. Aiden and Meg catch up with me on the other side of Walnut.

"Lizzy," says Meg, "Wait. Lucy and Benjamin are watching Sarah. They would have taken her back to our house at the first sign of trouble. I'm sure of it."

"But they don't have a key. They may be trapped in the middle of the riot."

"No one said anything about a riot," says Aiden, taking my arm.

"No one has to say it." I pull myself out of his grip and race to the end of the block. Damn these slippers. They're going to fall off my feet, and I'll have to run barefoot through the muck in the streets.

By the time I reach the corner, I'm winded. This ungodly corset is squeezing the breath out of me. How will I ever make it to Lucy and Benjamin's? At least the slippers are still on my feet.

Aiden and Meg catch up to me. "It'll be safer if we stick together," says Aiden. "Let's go home first. If they're not there, we'll head for Lucy's."

We head south on Seventh Street, paralleling the fire trucks racing down Eighth. The smoke thickens as we cross Locust, Spruce, and Pine streets. We're jostled by men and women—mostly men—carrying stones, bottles, anything they can use as weapons. Impeded by neither slippers nor corsets, even the women race past us.

On our street we can feel the heat from the fire several blocks south of us. Meg agrees to stay at the house in case the three of them show up. I race up to my room to exchange my slippers for boots, but it will take too long to remove my ragged gown and corset. I toss my cloak on the bed, hurry downstairs, and we're off again.

As we get closer to Lucy's street, our path is blocked by fire apparatus, although it appears the firemen are battling each other instead of the flames. We take the back alleys to get to St. Mary's Street.

"It's the Moyas that done it," someone yells. "They're shooting anyone who tries to put out the fire."

Moyamensing. Bull McMullen's hose company. Timmy used to ride along with his cousin. He loved to brag about it. Could he be here in this crowd? If he caught sight of Sarah...Stop! I must not let my imagination get the better of me.

Two of the Moyas attach their equipment to the only fire plug on the block, while the rest of their men stand around, their hoses idle. I try to see their faces, but there's too much smoke. The California Hotel is half consumed by flames, as are the surrounding homes.

A block away, another company, the Lafayette, has taken control of the plug, and the men are pumping away, sending streams of water through the hose. As we run past, we hear their song.

Fire-fire-fire!

Hark! 'tis the dreadful cry.

The Lafe boys are on the ground

To conquer or to die.

The mob closes in. Armed with knives, pistols, and brickbats, they attack the firemen, cut their hose, and drag their equipment away as we race down the alleys to Lucy and Benjamin's house, which is two blocks from the California. Their rowhouse stands in the middle of a block that until today was neat and well-kept, despite its unfortunate location not far from the shanties. They could have moved farther north to an area that had attracted middle-class Black families, but Lucy chose to stay in her parents' home, and today she is paying the price for that decision. Young rowdies, some carrying torches, are roaming the street, vandalizing houses and attempting to set anything that can burn on fire. One of them, close on the heels of a Black man, tosses a rock, which just misses the poor man's head. All the while, the odor of smoldering rubbish fires and burning wood chokes us. *It's happening all over again.*

The windows of the once spotless Washington-Jacobs house are shattered, and the front door is wide open. Standing amidst overturned furniture and broken crockery, we call out, but no one answers. I race upstairs and check every room, hoping against hope that they might be hiding in a closet or dark corner. But the house is empty.

"Aiden, what do we do?"

Meg answers for him. "Lucy and Benjamin would have moved heaven and earth to keep Sarah safe. They've got to be hiding somewhere. We can't do anything more, so let's get out of here." Aiden nods in agreement.

"I don't know. That mob is out of control," I observe, undecided about what to do next. "If they spot a Black man with a mulatto woman and a white child..."

We find rags to cover our mouths and noses and make our way to the front door.

"What's that?" I point to brownish-red stains on the floor by the front door. "I think it's blood. And look here, bloody fingerprints on the door and the doorframe. Oh, Aiden," I wail.

"I'm sure they're all right," he says once we're outside, although his voice lacks conviction. "Look. it's the militia." Men in uniform are marching up the street in our direction. "And the cavalry. They'll get all this under control." He grabs my arm. "No point standing around. Nothing we can do."

"Please, Aiden. We can't stop now." The rags do little to protect us from the smoke, and our words are punctuated with coughs.

"They'll find us when things have calmed down. Let's go home."

Reluctantly, I agree, and the three of us head home. Once there, we take turns pacing, sit, pace again, and look out the window from time to time, although the smoke makes it hard to see anything. The waiting is torture.

I take off the accursed corset and exchange my tattered gown for a day dress. At my seat by the window, I try to keep my eyes open, but drift off. A loud banging at the door startles me awake. It's Benjamin, covered in soot, bruised, and...alone. After he stumbles inside, I take a quick look up and down the street for Lucy and Sarah, but no one is there.

"Where are they?" I ask, but Benjamin is swaying on his feet. I lead him to the sofa and pull up a chair to face him.

"Where are Lucy and Sarah?"

He opens his mouth to answer, but all that comes out is a fit of coughing. Meg rushes in with a pitcher of lemonade. Once he has drunk his fill, he looks at me with bloodshot eyes, and I repeat the question.

"I don't know." He shakes his head. "I don't know. It was...we were separated...my responsibility to protect..."

"Here's something stronger," says Aiden, handing him a glass of whiskey.

Benjamin drains the glass. "Thank you." He hands Aiden the empty glass, which he immediately refills.

"Benjamin, what happened?" I hug myself hard, anticipating the worst.

"I cannot say where they are." His eyes fill with tears. "I..."

Meg fetches a handkerchief, and he wipes his eyes.

"We should have left home when we heard the first fire engines. But how were we to know there was violence brewing in the streets? When we heard the angry voices of the rioters and the sound of breaking glass getting closer and closer, we huddled down in the corner of the back bedroom. By the time we realized we were foolish to stay so long, they broke into our house, and it was too late for us to escape. We prayed they wouldn't come upstairs. We could hear them breaking anything they could get their hands on, but thankfully they never climbed the steps.

"We were very careful when we left the house—tried to stay in the shadows. We planned to use the back alleys to find shelter. We didn't know if you were back from the theater, so we decided we'd try to get ourselves to the Still's house, but"—he pauses to take a few sips of whiskey— "a man in the crowd spotted me and yelled to his mate to bring a bat and they'd take care of the n——. Thankfully they didn't see Lucy, who was standing behind me with Sarah in her arms. I begged her to run. She hesitated, then took off. The two men grabbed me, and I thought that was the end of me. But God must have been with me, because at that moment a burning plank from one of the houses fell on the arm of one of the men, and he ran off screaming bloody murder. As I struggled with the other man, I spotted someone chasing Lucy and Sarah."

"Benjamin, was it someone from the fire company?"

"I couldn't tell. By the time I got free, they had disappeared. I ran up and down the streets looking for them. I went to the Still house, but they weren't there. I have to believe they're hiding somewhere safe. Lucy can pass for white, and even those brutes wouldn't hurt a white woman and child, would they?"

The four of us pass the remaining hours of the night and early daylight hours trying to eat, trying to sleep, succeeding at neither. Later that morning, I pick up the kettle to boil water for tea, when there's a knock at the door. The kettle hits the floor with a clang, and we rush to the door.

There before us is a beautiful sight. A smiling Lucy with Sarah in her arms, both a little bedraggled but unharmed. I grab Sarah from Lucy's arms and hold her tight to my chest, bathing her in my tears of relief.

Benjamin embraces Lucy, clasping her in his arms and smoothing her hair.

"There, there," I murmur to Sarah. "You're with mama now." I don't want to let her go, and rock her as Meg retrieves the fallen tea kettle. Sarah's eyes are wide. She looks dazed. I feel I should be able to read her emotions, since I'm her mother. But all I can do is rock her in my arms.

After a time, once we've had a chance to collect ourselves, we sit around the dining-room table so Meg can serve us all some food. Suddenly Sarah bursts out crying.

"What's the matter?" I ask. But she pulls away when I try to comfort her.

"Cora. I...need...Cora."

"Cora? Oh, your doll. Poor Cora." Her doll probably got lost in all the confusion and wouldn't easily be found.

Sarah is sobbing so hard she can barely catch her breath.

"Oh, love, we'll get you a new doll," I say in soothing tones.

"No, I want Cora. I need Cora," she protests.

"We've been up all night," says Lucy. "Why don't you put her to bed, and I'll tell you what happened to us."

I take Sarah upstairs and dress her in her nightclothes, as she continues to sob and murmur her doll's name. I tuck her into bed and rub her back. After a while, she puts her thumb in her mouth and falls asleep.

Downstairs, we gather in the living room to hear Lucy's story.

"We spent the night with William and Leticia Still, but getting there wasn't easy."

"And Sarah?" I ask. "She must have been scared to death."

"I am sure she was, although she didn't utter a word. Just an occasional whimper. We had her wrapped in blankets and I held her against my chest so she couldn't see anything when we ducked out of the house—but she could hear everything. And it was frightening. There were ruffians everywhere. Screaming and yelling curses. It is a good thing she is too young to understand the hatred that ignited this conflagration. At least I hope she is."

"When Aiden and I searched your house, we found blood at the front door. Whose was it?" I ask.

"Benjamin cut himself trying to remove some of the broken glass from the front window and the door, so we went out the back."

Benjamin takes her hand. "I saw someone chase you as you ran off with Sarah."

"Yes. A man standing by the fire engines spotted me and yelled. Then he came after us. I ran as fast as I could, but I could hear him getting closer. And then he was running beside me. He reached out to grab Sarah, when someone yelled, 'Doyle. Get back here!' He tugged at Sarah while I held her close. 'Doyle, I mean it! Stop chasing the ladies and help us here. We let you ride so you can pull your weight.'"

"That madman," I say, a bitter taste in my mouth. "That evil, sick man. Ever a source of torment."

Lucy reaches out to comfort me, gently patting my shoulder before she continues. "We made it to the Still house where we stayed the night, although I hardly slept a wink."

"Poor dears, the both of ye," says Meg. "All wrung out. Ye can stay here as long as ye like. There's room on the third floor, although the amenities are somewhat lacking."

"That is kind of you. Benjamin, shall we stay here until tomorrow?"

"Yes, right now sleep would be a blessing. Tomorrow we can take up Mr. Still's invitation to stay with him until our house is habitable again."

"I'll help you make the repairs," says Aiden.

"Thank you, that would—" Benjamin's words are interrupted by a yawn.

"That's all settled, then," says Meg. "I'll take ye upstairs and ye can get some well-deserved sleep. Follow me."

"You must be exhausted," I say to Aiden. "I know I am. Let's speak no more of this. I can hardly keep my eyes open. Why don't we go upstairs too and get some sleep."

We retire to our bedrooms, but I don't think either of us slept a wink.

CHAPTER 50

I buy Sarah a new rag doll, hoping it will make it easier for her to bear the loss of her beloved Cora. She has blue eyes, sweet red lips, and braided yellow wool hair. Meg sews her a calico dress with a matching cap and red apron. But Sarah's eyes don't light up when I give her the new doll. She thanks me politely and dutifully carries it around with her all day. But that evening she puts it on the shelf, where it stays. And she continues to murmur "Cora" in her sleep.

I know she has gone without so much during her short life, and I would like to ease her way now; but when I embrace her, she still stiffens in my arms. I counsel myself to be patient and not force my affections on her, exhibiting the same restraint I exercise when planting seeds in our tiny front garden: covering the seeds with soil, watering them, rejoicing when the seedlings emerge, and protecting them until they can stand on their own. Love can be like that.

I know that the damage you suffer when you are deprived of love is always with you. I will carry the scars from my mother's rejection till the day I die. But they faded with the passage of time. And unlike Sarah, I was nurtured by a loving father and brother. I even remember a few words of a lullaby my mother sang to me and have a vague recollection of sitting on her lap, curled against her chest as she rocked me; so it is likely my mother showed me a modicum of affection during my early years.

But my poor Sarah has been unacquainted with love until now. She experienced only hardship, indifference, and dislocation. Can you ever be whole when you've never experienced love early in life?

Lately, Sarah has taken an interest in books. She finds a McGuffey's reader on the bookshelf in the living room, and I watch her turn the pages and trace the letters of the alphabet with her finger. From time to time I sit down beside her on the floor and teach her the letters. She repeats each one in a serious little voice and soon has them memorized. This gives me such pleasure that I consider the possibility of pursuing a job as a teacher. I want to contribute my fair share to the household and have considered various occupations, like working as a seamstress or even taking in laundry. But teaching would be the most gratifying and would allow me to pass on what I've learned to others.

Sarah finds the *Anti-Slavery Alphabet* book and begins tracing the elaborate letters. As we go through the book together, I look at some of the rhymes that accompany the letters but do not read them aloud. She is too young, and they are too raw.

"**K** is the Kidnapper, who stole
That little child and mother—
Shrieking, it clung around her, but
He tore them from each other."

"**W** is the Whipping post,
To which the slave is bound,
While on his naked back, the lash
Makes many a bleeding wound."

Sometimes I watch from the other room as she selects a book and slowly turns the pages, even though there is often not much for her to see besides dense text and an occasional illustration. For some reason she is quite taken by the *House-keeper's Almanac and Family Receipt*

Book, an odd choice for someone her age. She spends a lot of time looking at the charts that show the phases of the moon and the aspects of the planets, as well as the little illustrations that accompany the descriptions of each month. The first time I see her looking through the *Almanac*, I sit down beside her on the floor, and she asks me to tell her what the words say. I go over the months with her and point to January.

"That's the month we're in now, so it's very..."

"Cold."

We look at the frosted windows.

"Freezing cold," she adds.

She wants me to tell her more words, and she listens intently, although it is dry reading, indeed: remedies for ailments from decaying teeth to cramps to nosebleeds; instructions for destroying cockroaches and cleaning wallpaper. And there are recipes, which she especially enjoys hearing.

She also delights in the stories I read to her at bedtime. From a copy of *Anderson's Fairy Tales*, I read and reread her favorites, "The Ugly Duckling" and "The Little Mermaid." Although bedtime is when I feel the most connected to her, she refuses to sit on my lap on the rocking chair while I read, preferring the distance of her own bed.

Tonight, when I'm tucking her into bed I ask her, "How would you like to pick out a new book for yourself?"

She sits up. "A new book for me?"

"Yes. And you can choose it yourself. Tomorrow I'm going to take you to a bookstore. I think you'll love it there. There are more books in a bookstore than you've ever seen in your whole life."

She slides her legs over the edge of the bed and says excitedly, "Let's go right now."

I chuckle. "I wish we could, but it's nighttime and the shops are closed. But I promise you we'll go tomorrow." I tuck her back in.

"When we find Cora, I'll read her a story from my new book."

CHAPTER 51

The next morning, Sarah wakes me up at dawn. "Lizzy." She taps me on the shoulder. "Lizzy, wake up." She is holding her best dress—pink calico trimmed with lace at the neckline—in one hand and a hair comb in the other. "Can you help me with my dress and pin my hair back?"

"Honey, it's early. The bookstore won't be open for hours."

"I want to get dressed now, Lizzy."

"All right. I see you want to look your best for all those books."

"Oh, yes," she says seriously.

I fasten her dress, part her hair in the middle, and use two combs to hold the sides back over her ears.

"I have an idea. Why don't we take a walk down to the river and see the skaters first? That way, by the time we get to the store it will be open."

After breakfast we bundle up in heavy coats, gloves, bonnets, and scarves. It is the weekend, so there are children everywhere, running around drunk on freedom, the crisp cold breeze turning their cheeks the color of ripe apples.

On our way to the river, we pass the husk of a burned-out house gutted by hatred, a victim of the recent riots. The front has collapsed, exposing what is left of the interior.

"Look, you can see all the way into its insides," says Sarah.

It looks like a wrecked dollhouse, with charred walls and broken furniture. In truth, more skeleton than dollhouse. There is a single picture hanging askew on the only remaining wall of what used to be the living room, a floral vase standing unmolested among the shards of the objects that once surrounded it. Something we shouldn't be seeing—a family's personal life in shambles, naked and exposed.

Although it's early in the day, it seems that half of Philadelphia is crowded onto the frozen Delaware, skating, sledding, or sitting on chairs watching the scene. Couples weave their way gracefully arm-in-arm through the crowd, the women in bonnets, the men in top hats. Two boys racing each other plow into a gentleman, who lands bottom first on the ice. A boy skates lazy figure eights, glancing at a girl standing nearby each time he completes a figure.

I notice a large man standing motionless in the midst of the swirling crowd, staring at me. Although he's some distance away and bundled up in a heavy coat, top hat, and scarf, there is no mistaking him. Timmy Doyle! He tips his hat. The icy air is no match for the chill that freezes the blood in my veins.

"Madman," I mutter. He's like a cat, playing with a mouse before killing his prey. *I will not let that happen.*

I grip Sarah's hand so hard she winces, and I pull her toward the street. "I'm sorry, but we have to go now."

"Are we going to the bookstore, Lizzy?"

"Yes. Let's hurry." I take a quick look back and he's no longer there. But he could be lurking somewhere in the shadows like he used to do when I was younger. I keep Sarah's hand firmly in mine, eyeing our surroundings as we make our way from the waterfront to Leary's Bookstore on Ninth Street.

When we step inside the door, Sarah's eyes widen. She utters a soft "oh" of wonder as she gazes up openmouthed at the towering shelves crammed with books of all colors and sizes, as if they were confections. I am so enchanted by the sight of her as she drags me from section to section that I forget our near encounter with Timmy Doyle.

"Ooo," she says, pointing up to a book with a blond curly-haired girl on the cover. Most books on the shelves are visible only by their spines, but here and there are some with their front covers on display. "She looks like a princess. Can you get me that book, Lizzy?"

"It's too high up for me. We'll have to find someone taller to reach it. Meanwhile, maybe you'll find other books we can reach." I point to books for children on the tables, but it seems Sarah is only interested in the books that are out of reach.

I am so focused on our quest that I am unaware of the presence of other customers in the shop until someone taps me on the shoulder. I turn around, startled, and there is Thomas. His face is only inches from mine.

I want to run away. I want to rush into his arms. The two opposing forces freeze me in place. Thomas' dark hair is tousled, and his cheeks are rosy from the cold. In his black overcoat with his top hat in his hand, and a smile so warm it could melt the Delaware, he looks perfectly splendid. My pulse quickens and I am afraid to touch him for fear of losing control of my emotions right here in the middle of Leary's Bookstore. I am flooded by memories of us lying together on the banks of the Schuylkill when he proposed, and the touch of his hands on my body, and my longing to surrender to him. My face is burning. What does he think when he sees my crimson cheeks? Can he read my mind? I must put an end to these foolish thoughts.

"I should have known we'd meet in a bookstore. How are you, Lizzy?"

"I...I'm..." The words are stuck in my throat.

He smiles and places his hand lightly on mine. "I know, Lizzy, I know. You don't have to say a word."

The feel of his hand on mine is like a homecoming. I...*No!* I pull my hand away from his. I must put an end to these feelings. He would not want to touch me if he knew all I had done, all that had been done to me since he'd last seen me. If he knew I'd tried to murder my unborn child, tried to kill myself. If he saw the scars of my madness. If he knew my shame.

His expression tells me he is seeing the woman I was, not the one I have become. He is seeing the tall, straight-backed, red-haired eighteen-year-old, threading her way around the tables at City Tavern, unsure of how she'd fit into his world, but sure of their love for each other, and confident she would find her way. He is seeing the proud, independent, determined Lizzy, eager to pursue justice, ignoring the hungry stares of the men as she walks by. No, I fear I am no longer that woman.

"I don't understand," Thomas says, scouring my face for a clue as to why I rebuffed him. Then he whispers, "This is your child, Lizzy, I would know her anywhere."

He kneels till he's eye level with Sarah. "Hello. My name is Thomas. What's your name?"

"I'm Sarah. You're very tall, aren't you?"

"Yes, very tall."

"Then you can reach the books Lizzy can't."

"I can certainly try. Why don't you show me what you want."

I watch her lead him, her hand in his. She points and he lifts her up to retrieve the book. They repeat this two more times before returning to me. He puts her down and kneels.

"Do you think your mommy will buy you these books?"

"You mean Lizzy."

"Yes, that's who I mean."

She reaches out and touches his cheek. What is it about Thomas that draws Sarah to him? Does he remind her of someone who showed her a rare kindness? Does she sense my feelings for him and act them out in a way I cannot? Or is it one of those magical connections that has no explanation, but just is? When she touches his cheek, I realize a heart can melt and break at the same time, as mine is doing now.

"Lizzy says I can buy one, but maybe there's a better one than these."

"There just might be. In fact, I think I know one you will love."

Silently I follow the two of them to the shelf with children's books. I want to tell him that he has performed a miracle, animating my Sarah. But even as my heart is overjoyed by their extraordinary connection, it aches with the knowledge that he and I will never be together.

Thomas picks out a book and kneels once again. "This one is called *A Wonder-Book for Girls and Boys.* And look at this." He opens the book to the frontispiece and hands it over to her.

"A horse with wings," she says, her voice flush with excitement.

"That's Pegasus."

"Oh, I love it." She clutches the book to her chest and turns to me. "Can we buy it, Lizzy?"

"Of course—I promised, didn't I?" My voice is harsh, which I regret, but the words have left my mouth. Sarah doesn't seem to notice, although Thomas looks pained.

I sweeten my voice. "Why don't you pick out a second book, and I'll buy that for you, too. Let's take another look."

Sarah looks up at Thomas. "I love books."

"I can see that," he says as I take her hand and walk through the aisles. He is waiting where I left him when I pay for the books, and the three of us walk out together as if we were a family.

I don't know what to say to him, so I shake his hand before we go our separate ways and tell him it was wonderful running into him like that. As if we were casual strangers. As if I had never accepted his proposal of marriage.

Sarah turns back and waves, but I keep my eyes on the sidewalk in front of me.

On the way home Sarah asks when we will see Thomas again. I give her a vague reply. It's best to leave her with hope, although I have no intention of seeing him again. I'm being selfish, disingenuous. Not long ago, I promised myself I'd sacrifice anything for Sarah's happiness. But making a commitment to Thomas, letting him think I was the same person he loved so many years ago...that was something I just couldn't do.

CHAPTER 52

"I don't understand why ye can't just talk to him," Meg says after I tell her my decision about Thomas after the encounter in the bookstore. "Why ye can't tell him what Northam did to ye, what happened to ye in prison. He loved ye then, he'll be loving ye now."

"I'm not the same person he knew, so why would he still love me. And the thought of saying those things out loud. The filth. The degradation. How I sinned, blasphemed God, cursed the Quakers. I...I just can't face him."

"What sin did ye commit?"

"I tried to murder my child."

"I don't understand."

"Madame Restell."

Meg crosses her arms and glares at me. "'Tis not a sin ye committed. Murder is a sin, and that's not something ye did." Her expression softens. "Lizzy, love, why don't ye have faith in the man ye loved. Tell him everything. He loves ye."

"Loved me. Past tense. I know you mean the best for me, but I just can't look him in the eye and tell him everything. There are things I have never told anyone—not you, not Aiden. That's my final word."

But during the weeks that follow, I can't get the image of Thomas and Sarah together out of my head. Nor can I erase the sound of his voice or the touch of his hand. After another sleepless night, I decide once and for all that the last words I said to Thomas would be my final *spoken* words, but perhaps not my final *written* ones. What if I let the journal I kept in prison speak for me? Other than the clothes on my back, my journal was the only possession I took home with me. And when Meg brought me up to my bedroom for the first time, I had slipped it into a dresser drawer beneath the undergarments she had purchased for me. I had forgotten about it until now. Reaching into the drawer, I pull out the journal, and lay it on the bed. I hadn't noticed how the muslin cover had become stained and torn over the years. The edges of the pages within are rough, as if chewed by an animal. I open it to a random page, and tucked into the crease is the letter Aiden wrote me shortly before my release.

"I cannot tell you how many letters I have written to you, knowing they would never be delivered. How cruel you must have thought me... *Yes, that was true.* "Not a day has gone by when I haven't thought of you..." *How those words eased my pain.* "Two weeks from now when the doors open and you step out into freedom, I will be waiting outside for you with open arms. Two weeks seems like a lifetime. But in the blink of an eye, we will be together. Your loving brother." *I could hardly believe it at the time, but the two weeks of waiting had, indeed, passed in the blink of an eye.*

I page though the entries, trying to imagine reading them through Thomas' eyes. The early ones are neatly written, mostly about my past life, written in detail so I wouldn't forget them. Interspersed are entries written in a rougher hand, describing my life in prison and the tyranny of silence. I'd have little trepidation showing those pages to Thomas.

But then comes the passage where I describe what Northam had done to me, and the entries where I cursed God and begged for release. And here is a page where I describe my feelings about Thomas and how my body felt when he touched me, and where he touched me, and how

I imagined it would be to lie with him as man and wife. I held nothing back, and my face burns as I read it. On later pages my thoughts become progressively less coherent. Sentence fragments, blood flowing between my legs, the bloody Schuylkill, "Shame," "Bastard," and "WHORE" writ large on several pages. Then page after page of jagged scrawls, like marks left by an animal. And finally, pages that are blank, save for bloodstains from my suicide attempts.

This is the journal of someone who was no less mad than her mother, who died in an insane asylum. If he knew how my mother's life had ended, would he not be afraid that I too would end my days in Blockley? But I am determined to send this to him. A final goodbye of sorts. Before wrapping the journal up to send to him, I write a note.

Dear Thomas,

After much anguish, I decided to send you the journal I kept in prison, so you can read about my sickness and my shame. About how I tried to take my own life. How I let Robert Northam take advantage of me, for surely a stronger woman would have fought back harder and avoided my fate. I am too ashamed and embarrassed to tell you all this myself, so I am letting the journal speak for me. What you find in here will disgust you.

I owed you an explanation for my behavior of late, which is why I am sending you this journal. Please do not return it to me, I am done with it. You are welcome to discard it as rubbish or burn it or dispose of it however you see fit. You can reply by post, if you are so inclined, but let me be clear that you have no obligation to me, and I am not expecting an answer.

I wish you happiness and long life. You deserve the best that life has to offer.

Lizzy

I tuck the note into the diary and wrap it in brown paper. Then I ask Aiden to deliver it to Thomas and convey the same instructions about its disposal that I included in my letter.

That chapter of my life is finished, and it's time for me to close the book.

CHAPTER 53

Although I do not expect Thomas to respond, I cannot extinguish the faintest glimmer of hope that he will. But it has been a week, so it's time to empty my heart of any romantic notions. I tell myself I am glad at least he didn't send my journal back to me. It is a blessing that I will never see it again.

I was hoping Sarah would forget him, but not a day has gone by when she hasn't inquired about "that nice Mr. Thomas." When she asks if we can go to the bookstore tomorrow, I suspect she is thinking of Thomas as much as she is of books.

"I think the bookstore is closed tomorrow." Which is not true, but why nurture her hopes about seeing Thomas again? "But I have another idea, and I think you are going to like it. A lot. Would you like to hear it?" I pause to pique her curiosity, and she catches the enthusiasm in my voice. Her eyes widen and she nods eagerly.

"Do you remember the cherry tartlets we had for dessert last week?"

"Uh huh."

"Of course, you do. You loved them, didn't you?"

Another enthusiastic nod.

"How would you like to go to the market tomorrow and visit the Pie Man?"

She leans down and whispers something into the crook of her arm, as if she's cradling something. Then she answers. "Cora says she wants to visit the Pie Man." Her lost doll is with her in spirit.

The noise and confusion of the outside world still frighten her (as it does me from time to time), and I would not be surprised if she changes her mind. But she tells me Cora really wants to visit the Pie Man. "She's a little scared," she says, "but I'll hold on to her real tight."

So that afternoon, Sarah, Meg, and I, plus one imaginary doll, take off for the covered stalls called the Shambles. We pass women chattering as they sweep their stoops and hang laundry, vendors crying out their wares, children throwing balls and playing hide-and-seek, girls rolling hoops, boys pushing and shoving each other. As we near High Street we are accosted by the din that accompanies the business of buying and selling. Although the market has been a bustling center for as long as I can remember, it was much smaller when I was growing up—just a few blocks of stalls along the wharf and down Second Street. But it has since grown like the beanstalk in Jack's tale, and now a line of covered sheds stretches along High Street from the wharf to Sixth Street.

Meg and I keep to either side of Sarah, walking as if we were a single unit to avoid being separated and to protect ourselves against pickpockets. Sarah walks silently between us, her eyes darting every which way as we are enveloped in the smelly, noisy world of commerce. We pass wagons hung with meats of every variety, carts piled high with loaves of bread, potatoes, cabbages, onions, crates of chickens, and other livestock. There's firewood and housewares, sugar, spices, and molasses from the islands—everything we could possibly want, spread out before us in overwhelming abundance. We point all of this out to Sarah, and she stares wide-eyed at the bounty that surrounds us.

The cries of the vendors are matched in volume by the patrons as they bargain for the best price. The streets reek of horse droppings, and we wrinkle our noses whenever we pass a fishmonger's stall. Dogs and cats wander underfoot, and smudge-faced urchins dart in and out among the patrons, racing between the stalls, stooping to snatch stray coins that drop from hands and purses, or reaching out to grab an apple or potato when the vendor is looking the other way.

We pause to look at some of the displays and watch a young boy grab an apple from a nearby cart. By the time the farmer calls out, "You there, you little guttersnipe. Come back here with that apple!" the boy has disappeared.

Finally, we make our way to the Pie Man's corner at Fifth and Chestnut. Someone bumps me from behind, hard enough to knock me off-balance, and I let go of Sarah's hand. Fists clenched, I turn and shout, "If you touch her, I'll...I'll..." but he is already off and running.

I calm my racing heart, turn and take Sarah's hand, trying to be as gentle as possible so as not to frighten her. "The problem with crowds, Sarah, is that people sometimes push us by accident." My purpose is to reassure her, but to my surprise, the look on her face is one of excitement, not fear.

"There he is!" She has spotted the Pie Man up ahead, and he is indeed a sight: top hat, formal suit, and a pastry tray suspended from a rope around his neck. Children are everywhere, munching on tarts and spitting out cherry pits.

"Cora is *very* hungry," says Sarah when we get to him. I give her a coin, which she hands to the Pie Man, and he hands her a tartlet. And for a miraculous moment, she is no different from the other children that surround us.

As I buy pastries for tonight's dessert, Sarah lets out a blood-curdling scream. "No! No!" I turn to her, anticipating God knows what. Her coat is open, and I see she has dropped the tartlet and is rubbing at her dress, which is stained cherry red.

"Bad, I'm a bad girl, a stupid girl!" she cries, hitting her chest. Addressing me she says, "Now you're going to beat me like Mrs. Doyle."

I pick her up. "No, honey. You're not a bad girl and no one is going to beat you. Ever! It's only a dress, and we'll wash it clean. Everyone gets stains on their clothing." She is inconsolable, so I open my coat and hug her tight, chest to chest; then I step back to show her the stain on my dress.

"See. My dress matches yours. When we get home, we'll wash both our dresses."

I'm hoping for a smile, but that is not forthcoming. By the time we arrive home, Sarah has crawled back inside herself.

CHAPTER 54

A week has passed since the incident with Sarah's stained dress, but my heart aches when I remember how she called herself a bad stupid girl and how she was afraid I would beat her like Mrs. Doyle did. Damn those people and what they did to my daughter. Damn Timmy Doyle and his sick obsession with me. Every time I leave the house, I fear he is lurking around every corner, behind every tree. I've been afraid to wander out by myself. I swear I will not let him imprison me with fear forever. I am done with prisons. But for now, I can't venture out alone, which is why I ask Aiden to accompany me on a trip to the market to buy a new cookpot.

"You needn't worry about Doyle when you're with me," says Aiden, as we put on our coats.

"I know, but you're not always here. How can I feel safe? How can I protect Sarah?"

"If I got my hands on him, I'd kill him."

"I would, too." I make a fist.

"Undoubtedly." He laughs.

"Seriously though, you must promise me you won't fight him. He's bigger and meaner than you, and you'd end up hurt, or worse."

"It won't be easy, but I promise. And don't forget, Lizzy, 'tis a good neighborhood we live in. We watch out for each other."

Soon after I moved in with them, Aiden told me that the "old-timers" on the block had lived here for many years and were in the habit of looking after each other. And as newcomers arrived, they did the same for them—watching their neighbors' children, caring for each other when they were ailing, and sharing food from their larders. Probably everyone in the neighborhood is familiar with my history. They know I spent years in prison, that my daughter has no father, and I keep company with a Black woman. But they always smile at me and greet me politely, despite what they might be saying behind my back. And when I take my daughter for a walk, they smile at her as well, often exclaiming about what a beauty she was.

"I've already talked to the neighbors," Aiden reassures me. "I've asked them to watch out for Doyle and let us know if they spot him. A lot of them know him already through personal experience or by reputation, so they'll have no problem warning us when he's around. Knowing the folks around here are keeping their eyes out for Doyle should make you feel safe—at least in this neighborhood."

"In *this* neighborhood, yes. But I cannot confine myself to this small world."

•   •   •

I have been out of prison over six months, but after the whirlwind search for my daughter and the joy of finding her, I now find myself in a dark place. Despite my efforts to comfort Sarah and strengthen my bond with her, I'm afraid we are no closer to each other than we were when I took her home. The specter of Thomas hangs heavy over me, and I haven't heard from him in the nearly three weeks since he received my journal. Although his silence is the answer I tell myself I want, I cannot deny that I continue to be disappointed.

And I fear I am becoming a burden on my family. I have not contributed a penny to the household since my return from prison. I must find a job, but what can I do? My sewing skills are lacking, despite the many hours I spent stitching in prison. Working as a maid is out of the question. I would like very much to be a teacher, but fear I lack the proper training. I was a good student, but I'm unsure that would qualify me to teach even primary school students. I'll have to push myself to start making inquiries.

Mr. Dickens expected great things of me, but I find it increasingly difficult to understand why. I continue to be a disappointment to myself, if not to others. I want to do more for the abolitionist movement, but it seems all I can do for them is bake cakes for the anti-slavery fairs. If I don't do *something* to change my lot, I may never emerge from this dark place.

•　　•　　•

Today Lucy and I are delivering old clothing to the Still house for his "passengers" to use on their journey north. I decide to ask Mr. Still if there is anything more I can do for the movement. He spends a few moments with me before Lucy and I start sorting the clothing.

I tell him I'd like to do more for the "railroad" than baking cakes and collecting clothing. After the riot I'd asked Aiden and Meg whether they'd be willing to hide fugitives—knowing they'd be taking a risk—and they had said yes.

"Would it be possible for me to shelter passengers?" I suggest. "My house has plenty of room for 'visitors,' and my family is amenable."

"I thank you for your offer, but we already have an extensive network in place. Most of our stationmasters are colored, because the runaways are less conspicuous that way. I assume your neighbors are white."

"They are."

"What would your white neighbors think if they saw colored people slipping in and out of your house?"

"Lucy and Benjamin are frequent visitors, and the neighbors are quite used to seeing them. But, you are right. They would not welcome such activity."

"Nonetheless, if we are ever in need of emergency shelter, I will consider your offer."

"Thank you, sir. I appreciate that."

Lucy and I are about to take our bundles of clothing to the back room to sort, when a Black man comes to the door. He is out of breath and sweating heavily, having obviously run some distance to get here. He hands Mr. Still a note.

"I was asked to deliver this message to you. It is of the utmost urgency," he says after pausing a moment to catch his breath. He leaves immediately thereafter.

As Mr. Still reads the message, his wife slowly makes her way downstairs with their new baby asleep in her arms and calls out, "What is it, William?"

"It's from a porter at Bloodgood's Hotel. He says a slave woman named Hanna and her two children are on their way to New York in the company of her master, a Mr. Wilson, and several companions. Wilson left Hanna in the hotel room so he could attend to some business, and she told the porter she was a slave who desired her freedom, although she had been forbidden by Wilson to talk to anyone."

"When are they departing?"

"Five o'clock ferry to Camden from the Walnut Street wharf." He looks at the clock. "It's two o'clock now, so we'll need to act quickly if we hope to rescue them."

"You will need help," says Mrs. Still.

"Indeed I will. Wilson and company will be keeping a close eye on Hanna. They might already be on board the ship when we get there, so we'll need a way to distract them."

Out of nowhere an idea comes to me. It is mad, but it would do no harm to ask. When I whisper my plan to Lucy, she looks at me wide-eyed before smiling and nodding in agreement. "I would join you," she says, "but I think the 'distraction' should be a white woman, especially if you have to climb on board."

"Mr. Still," I say, "I think I can help you." I tell him my idea, and after a little persuasion, he agrees.

"I can put a costume together with some of the clothing on hand. But someone will have to get me the apples." What have I done? I can hardly believe I volunteered to do such a thing. But as we look through the clothing to find something that fits, I realize I'm feeling alive for the first time in weeks.

My hair is fastened tight under a bonnet pulled low over my face, and I have a basket of apples hanging from a rope around my neck when I arrive at the wharf with Mr. Still and a white lawyer named Thompson, who is active in the underground railroad. We spot Hanna and her sons on deck and know we must make haste.

"Apples!" I call out, as we push our way to the front of the crowd lining the wharf. "Fresh and delicious." I grab an apple from the basket that is strung around my neck and hold it out, although I am moving too fast for anyone to make a purchase. "Who doesn't like a juicy apple?"

We climb the steps to the deck—the Black man, the white man, and the apple peddler—and the people on board turn to watch us, including two men in tall hats who are standing near Hanna and her children. One of them is restraining Hanna, while the other has his hands on the shoulders of each boy. I slip off the rope that holds the basket of apples around my neck and grab the handle.

Mr. Thompson yells out to Hanna. "Do you want your freedom?"

"I do, but I belong to this man, so I can't be free."

"Yes, you can," says the lawyer, who has now positioned himself in front of Hanna.

Mr. Still is inching his way toward the boys.

Wilson, tightening his hold on Hanna's arm, says, "The woman speaks the truth. She is my property."

"No, she is not. I am a lawyer and I have just informed her of her rights." And with that, Mr. Thompson grabs Hanna and pulls her away from Wilson, while at the same time Mr. Still takes hold of the two boys and rushes them down the steps. Mr. Thompson tries to put some distance between himself and Wilson, but Wilson and his companion are getting closer. When they are almost upon her, Wilson reaches out to grab her and...

Now! I empty the contents of my basket at Wilson's feet. He falls as I run toward the steps, and the men in the tall hats stumble. A stranger grabs my arm and yells, "You have no right to deprive the man of his property."

"Get your hands off me!" I yell, pulling myself from his grasp and flinging my basket in his face. *No man will ever touch me like that again.*

I run down the steps and follow Thompson and Hanna through the crowd to a carriage where Mr. Still and the children are waiting for us. As we drive off, Mr. Still says something to me, but I hear nothing except the sound of my pounding heart.

Afterward, still wearing my ridiculously oversized bonnet and skirt, I tell Aiden and Meg about what just happened. I reach into my pocket for the apple that has somehow found its way there, and tell them how much I had surprised myself doing what I did. Meg says she's not at all surprised, and Aiden agrees. I am learning what I am capable of and how others see me, and I blush with pleasure at the thought.

Once in bed, I find myself too excited to sleep. I sit up and look over at Sarah, sound asleep in her bed. I decide not to tell her about my "adventure" just yet. A little girl her age would likely find my story confusing. It will probably make more sense to her when she's older. Perhaps it will serve someday to show her how even the most ordinary woman can take risks and make a difference—although I struggle to think ahead while there are still so many mountains to climb.

I take great satisfaction knowing I helped a slave cross over to freedom. I am feeling stronger in the face of my audacity, and without a husband—for after losing Thomas, I have no desire to marry—I will need enough strength for two.

CHAPTER 55

The next day I sleep later than usual. When I come downstairs, Meg is preparing a Sunday breakfast of eggs and sausages with Sarah as her little helper. I offer to take over, but Meg tells me I earned a day of rest and should just relax in the living room with Aiden, who is reading the paper.

I pull my copy of *American Notes* from the bookshelf, and after running my fingers over Mr. Dickens' inscription to me, I turn to the chapter about the penitentiary. I do not get very far before there's a knock at the front door. I open it, and before I can say a word, Thomas has enfolded me in his arms and is kissing my face, my neck, murmuring, "I'm so sorry, Lizzy," and I am kissing him back. And I don't care that the door is open and the whole world is watching. And I don't care that Aiden and Meg and Sarah have gathered around us. And I don't care that the neighbors are watching. Because at that precise moment, everything around us has ceased to exist except Thomas and me.

Gradually the laughter and exclamations of my family and the people peering through the curtains of their front windows penetrate our private world of two. Thomas retrieves my journal from his bag, and the two of us sit on the couch, our legs touching. Meg and Aiden pull chairs up, and Sarah stands between them. Thomas lays the journal down next to him and turns to me.

"The day Aiden delivered your package, my father suffered an attack of apoplexy. I was consumed with the state of his health and the business affairs that had to be handled in his absence, and I forgot everything else. It was only when his condition improved that I remembered Aiden's delivery. I am so sorry, Lizzy. I should have attended to your package the moment Aiden handed it to me." He takes my hands in his. "You mean everything to me. You have from the moment I met you."

"Finally," whispers Meg.

As my tears flow, I feel a tiny hand squeezing into the space between Thomas' hand and mine. My Sarah standing in front of my Thomas. Yes, *my* Thomas. He pulls her onto his lap and she snuggles into his chest.

"I read every word of your journal, Lizzy. All you suffered. No one should have had to endure what you did. You wrote in your letter that I would be 'disgusted' by what was in the journal. Nothing is further from the truth. I am disgusted by what they did to you. You asked why you had to pay so dearly for a debt you didn't owe. You said you were ashamed. But it's the people who did this to you who should be ashamed."

He was quoting from my journal, my words to the priest the first time he visited me in prison. As I sit on the couch, surrounded by my family, I can already feel the healing effect of Thomas' love on me and Sarah.

CHAPTER 56

The next day, Thomas and I cross the suspension bridge over the Schuylkill, as we did years ago. This time it's late winter, not spring, but that does not stop us from spreading our blanket in the same spot, with a view of the waterworks gleaming on the opposite shore like a magical kingdom, as it did then. Thomas tells me he hasn't been back here since that last afternoon we spent together.

"I wanted to keep the memory of this place fresh and unspoiled. It was a beautiful moment, planning our future together. I never understood why you—"

I put my finger to his lips. "It's time for me to tell you the whole story." Although he knows much of it from my journal, he didn't know what happened with my mother, how she went mad, how she made me believe I had murdered my baby and sent me to prison, how we found Sarah.

"That night at City Tavern where we dined with Aiden and Meg gave me the confidence to believe that everything would work out. I even believed that when I took you to meet Ma, crazy as she was, she would see what a fine match we'd make, and she would gladly give her blessing. But I never got the chance. The very next day, Robert Northam forced himself on me and—"

"Northam. That bastard. If I'd known, I would have..." He takes a deep breath and lets it out with a sigh. "Were he not dead, I would kill him myself."

"That monster is dead?"

"Yes. I'm surprised Aiden didn't tell you."

"I'm not. So much has happened since I was released from prison, the subject of Northam never came up."

"He died three years ago. He either committed suicide or was murdered, it's not clear. They discovered he'd been frequenting a house of ill fame, where he inflicted such damage on the woman he was 'seeing' that she could no longer...ply her trade. The madam was so incensed she spoke to the press. It all became public, and there was quite a scandal. Northam's reputation was shattered and his finances decimated. Had he lived, it isn't clear how he would have survived. His wife was the initial suspect until they found evidence that one of the women at the brothel was responsible. In the end they could prove nothing, and no one was charged."

I hope he went to his grave with my mark on his cheek.

"What's the matter?" he asks.

"It's not important. What is important is telling you the truth about why I didn't want to see you again. Once I was...defiled, I didn't believe I was worthy of you."

Thomas takes my hands in his.

"I'm sorry, Thomas, but that's how I felt. You are a fine gentleman, and I believed you deserved an unspoiled partner. I was ashamed to tell you what had happened to me."

He squeezes my hands and slowly shakes his head.

"So instead, I told you I feared I'd always be an outsider in your world. And because I still loved you, I could never see you again, lest I be tempted to change my mind."

"Lizzy, when you were gone, I tried to get on with my life. I had relationships with women, one of them serious. But I stopped short of proposing because every time we were together, I thought of you. In my life, in my bed. I don't want to make 'amorous congress,' Lizzy, I want to make love. So, I ask you the same question I asked the last time we were here. 'Lizzy O'Meara, will you marry me?'"

And here on the banks of the Schuylkill, I finally say yes. And once again we kiss as we did that first time so many years ago. And I remember how I wanted to surrender to him. And I remember when I was in prison imagining what it would be like to make love to him, and how I wrote about it in graphic detail in my journal. And how Thomas had read that journal. And I know where I want to be at this moment.

CHAPTER 57

Thomas owns an apartment on Spruce Street, and I tell him that is where I'd like to go with him. Now. I am brazen, and I don't care.

I don't remember the carriage ride or climbing the front steps. But I follow him as he unlocks the door, and lights the fire, and leads me to the bedroom. He unhooks the front of my dress and watches as I let it slip to the floor. I shiver as I stand before him. I do not cover myself with my hands as his eyes linger on my nipples, which have become hard, straining through the thin fabric of my chemise. He takes off his shirt and trousers, and although I had been "intimate" with a man before, everything had been hidden. Now, even though Thomas is still wearing his drawers, I can see what desire looks like. He leads me to the bed and lays down beside me, but when he reaches over to touch me, I flinch, suddenly engulfed in a flood of painful memories.

"We don't have to do this if you're not ready," he whispers.

"I want to do this." My voice trembles.

"If you're sure, take my hand when you are ready and let me know what you want."

I inhale, aware of every inch of my body. Then I take his hand and place it between my breasts. He moves it slowly over one breast, along my hip, and down my thigh until he reaches the hem of my chemise. I help him pull it up over my shoulders, and he tosses it off the bed. Then he takes my breast in his mouth, and I gasp. I had heard that this act was a part of lovemaking, but until now the last time I was conscious of mine was when they were filled with milk and aching because there was no baby to nurse. But here is Thomas sucking my nipple, then the other. *The feeling is too much to bear. And not enough.* I take his hand and move it between my legs, keeping my hand on his as he rubs me there, and I feel wetness.

I take off my pantelettes and he pulls off his drawers.

"Wait," I whisper as he reaches for me. I sit up and look at his strange and wonderful body as he lies beside me motionless as a statue. Yes, I had been with a man, but I had never *seen* a man. "You are beautiful, Thomas," I whisper.

"And you are a marvel," he says, gazing at my nakedness.

Thomas is as tender and cautious with me as if I were a virgin; and in the matter of love, I am indeed a virgin. As we move together, I press him hard against me to let him know I'm ready, and he enters me. I expect to feel pain, since that's what I experienced in the past. But this sensation—*this*—is the opposite of pain. We move together as the sun streams in through the window, blessing our union. When we have both found our pleasure and he is still inside me, I think: So this is how it feels to be loved. The physical act unleavened by love is painful, bitter, hard, dry, like stale bread. With love comes sweetness and softness.

Perhaps I should be worried about becoming pregnant, but I know it is not the time of the month when this is likely to happen, so I put that thought out of my mind.

Afterward, we sit on his bed, talking about what it will be like to live our lives together. I tell him it all seems so perfect were it not for Sarah's distress.

"Sarah spent so many years with no mother, no family," he says. "When we are a family, we will give her what she never had."

"Perhaps."

"Yes, the two of us will heal her."

CHAPTER 58

This time of year, when spring struggles to emerge from the gloom of winter, and the skies are mostly heavy and gray, I am heartened whenever the sun makes an appearance. So it is with Sarah. I am encouraged when she opens up, albeit only briefly. Helping me bake a cake when Thomas is coming to dinner. Smiling at Aiden when he gives her a little wooden animal he has carved for her. Adding a book to the growing collection on her bookshelf.

Soon after our reunion, Thomas and I take Sarah to the bookstore to let her select another book. After much deliberation, she chooses *A Christmas Carol*—this after Thomas recites some of its most well-known lines with an exaggerated British accent and a dramatic flair I didn't know he possessed. She laughs when he pronounces Marley dead as a doornail, and she repeats Ebenezer Scrooge's "Bah humbug," imitating Thomas' delivery.

And she has made a friend. Until recently, Sarah paid no attention to the neighborhood children when we took walks together. I told her their names as we passed them and asked her if she wanted to play with them, but she shook her head, eyes downcast, clutching my hand. Gradually, though, she began to pay attention to the surrounding activity.

The little girls laughing as they played with their dolls, or joined hands and skipped down the street. But still she clung to my hand.

That is, until she met Meghan, the five-year-old daughter of the McCarthys, who live two doors down from us. I don't know what it is about Meghan. Perhaps it's her red hair and shy smile—the two girls bear a remarkable resemblance to each other. One day, Sarah asks me if she can play with Meghan, but only if I watch. She brings out the rag doll I'd bought for her as a replacement for Cora—a doll that has been gathering dust on the shelf since she put it there three months ago. They play with their dolls on the stoop, quietly at first, then making up little stories about them and acting out scenes. And today—for the first time—Sarah is playing with Meghan at her house under the watchful eye of Mrs. McCarthy. Her new friend is her first connection with the world around her. I am hopeful this is a new beginning for her.

But my optimism is short-lived. The next morning, as Meg and I are washing the dishes from breakfast, I notice that Sarah is not in the living room, where she usually plays after breakfast. Perhaps she's upstairs, but when I check the bedroom, she's not there either. Her doll is lying on the floor, as are her books, although *A Christmas Carol* is not among them. Meg and I search every corner of the house, and my anxiety grows with each empty room. She's gone. Where? Why?

I look up and down the street, but she's not there. She's not at the McCarthys' either. But a neighbor down the block cleaning her stoop tells me she saw Sarah running down the street carrying a book. She points me in the direction she was headed. Meg has joined me, and we ask everyone we pass whether they saw a little red-headed girl running down the street. Enough of them have seen her that we can trace her path. We race past a man coming out of a tavern, barely noticing the voices of the men spilling out of the open door—men who have already drunk many a pint although it's barely noon. We step around a little boy playing with a wooden boat in the gutter. We continue, all the while anticipating the sound of that sinister laugh, until we find ourselves a block from Lucy's house.

"How could she possibly remember the way?" I ask.

But remember she did, for at that moment Lucy steps outside her door, holding Sarah's hand. Sarah is clutching *A Christmas Carol* to her chest and sobbing.

I fall to my knees and hug her. "Oh, baby. Why did you run off?"

"Cora," she wails.

"What about Cora?"

"I wanted to find her and read her my book. Cora is my best friend in the whole world."

"Oh, Sarah," I say softly, still on my knees as my daughter sobs against my chest. Although Sarah had made a new friend, she could never forget the connection she lost to the one constant in her life.

CHAPTER 59

Spring has finally arrived. The dull brown trees have begun to dress themselves in their spring greenery. Crocuses, irises, and daffodils color the drab city landscape. Soon the lone cherry tree on the block will bloom. Cherry blossoms are beautiful, but they still remind me of Cherry Hill Penitentiary. Although the memories persist, they are slowly fading because I now live in a world where cherry trees bloom in freedom. Thomas and I are to be wed in six months, and we will surround Sarah with love. Like the earth in spring, I am being reborn.

This morning I am alone in the kitchen and delighting in this new season as it transforms the backyard. Meg is visiting a friend, Sarah is with Meghan at the McCarthys', and Aiden is running an errand. He told me where he was going, but I was daydreaming and didn't pay attention.

I am enjoying the quiet, my mind filled with images of flowers, of the simple but elegant wedding dress Meg is making in gray silk, of how pretty Sarah will look with her hair tied back with a pink ribbon, of—

A creak of a floorboard in the parlor. So much for my communing with the quiet blush of spring's splendor. "Aiden? You are back already...from wherever you said you were going? You have interrupted my glorious solitude..."

But there is no acknowledgment, and yet I know someone is there.

"Aiden, is that you?" I call, louder now, crossing the kitchen to enter the dining room. Still no answer. Hmm. Maybe... "Meg?"

As I enter the parlor, a different voice speaks, and a dreaded face greets my eyes. "Red. There you are. Still the prettiest girl in the city."

Timmy Doyle is standing by the door, a bouquet of flowers in his hand. "For you," he says, extending his arm.

Surely this is a dream. Timmy Doyle offering flowers. Timmy Doyle smiling and not smirking.

"I'm here to apologize. I ain't been nice to you, Red. But since I started going to church, I done confession, and I told the priest I would make...amens. So I'm doin' like I promised him."

Can someone that evil change? Did he uncover an inner light? But there is something odd about his speech—slow, halting. He stumbles, and I realize it's not sincerity speaking, but whiskey.

I retreat a few steps, but he follows me. Nearer to me now, I can smell the liquor on him.

"Roses are red, like your hair, Red." He chuckles as he comes still closer, pointing the flowers at me like a pistol.

"Take 'em. Go on now, they're for you, Red—"

I can retreat no further. My back is now against the wall that separates the parlor from the dining room. His face is inches from mine. His breath reeks. I struggle, gasping for air.

"Take 'em, I says!" He throws the flowers in my face, and they fall to the floor. Then he grabs my shoulders. "Fooled ya, Red. I been watching the house, on the sly since I know the neighbors been lookin' out for me. Waitin' to get you alone. And now I'm gonna do what I been waiting to do all these years." He presses against me, lifting my dress, running his hands up the inside of my thighs.

Not again, dear God. Please, not again.

I find my voice and scream, trying to push him away, but I'm no match for him. He covers my mouth, pressing it with one hand, ripping at my undergarments with the other. I reach down to grab his arm, but he twists my wrist with such force that the pain is excruciating...I'm afraid he's broken it. I feel him wedge himself between my knees, his one leg, then both, and now he presses his groin closer, closer, closer, inching his way forward while he unbuttons his pants. I try to bend a knee to kick him, but his legs, his groin, his manhood, all press against my lower half. I bite the palm covering my mouth and he yelps but does not move his hand.

"Oh, you little she-devil. I always knew you were a wild one."

A noisy door hinge announces itself. It's the front door sweeping open.

"Doyle, you bastard!"

It's Aiden.

"Get away from my sister or I'll kill ya!"

My brother pulls at my assailant, but Timmy is so intent on his mission he doesn't budge. I see Aiden's face, red as a flame, over Timmy's shoulder. He grips Timmy's hair and rips at it so violently that a clump comes out in his hand. Timmy turns and faces my brother. I wriggle out from behind him.

"Run, Lizzy, I'll take care of him. Get the hell out of here!"

I run, but not out of the house, only as far as the dining room. I can't leave, would never leave my brother alone with Timmy Doyle, but I don't have the voice to tell him. I move farther back into the dining room but stay close enough to help him.

"O'Meara, you bastard!" Timmy screams, his voice loud but unsteady. "I hear you been talking about me to the neighbors, spreading lies, about how I been fucking their wives."

"I never said a word about that, Doyle. I didn't have to. People told me all kinds of stuff. Seems you've been having a good time with other men's women."

"That's a fucking lie, O'Meara. And you're going to pay."

Timmy is facing away from me, but I can see him reach into his pocket.

"Aiden...he's got a gun!" I scream.

Aiden backs away, but the words are barely out of my mouth before Timmy has pointed a pistol at my brother. There's no way this shot can miss at this distance. He sways, his hand shaking from the booze.

Crack! The bullet hits the wall.

Timmy closes the gap between himself and Aiden. "The next one won't miss, you bastard. And after I finish you off, here's what I'm going to do to your sister—"

Aiden pushes out his chest, defiant, but also smart. "Sure, why don't you tell me."

Good, Aiden. While Timmy is talking, he won't be shooting.

Timmy bellows his diatribe at Aiden, describing the details of the acts he plans to perform on me, but I don't hear his filthy words as I canvass the room, my eyes darting, searching...*Ah, this will do.* I grab the brass oil lamp from the table.

Aiden sees me, but quickly lowers his eyes so as not to give me away. I raise the lamp then realize the danger. The gun might go off when he feels the blow. But I need to act...

"Timmy! Stop. I...I'm ready for you, darling, come here..."

As he turns away from Aiden, I slam the lamp against the back of his skull, a crushing blow as a bullet fired from his pistol shatters the front window. Timmy slumps to the floor, blood flowing, pooling under his head, the red puddle expanding.

Everything happens so quickly I can hardly describe it. A neighbor who heard the shot rushes in and kneels over Timmy. He and Aiden check for signs of life, but in my heart I know he's gone. Timmy Doyle, my lifelong tormentor, is dead. I am still clutching the bloody lamp in my hand. Aiden relieves me of it and puts it on the floor. Before the neighbor can rush out to the stationhouse to summon the police, I ask him to stop at the McCarthys' and tell them what happened so they can keep Sarah away from the house.

Then it's all a jumble. Two policemen arrive, ask questions, the neighbor says he saw everything and will testify that we acted in self-defense if there's a trial. I tell Aiden I'm afraid of what McMullen will do when he hears we killed his cousin.

"Mr. Baldwin is a good friend of the mayor," Aiden says, "and the city now controls the police force, not the aldermen or sheriffs."

I don't understand all that he's implying, but it seems to mean that William McMullen has no special power over us anymore. I let go of my emotions and my eyes overflow in a torrent of tears as Aiden reaches out to comfort me.

Meg comes home. The body is removed, the floor is scrubbed. By evening our house is in order, as if nothing has happened. But everything has changed. Timmy Doyle is gone forever.

While there will be no conviction, and I experience no guilt, I will need to accept that I have killed a man.

"We will shed no tears for Timmy Doyle," I say to Aiden before going up to bed.

"A fitting epitaph for the bastard," he says.

I cannot disagree.

CHAPTER 60

Sarah does not know exactly what happened, but she overhears bits and pieces of conversation. Something violent has happened, and it happened in our house. Although we try to hide our emotions, she is sensitive to them, and reflects them back to us. Outside, in the neighborhood, people whisper and point when they see us.

Sarah no longer goes out to play and she barely looks at her books. She takes the doll down from the shelf, then puts it back. It offers no solace. It doesn't even have a name.

We continue our bedtime ritual. Every night I sit in the rocking chair while she sits in her bed, and I read to her. She listens to the stories and looks at the illustrations when I show them to her, but when I ask her if she liked the story or what was her favorite part, she answers halfheartedly. And so it goes.

Tonight, I open *Anderson's Fairy Tales* to a new story and start to read, but my heart isn't in it. *Is this how it's always going to be? Sarah in her bed, me on the chair, an ocean between us? An ocean between her and the world?* I stop reading and close the book. Sarah looks at me puzzled, as I rock. I close my eyes, and the seeds of a story take root. I am not sure where it comes from or where it's going. But I open my mouth, and the words spill out.

Once upon a time there was a little girl. Her name was Miriam, but everyone called her Mimi. She lived with some other children and grownups far away in a place called Alabama. She lived on a plantation where everyone worked all day in the hot sun, picking cotton. Mimi was very sad because she didn't have a mother.

Her uncle told her, "Mimi, you *do* have a mother. But she had to leave you when you were a little baby."

"Why did she have to leave me?" asked Mimi.

"Because someone told her they were going to take her away to live on another plantation."

"Were they going to take me away too?" asked Mimi.

"No," replied the uncle. "Only your mama."

"Then why didn't she take me with her anyway?" Mimi cried. "If she loved me, she would have taken me with her."

"That is not true," said the uncle. "It was because she loved you so much that she left alone. You see, it was too dangerous for her to take you because you were so little. So she decided to take the underground railroad by herself, and when she got to Philadelphia, she would send for you."

"But she didn't send for me," said Mimi, weeping. "So she doesn't love me."

"Oh, yes, she does, Mimi. Your mama cried and cried the night she left, but you don't remember because you were just a baby."

The uncle would rock Mimi at night and tell her that soon he would take her on the underground railroad to her mama.

"I don't believe you," said Mimi. And she cried herself to sleep.

Then one day, the uncle said to her, "Mimi we have to leave here tonight. If we don't, someone is going to take you to another plantation, and I won't see you again. So tonight we're going away."

They packed up their few belongings and set out in the middle of the night through the forest.

Sarah sits up in bed, takes her thumb out of her mouth, and asks plaintively, "Did Mimi take her doll with her?"

"Yes, of course she did. But she lost her in the woods, which made her very sad. Would you like to know what happened next?"

Sarah nods and puts her thumb back in her mouth. I close my eyes to "see" what comes next, and once again the words tumble out.

It was dark and scary, and Mimi was scared, but the uncle told her not to be afraid, they would get there soon.

"Where are we going?"

"To the underground railroad."

"Oh," said Mimi. And they walked on for many hours until they came to a little house in the woods.

"There it is," said the uncle. "The railroad station."

"No, Uncle, you're wrong. That's not a railroad station," said Mimi bursting into tears. "That's just a house. Where are the railroad tracks and the trains? Are they all underground?"

"No. This is a different kind of railroad. There are no train cars, just people who take you from place to place on your way to your mama. And even though it's not underground, it's secret, which is the same thing."

They go in the house and a nice man feeds them. There's another little girl in the house. She's crying.

"Why are you crying?" asks Mimi.

"Because I miss my mama," says the little girl.

"I miss my mama, too," says Mimi. "I thought I was the only little girl in the world who didn't have a mama."

I feel a hand on my leg. I open my eyes, and there is Sarah, looking up at me.

"Would you like to climb up on my lap?"

Sarah nods, and I help her up. She lays her head against my chest. I want to stroke her red curls, embrace her, but instead I simply wrap my arms around her waist to support her. I could stay like this forever, rocking, my daughter's warm breath on my neck, her little body against mine. But there is more to the story.

Even though the food at the farmer's house is delicious, Mimi cries herself to sleep. How can I get to my mama, she wonders, if there's no railroad and no train?

The next day, a man pulls up with a cart loaded with hay. Get in, says the farmer. Mimi and her uncle crawl into the cart under the hay.

"We have to be quiet," says the uncle. "Some people might be looking for us, and we don't want them to find us."

Mimi is quiet as a mouse as they clippity-clop all day to the next house. The next day they crawl into a cart full of cotton. Though the cotton tickles her nose as they ride to the next house, she presses her fingers to her nose and mouth so she won't sneeze. And so it went day after day as they traveled north on the underground railroad that isn't underground and has no trains until they finally arrived in Philadelphia.

"This is our last stop," says the uncle. "There is a surprise waiting for you at the station," he says as they hurry up the front stoop and open the big wooden door. A woman is standing just inside the door, with tears streaming down her cheeks and the biggest smile Mimi had ever seen.

"Who are you?" asked Mimi.

"I am your mama," says the woman, scooping her up into her arms. "And I will never leave you again."

"Do you promise?" asks Mimi.

"I promise," says Mama.

When I finish the story Sarah takes a deep, satisfied breath and stays nestled on my lap. I rock her until her breathing is even. Then I pick her up as gently as I can and set her down on the bed.

"Did Mimi find her doll?" asks Sarah, her voice little more than a whisper.

"No, she didn't. But her mama bought her a new one."

She smiles and closes her eyes.

•　　•　　•

Early the next morning, while Sarah is still sleeping, I hurry over to William Still's house. Lucy is there, having spent the night assisting Mr. Still with the latest arrivals. I ask her a question and I'm pleased with the answer.

Then I speak to Thomas.

"Of course I'll come with you," he says. "After all, in six months she will be my daughter, too."

CHAPTER 61

I hold one of Sarah's hands and Thomas holds the other as we walk to the Still house.

"Did you know that Aunt Lucy works at an underground railroad station?" I ask. Her eyes widen. "Well, she does. And I have worked there, too."

"You have?" Her eyes grow even wider.

"Yes. And someday you will, too. There is still so much to be done. Are you excited about your surprise?"

"I don't know. I think so."

A carriage is waiting outside the Still house, and we arrive just as Lucy is escorting a young Negro couple and a little boy to the vehicle. Although it's not chilly this morning, the three of them are wearing heavy coats for their trip north. After the man helps the woman and child into the carriage, he turns to Lucy.

"We is so grateful for all you done for us." His voice breaks as he shakes her hand.

"I wish you Godspeed, John. Take care of Martha and Peter, and send word when you have arrived."

"Where are they going?" asks Sarah as the man climbs into the carriage and they drive off.

"To Canada."

"Where is that?"

"Far away from here."

"Will they have to hide under the hay?"

"I don't know. Why don't you ask Lucy when we go inside?"

"I know this house. This is where I hid with Aunt Lucy that night."

"You didn't know you were hiding in an underground railroad station, did you?"

"I was?"

"You certainly were."

When we're inside, Sarah looks around and says, "There is still so much to be done."

She cannot possibly know what I meant when I said those exact words earlier. Or maybe she does.

Thomas says he will stand aside, because he knows that what is about to happen is a special moment between two dear friends and a little girl.

Lucy knew about the story I'd told Sarah, so she wasn't surprised when my daughter asked her about the hay and then added, "I hope you told them to be quiet, Aunt Lucy."

The Stills' living room is dimly lit, as always, and warmed by the glowing embers in the hearth.

"It is so quiet this morning. Are we the only ones here?" I ask Lucy.

"Mrs. Still is sleeping upstairs. There were a lot of comings and goings last night. Mr. Still is out hiding his journal in his secret spot, but he'll be back soon. I know he's looking forward to meeting this special little girl."

"Lucy, I think this is a perfect time to give Sarah her surprise."

"Yes, perfect. I'll go fetch it."

Sarah and I sit together on the couch, while Thomas takes a seat on a nearby bench, watching us. "Remember I told you that Lucy and I were best friends since we were little girls. I think Lucy must have known that someday I'd have a little girl, because she kept something I gave her a long time ago. Now we want to give it to you."

Sarah can't take her eyes off the cloth sack Lucy carries downstairs. I tell her she's going to love the surprise Lucy is about to give her, but now I'm not feeling so confident. After all, it's still just a rag doll, although Lucy had transformed her as best she could, using Sarah's lost doll, Cora, as a model. She had copied Cora's features but freshened them up. A ruby red bow-shaped mouth replaced the faded outline of the original. The doll Sarah had carried with her wore a lace-trimmed petticoat that was stained and torn. This doll wears a new petticoat identical to the original, minus the stains and tears.

In a sense, this new version of Cora is a reflection of Sarah's transformation. Still, my misgivings grow when Lucy pulls the doll out of the sack and holds it out to Sarah. Why had I been so naïve as to think this would be the perfect gift?

"You like her?" Lucy asks, still holding the doll.

Sarah cocks her head and bites her lip as she contemplates the doll. I hold my breath.

"Can I hold her?"

Lucy hands her the doll, and she cradles it in her arms just as she cradled Cora.

"What's her name?"

"What do you think it is?" I ask.

"Cora," she answers without hesitation. "Cora O'Meara."

"Why, that *is* her name. How did you know?"

Sarah smiles. Then she jumps down from the couch. "Come with me, Cora, I'll show you around the room. Did you know this is an underground railroad station?"

AUTHOR'S NOTES

One of the reasons I love reading historical fiction is that a well-told story often motivates me to learn more about the history behind the fiction. I want to know where the author has taken liberties with the history in service to the narrative.

Locked in Silence is a work of fiction, and the main characters are the product of my own imagination. I have tried to portray historical characters and events as accurately as possible. For example, Matthias Baldwin was the founder of Baldwin Locomotive Works, one of Philadelphia's biggest and most successful businesses. He was known for his philanthropic and abolitionist views. William Still, a prominent though often overlooked abolitionist leader, documented the stories of hundreds of slaves he helped to escape north in violation of the Fugitive Slave Act. To avoid arrest, he hid his notes in a nearby cemetery.

There were times, however, that I found it necessary to exercise creative license, as noted here.

1. When Eastern State Penitentiary opened in 1829, the rules of solitary confinement and silence were strictly enforced, as described in the novel. During subsequent years, the institution relaxed some of the restrictions, though conditions would still have been extremely harsh in 1848 when Lizzy was incarcerated. Also, the women were housed

separately from the men, and the few women in residence during those early years were mostly poor and Black.

2. Though Timmy Doyle is a fictional character, his cousin William "Bull" McMullen was a major figure in Philadelphia politics. A street fighter during his early years, McMullen became a powerful political boss representing the people of Moyamensing, who kept him in office from 1856 until his death in 1901.

3. Lucy Washington is a fictional character, but her "Uncle" Robert and "Aunt" Harriet were abolitionists and active in anti-slavery groups. Robert Purvis was president of the Pennsylvania Anti-Slavery Society; and his wife, Harriet Forten, founded the interracial Female Anti-Slavery Society.

4. Madame Restell, a notorious abortionist of the nineteenth century, would have sold her abortion and birth control powders at her clinics, and they most likely would not have been available at pharmacies. Also, it's likely that Madame Restell herself, rather than a man, would have performed the procedure. She had better outcomes than any of her male or female competitors.

5. Charles Dickens visited Eastern State Penitentiary in 1842. I changed the date to 1848 to coincide with Lizzy's incarceration. And I moved up the date of his American reading tour, which took place in 1867, to incorporate it into the story.

6. The notorious *Guide to the Stranger* was published in 1849, not 1848.

The following books were extremely helpful in my research for this novel.

Biddle, Daniel L., and Murray Dubin. *Tasting Freedom: Octavius Catto and the Battle for Equality in Civil War America.* Philadelphia: Temple University Press, 2010.

Southwark, Moyamensing, Weccaccoe, Passyunk Dock Ward for Two Hundred Seventy Years. Philadelphia: The Quaker City Publishing Company, 1892.

Clement, Priscilla Ferguson. *Welfare and the Poor in the Nineteenth-Century City: Philadelphia 1800-1854.* Cranbury NJ: Associated University Presses, 1985.

Clark, Dennis. *The Irish in Philadelphia: Ten Generations of Urban Experience.* Philadelphia: Temple University Press, 1973.

Johnston, Norman, Kenneth Finkle, and Jeffrey A. Cohen. *Eastern State Penitentiary: Crucible of Good Intentions.* Philadelphia: Eastern State Penitentiary Historic Site, 2010.

Tomek, Beverly C. *Slavery and Abolition in Pennsylvania.* Philadelphia: Temple University Press, 2021.

ACKNOWLEDGMENTS

Writing is a solitary activity, but it takes a village to craft the words, phrases, sentences, and chapters into a compelling story. And I am grateful to my "village,"—that is, everyone who has helped me on this journey.

First, heartfelt thanks to the members, both present and past, of the Bucks County Writing Workshop and its intrepid leader, Don Swaim. You are a wonderful group of writers whose comments and suggestions helped me shape this novel. The unfailing encouragement of every one of you has meant the world to me. Special thanks to Bill Donahue for helping me navigate the challenging world of book submissions and to Chris Bauer for his suggestions on adding spice and suspense to action scenes.

Thank you Lindsey Allingham for reading the first draft of this novel. Your ability to create strong women and convey emotional depth set me off on the right track. And thanks to the readers of later drafts: Ef Deal, Jackie Nash, and Jim Kempner. Each of you had excellent suggestions that made me rethink and rewrite parts of the story. Jim, I especially appreciate your help in detecting and fixing plot holes.

Joslyn Pine, you are an editor extraordinaire. Thank you for catching errors and inconsistencies that would have been embarrassing if they'd made it into print.

Just as I was about to start this project, the pandemic hit, closing libraries and other research institutions. Being new to historical research, I was at a loss as to where to begin. So I owe a big debt of gratitude to Nancy Halli, who got me started by providing me with an extensive list of online sources and introducing me to a treasure trove of material. And thank you, Becky Caracappa for putting me in touch with Nancy.

I am fortunate to live near a number of excellent historical societies, and I am grateful for the librarians, staff, and archives I came to rely on. My thanks to The Library Company of Philadelphia, America's first successful lending library and oldest cultural institution, founded by Benjamin Franklin in 1731; Emily Pope at The Doylestown Historical Society; the staff of the Historical Society of Pennsylvania, in particular Anthony DiGiovanni, who was able to track down even the most obscure material I requested; Jesse Crooks at the Mercer Museum; David B. Roland at the Old York Road Historical Society; and Damon McCool at the Eastern State Penitentiary Historical Site.

Thank you to Black Rose Writing for believing in this book.

Finally, a special note of love and gratitude for my husband, Jim, who let me "do my thing," and who almost always stopped talking to me when I was writing.

ABOUT THE AUTHOR

Natalie Zellat Dyen began writing humor pieces and essays for newspapers while working as a technical writer. Since turning to fiction, her work has appeared in a number of publications including: *Philadelphia Stories, The MacGuffin, the Schuylkill Valley Journal, Willow Review, Alternative Truths: Endgame, Jewish Writing Project, Damselfly, Every Day Fiction,* and *Neshaminy: The Bucks County Historical and Literary Journal.* Her short story collection, *Finding Her Voice,* was published in 2019. She lives in suburban Philadelphia with her husband.

NOTE FROM
NATALIE ZELLAT DYEN

Word-of-mouth is crucial for any author to succeed. If you enjoyed *Locked In Silence*, please leave a review online—anywhere you are able. Even if it's just a sentence or two. It would make all the difference and would be very much appreciated.

Thanks!
Natalie Zellat Dyen

We hope you enjoyed reading this title from:

www.blackrosewriting.com

Subscribe to our mailing list – *The Rosevine* – and receive **FREE** books, daily
deals, and stay current with news about upcoming
releases and our hottest authors.
Scan the QR code below to sign up.

Already a subscriber? Please accept a sincere thank you for being a fan of
Black Rose Writing authors.

View other Black Rose Writing titles at
www.blackrosewriting.com/books and use promo code
PRINT to receive a **20% discount** when purchasing.